W9-BRP-536

The gunner in the Mercedes van cut loose with another burst

Bolan's assault rifle spit flame, and the chase car's left headlight exploded. His volley was too low and too far to the right as Grimaldi swerved to avoid incoming bullets, spoiling the Executioner's aim.

He fired another short burst, strafing the van's narrow grille. The fusillade wouldn't stop the Mercedes immediately, but an overheated engine could slow them in the short run.

They had reached the last paved road before the riverbank, crossing from east to west, while north-south drivers blared their horns, shook fists and shouted curses in the Audi's wake.

Road rage. Damn right.

The van was crossing the river, pursuing them, with the biker trailing it, decelerating now that he knew where the fight was headed. Bolan hoped the guy would be smart, turn back and live to see another day...

But that wasn't Bolan's call. He had four men to take out, at least, before they finished him.

DON PENDLETON'S MACK BOLAN

DEAD RECKONING

A GOLD EAGLE BOOK FROM
WORLDWIDE®

TORONTO • NEW YORK • LONDON
AMSTERDAM • PARIS • SYDNEY • HAMBURG
STOCKHOLM • ATHENS • TOKYO • MILAN
MADRID • WARSAW • BUDAPEST • AUCKLAND

If you purchased this book without a cover you should be aware
that this book is stolen property. It was reported as "unsold and
destroyed" to the publisher, and neither the author nor the
publisher has received any payment for this "stripped book."

Recycling programs
for this product may
not exist in your area.

First edition October 2015

ISBN-13: 978-0-373-61580-3

Special thanks and acknowledgment to
Mike Newton for his contribution to this work.

Dead Reckoning

Copyright © 2015 by Worldwide Library

All rights reserved. Except for use in any review, the
reproduction or utilization of this work in whole or in part
in any form by any electronic, mechanical or other means,
now known or hereinafter invented, including xerography,
photocopying and recording, or in any information storage
or retrieval system, is forbidden without the written permission
of the publisher, Worldwide Library, 225 Duncan Mill Road,
Don Mills, Ontario M3B 3K9, Canada.

This is a work of fiction. Names, characters, places and incidents are
either the product of the author's imagination or are used fictitiously,
and any resemblance to actual persons, living or dead, business
establishments, events or locales is entirely coincidental.

® and TM are trademarks of the publisher. Trademarks indicated
with ® are registered in the United States Patent and Trademark
Office, the Canadian Intellectual Property Office and in other
countries.

Printed in U.S.A.

Justice delayed is justice denied.
                          —William E. Gladstone

Justice may be late sometimes, but it's inevitable.
I don't judge my targets. I am their executioner.
                          —Mack Bolan

For John Christopher Stevens and Sean Smith

PROLOGUE

Zarqa, Jordan

The mob was heating up outside. Its rhythmic chanting of the past two hours had given way to random shouts and jeers from individuals amid the larger, heaving mass of human fury. Rocks were flying, and if experience was any guide, Molotov cocktails wouldn't be too far behind.

Mark Hamilton stood watching on a closed-circuit television, since the US consulate had no external windows. It was basically a bunker, the design dictated by security concerns, with eight-foot concrete walls around it, topped by razor wire.

That wouldn't stop the mob, if its excited members were determined to get in.

"Still no police?"

Hamilton turned to face his aide, Arnie Connelly. "Not yet."

"Jesus, how long does it take?"

Hamilton shrugged. They both knew members of Jordan's national Public Security Force should have shown up by then, if they were coming. Their headquarters, another bunker, stood roughly half a mile from the consulate, a five-minute drive at rush hour, even without lights and sirens.

"They're hanging us out to dry," Connelly said.

"We're not hung yet," Hamilton answered, trying to sound confident.

The trouble, this time, had blown up out of nowhere. Back in the States, in some southern backwater, a crackpot preacher short on congregants and craving national publicity had hatched a plan to gain recruits and pocket their donations with a protest against Islam. Picking up a couple dozen copies of the Koran—likely the only ones for sale in his reactionary cotton-picking state, Hamilton suspected—he had invited all and sundry to a grand book-burning ceremony, featuring a barbecue, a bluegrass band and his incessant pleas for money to support his "great, important work."

Predictably, the Muslim world had gone insane.

Now, here he was with Connelly, one other staff member, and two US Marines, manning a bunker in the middle of the night, a lynch mob at their gate.

Great time to be a diplomat.

Most people in the States couldn't explain the difference between an embassy and a consulate. Embassies were the larger, more important facilities, defined as permanent diplomatic missions, generally located in a foreign nation's capital city. Consulates, by contrast, were smaller outposts, normally sited in tourist cities, where they handled minor problems involving visas, travelers' problems, and wheedling complaints from expatriates. They had smaller staffs, fewer guards, less prestige.

Zarqa was not a tourist town, per se. There were no tourist towns in Jordan, at least so far as jet-setting Americans were concerned. Zarqa *was* Jordan's second-largest city, with a population of 481,000, and housed more than fifty percent of all Jordan's factories, fouling the air till it hardly lived up to its own name's translation: "the Blue

One." Zarqa also moved about ten percent of Jordan's exports—leather goods and clothing, chemicals and pharmaceuticals.

That meant that while sun-baked foreign tourists were in short supply, the city saw its share of Western businessmen, wheeling and dealing in suits that cost more than Hamilton earned in a month. Few of them visited the consulate, preferring to discuss their needs with the ambassador in Amman, but Hamilton was there, in case one of their trophy secretaries lost her purse and didn't think the native cops were suitably outraged.

"What's Rigby doing?" Hamilton inquired.

"Burning a lot of papers."

"Shit!"

Hamilton left his aide staring at the monitors and went to find Cale Rigby in his office. Rigby was supposed to be a cultural attaché, which was not-so-secret code for CIA. Their spook in residence, he was involved in God knew what, lording it over Hamilton and Connelly as if *he* were the consul, and the pair of them were just his flunkies.

Then again, given the climate of the times and the leanings of the State Department back in Washington, he might be right.

Hamilton didn't knock before he entered Rigby's office—still the only one he'd ever seen that had its own incinerator in one corner, with a stovepipe routed through the outer wall. Rigby was sitting in his roller chair, with the incinerator door open in front of him, feeding the flames with documents one handful at a time.

"You think we're that bad off?" Hamilton asked.

The CIA man didn't bother facing him. "We could be screwed," he answered, "but it doesn't matter. This is protocol."

"All of your hard work, up in smoke."

"No sweat. It's all on file at Langley, anyway."

The first shot sounded like a firecracker outside, but Hamilton could tell the difference. His bunker had been strafed and stoned before, though never by a mob this size, so furious.

"Better go check that out," Rigby advised, dropping another wad of top-secret reports into the fire.

THE FIRST SHOT was a signal, nothing more. Saleh Kabeer checked his Rolex watch and saw that it came right on time. He trusted other members of his team to hear and carry out the orders he had drilled into their heads over the past two weeks, in preparation for this moment.

He was grateful to the backwoods bigot in America who had devised a plan to outrage all of Islam at a single stroke. Without him, Kabeer would have had to plan a local incident himself, whip up the necessary anger to collect a mob and go from there. This stroke of luck, headlined and amplified by Muslim news outlets from Nigeria to Indonesia, was surely a gift from God to aid his endeavor.

Given the time and opportunity, Kabeer thought he might send the scrawny Crusader a fruit basket, as thanks. Of course, the fruit would all be poisoned.

Kabeer was supervising the attack, which he had also planned from its beginning as a spark of rage against the West. His group was not yet large enough to tackle major targets, but this would be a decent start. His young men were the best, most dedicated he could find, all disillusioned by the endless talk and feeble action from al-Qaeda and al-Gama'a al-Islamiyya, craving battle and glory.

Starting this night, their wish would be fulfilled.

"JESUS! YOU SEE THAT?" Connelly blurted out.

It was impossible to miss. Someone had thrown a grappling hook over the razor wire topping the consulate's south wall and was hauling in its line, ripping the coiled wire from its moorings. "And there's another one!"

He turned and followed Connelly's finger, pointing toward the west wall's monitor. Same thing and same result. Within another minute, maybe less, the north and east walls both had broad gaps in their curly razor wire. A moment after that, he saw the ladders going up. Dark, nimble figures scrambled over, dropping down inside the walls.

Welcome to US soil, Hamilton thought. For whatever that's worth.

Not much, this night, with no police in evidence and only two Marines to guard the consulate. He'd issued orders not to fire on anyone unless the building was invaded, then use common sense in self-defense. Hamilton knew Marines were tough, but two of them could no more stop a mob of hundreds—was it thousands, now?—than they could stop a tidal wave with sandbags and harsh language.

Five men altogether, in the consulate, and what would happen if he broke out extra guns for Connelly and himself? Would it make any difference to the inevitable outcome?

Hamilton had already phoned the embassy, not once, but half a dozen times. Their answer was the same each time he called: *Hang on. Help's coming.*

So was Christmas, but the way things looked right now, Hamilton doubted he'd be celebrating it. More likely, he would be the ghost of Christmas past.

"Look! That guy's got a rifle!"

By the time Hamilton turned, the man Connelly had seen was on the ground and out of sight. Another one came close behind him, though, and this one definitely had some kind of military rifle slung across his back, together with a heavy-looking satchel.

Ammunition? High explosives? Hamilton was betting that the gunman hadn't scaled their wall to drop off a petition or his dirty laundry.

"We need to get out of here!" Connelly said.

Too late, Hamilton thought.

"And go where?" he inquired.

"Pile in the Hummer," Connelly answered. "Rush the gate. Whoever tries to stop us, run them down or shoot them. Make it to the embassy."

That might work, in an action movie, but the gates were fortified to keep a semi tractor rig from smashing through. The Hummer in their motor pool could take down a few rioters, but it could never part the human sea outside their walls. It was a fantasy.

"You want a shotgun?" he asked Connelly.

"What? Um...well..."

A flash of light on one monitor screen, accompanied by thunder in the building, told Hamilton that the bunker was breached. They had minutes left, maybe seconds, before the mob reached them. Hamilton turned to his aide, hand extended, smiling into Connelly's pallid, panicked face.

"It's been good working with you, Arnie," Hamilton declared. Connelly was stunned, too terrified to answer, much less shake his hand.

"Um...um..."

Shouting and gunfire erupted in the hallway, drawing closer by the second.

Calm now, Hamilton turned toward the door he'd locked behind him, coming back from Rigby's office. Thinking of his wife and daughter, he put on a smile and waited for the end.

CHAPTER ONE

Ciudad del Este, Paraguay

"It's freaking hot down here," Jack Grimaldi complained, lifting off his baseball cap to draw a handkerchief across his sweaty brow.

"It's South America," Mack Bolan, aka the Executioner, answered from the meager shade cast by his Tilley hat.

"Hot," Grimaldi echoed. "Like I said."

They were on Avenida los Yerbales, near the sprawling greenery of Parque Jose Asuncion Flores, looking for a man who dealt in death. Their quarry didn't advertise himself that way—in fact, his neighbors knew him as an importer of farming implements and sporty motorcycles—but behind the public face, familiar from his television commercials, the guy pursued a thriving trade in weapons.

Paraguayan law mandated record keeping for acquisition, possession and transfer of all privately owned firearms, yet no statute regulated activities of arms brokers or transfer intermediaries. Authorities claimed that one million guns, both registered and otherwise, were owned by Paraguay's people.

"We're here," Grimaldi said, standing at ease while foot traffic eddied around him.

Bolan eyed the tractor showroom, looking for a trap, and came up empty. The interior was air-conditioned, almost frosty next to the oppressive humidity outside. Before they'd had a chance to look around, he saw the owner moving toward them, flashing the electric TV smile.

"Good day, gentlemen. How may I serve you?" the dealership owner said in Spanish.

Bolan bit the bullet on the coded answer and replied in English. "We're concerned with pest control."

The famous smile lost just a hint of luster, then came back full-force.

"Of course, if you will follow me." Crossing the showroom, heading for a storage area, the man called out, "Antonio! You have the floor."

In the back, he led them to a steel door, tapped out numbers on its keypad, then they descended to an air-conditioned basement. The "armory" contained a cornucopia of killing hardware racked or hung on walls, some of the larger pieces free-standing on tripods. Crates of ammunition made a double row running the full length of the space, stacked chest-high beneath fluorescent lights.

"Gentlemen, what I have is yours," he said, then added, "For a price, of course."

"Of course," Bolan acknowledged.

He was flush with cash from his last mission in the Bahamas, liberated from a narco-trafficker who didn't need it anymore. The mony had been converted into Paraguayan currency at the going rate. Browsing, Bolan chose a Steyr AUG assault rifle, backed up by a Glock 22 autoloader in .40-caliber S&W. Grimaldi agreed with Bolan on the Glock but picked a Spectre M4 submachine gun for his lead weapon. Suppressors all around, with ample extra magazines and ammunition to feed their deadly tools.

Bolan switched next to heavy hitters, picking out a Neopup PAW-20 grenade launcher. Designed and manufactured in South Africa, the Neopup fired 20 mm point detonating rounds from a 7-round detachable box magazine, with an advertised effective range of 400 meters. For closer work, he took a case of U.S.-made M-67 frag grenades, in standard use throughout the Western Hemisphere and well beyond.

For cutting tools, Bolan bought an all-steel Randall Model 18 survival knife with a 7.5-inch blade honed to razor sharpness. Grimaldi made do with a six-inch Italian switchblade, basic black.

"Reminds me of the old home neighborhood," he said, wearing a crooked grin.

With pistol shoulder rigs and other stray accessories, the price was staggering—at least, in Paraguayan currency. Bolan paid up in one-hundred-thousand guaraní banknotes, significantly lightening his roll, but leaving plenty for their travel and emergencies. Bidding the tractor man farewell, they lugged four heavy duffel bags back to their rented Hyundai Accent.

"Next stop?" Grimaldi asked, when he was at the wheel.

"Lay of the land," Bolan replied.

Ciudad del Este was Paraguay's second-largest city and capital of the Alto Paraná Department. It was a chaotic, crowded place, hosting thousands of foreign tourists per year. Visitors were drawn by counterfeit Viagra, exotic pets, pirated CDs or DVDs, and weapons like the stash riding in the backseat of Bolan's rental.

None of that had drawn the Executioner to Ciudad del Este.

He was looking for specific men, and he had payback on his mind.

BOLAN'S TARGETS HAD chosen Paraguay for its place on the Triple Frontier. The name referred to a tri-border region where the Iguazú and Paraná rivers converged, bringing Paraguay into kissing contact with neighbors Argentina and Brazil. The US State Department claimed, with evidence to back it up, that thousands of Lebanese inhabiting the region funneled cash to terrorist groups including al-Qaeda, Hezbollah, Islamic Jihad and Egypt's al-Gama'a al-Islamiyya. That was possible, in part, because Paraguay, for all its pious claims of dedication to the war on terrorism, had no laws against financing foreign insurrectionary groups. Such laws as did exist, meanwhile, were hamstrung by the country's rank political corruption and its weak judicial system

The men Bolan was hunting were among the world's most wanted fugitives. *Un*wanted might have been a better way to phrase it, since no country publicly supported them or made them welcome as official refugees. The FBI had placed three-million-dollar bounties on their heads, sixteen in all, for a payday of forty-eight million if someone could bring them together in one place, then blow the whistle.

So far, there'd been no takers.

Bolan didn't hunt for money, and his lead to Paraguay had come around the hard way, through concerted effort and relentless digging, biometric facial recognition software and the spiteful word of an informer who had lost his woman to a fugitive's seductive charm. In

Washington, there'd been discussion of a covert military op—deploying navy SEALs, maybe a killer drone—but either one could backfire, big-time, in the theater of bitter politics. Americans had come so far from a consensus on the simplest things that no one cared to risk an act of war in South America.

Enter the Executioner.

"Are we firm on this address?" Grimaldi asked, wheeling the Hyundai along Calle Victor Hugo Norte, less than a quarter-mile west of the Rio Paraná and the Brazilian frontier.

"They were confirmed here yesterday," Bolan replied. "Hanging with Hezbollah."

"A meeting of the minds?"

"Or something."

Hezbollah was well entrenched along the Triple Frontier, collaborating with similar groups on occasion, skirmishing with them when tempers flared over logistics or fine points of Muslim doctrine. They were Shi'ites, modestly labeled the Party of God, and if a person bought that one, he or she might also believe that Jesus smiled upon the Ku Klux Klan.

One thing about extremists, Bolan had discovered during years of hunting them. Most could be flexible enough to deal with kindred souls of alternate persuasions in the short-term, if it profited both sides.

Sometimes, like now.

The target was a former tenement that Hezbollah had purchased from its slumlord owner for a song, assisted by the standard offer he couldn't refuse, then remodeled into two-bedroom apartments with a storefront office at street level, serving double duty as a mosque and faith-based charity soliciting donations on behalf of Middle

Eastern refugees. The mosque preached war against the West; the money donated for displaced persons went, in fact, to Hezbollah's war chest. As for the eighteen apartments, six to a floor, they housed members of Hezbollah and anyone they favored with accommodations for a stopover.

How many gunmen could a two-bedroom apartment hold? Plenty.

Say, four on average, and the total was over seventy. If they were really crowded in, it could be double that, without counting the mosque and office space downstairs.

A simple way would be to bring the whole place down. Strategic high-explosive charges, detonated simultaneously or in swift succession, could collapse the building with all hands inside, ensuring that they didn't live to fight another day. It was effective but completely indiscriminate.

And Bolan needed to be sure that certain targets were included when he made his sweep.

Three names, three faces were to be scratched off Bolan's list. But first, he needed further leads to their associates, directions to wherever they had burrowed in, waiting to surface once the present storm had passed.

None of the men he hunted would be likely to cooperate. Bolan took that for granted and had come prepared— both physically and mentally—to do whatever might be necessary. Torture wasn't something he condoned or trusted, having seen men lie outrageously to stop the pain, say anything their tormentors desired to make it end.

But the flip side of that was his determination not to take "no" for an answer.

"Ready?" Bolan asked.

Grimaldi nodded, then answered, "As I'll ever be."

GRIMALDI WAS READY for damn near anything. He hadn't flown forty-seven hundred miles to sit on the sidelines and watch Bolan do all the work, or to gripe about odds that were stacked against them. That was the name of the game as he'd learned years ago, when Bolan had snatched him out of his old life—long story—and set Grimaldi on a new path unexpectedly.

For the better, sure, but not without risks.

And what was life without risk?

Their plan was relatively simple when they'd sketched it: breeze in through the building's office space and make their way upstairs from there, in broad daylight, three specific faces foremost in their minds while they were taking out the trash. Spare one or more of those until they could be squeezed for information, preferably at another site, removed from what was bound to be a bloodbath. When a plan like that was put into practice, though, there was a tendency for things to go to hell.

The good news: everyone inside the building should be hard-core Hezbollah, except the trio at the top of Bolan's hit list. Once they got inside, it was a free-fire zone, no quarter asked or offered, and their sole constraint was time. How long before police arrived to intervene, assuming that they came at all?

The Paraguayan National Police had roughly 22,000 officers nationwide, spread over 157,000 square miles of city and jungle, riding herd on nearly seven million citizens, plus tourists, drifters and the like. Police might show up at a crime scene late or not at all, depending on the victims' status in society.

With Hezbollah involved, who knew what might go down?

Grimaldi double-checked his submachine gun, with its casket magazine containing fifty 9 mm Parabellum rounds. The Spectre M4 had a double-action trigger, which allowed the safety to be disengaged without a risk of accidental firing under any normal circumstances, and a shrouded barrel to facilitate cooling. He'd have to watch it, or the cyclic rate of fourteen rounds per second would devour a magazine in nothing flat. But Grimaldi had used the gun before and liked its feel, its firepower and its reliability. The suppressor he had screwed on to its threaded muzzle would prevent the gun from climbing in full-auto mode, as well as muffling the racket that it made.

Rain had begun to drizzle, which was normal for the tropics, handy for the lightweight raincoats Grimaldi and Bolan wore to hide their weapons as they moved along the sidewalk toward their target. Hezbollah had no men on the street that the Stony Man pilot could see, and there was no sign of surveillance cameras around the entrance to their ground-floor offices.

Apparently, they felt secure enough in Paraguay to drop their guard a bit.

Strike one.

The door, all glass, allowed a clear view of the office—or at least its front reception area—from where Grimaldi stood outside. There was a young guy sitting at a desk, directly opposite the door, with no one else in sight. He might be armed, but at the moment he was busy talking on the phone, half turned in profile to the street, oblivious.

Strike two.

When Bolan gave the door a push, it opened at his touch.

Strike three.

A little chime went off as Bolan entered, with Grimaldi on his heels. No doubt it was supposed to warn whoever occupied the office that they had a walk-in, and it brought the young guy's frowning face around in time to see two silenced weapons pointed at him. Blurting something in Arabic, he dropped the phone and shoved a hand into the knee well of his desk, maybe for a weapon or a panic button hidden under there.

He never made it.

Bolan's Steyr AUG coughed out a single round and granted the Hezbollah's receptionist the martyrdom he may have dreamed about when he signed on to be a terrorist. The exit wound sprayed abstract art across a filing cabinet behind him, and he slithered out of sight beneath the desk.

ABDULLAH RAJHID WAS tired of being cooped up in the small apartment, only seeing sunshine through his window or on those occasions when his hosts allowed him access to the building's roof. He understood that he and his two roommates were on every watch list in the world, their faces posted on the internet with prices on their heads, but he was sick and tired of hiding.

He was sick and tired of Paraguay.

Sitting on a sway-backed sofa in his underwear, Rajhid ticked off the things that irritated him about the country he'd been sent to as a fugitive.

The weather. He was used to heat, of course, but Paraguay's humidity was killing him. It sapped his energy and made him feel exhausted from the moment he awoke each morning to the final hour when he dragged himself to bed.

The insects. He had lived with desert scorpions and spiders all his life, and cockroaches, but those in Paraguay were monsters, grown unnaturally large, and they could turn up anywhere. Just yesterday, he'd found a black, five-inch scorpion hiding beneath his pillow when he went to bed, a shock that left him wondering if one of his so-called protectors might have placed it there to rattle him.

And Hezbollah. That was another thing. Its members, with their clique in Paraguay, had treated Rajhid almost like a leper from the moment he arrived with Walid Khamis and Salman Farsoun. It was as if they thought their little private army was the only group entitled to make war on the Crusaders in the name of God. Rajhid wrote it off to jealousy, but he resented being forced to smile and thank them for their hospitality. The war was going on without him, and he wanted to get back to it.

The food. Now, there was one thing Rajhid did enjoy. They all avoided pork, of course, but he was very fond of *pira caldo*, Paraguay's fish soup; the great *asado* barbecues; the *kiveve* made from pumpkins; and the *lampreado*, fried cakes made with manioc. Rajhid had put on weight since landing at the hideout, but he tried to keep it down with exercise, the only form of entertainment granted to him, other than a television set that played three channels, none of which he understood.

He hoped Khalid would reach out to them soon. Rajhid and his companions needed *action*, not the world's worst-ever tropical vacation, locked up in an apartment and eaten by mosquitoes, while they never even got to glimpse the rain forest.

Khamis was snoring in one of the apartment's two bedrooms, while Farsoun was in the small bathroom, door closed for privacy. Rajhid was field-stripping a MAC-10 machine pistol, its components spread out on a coffee table just in front of him, and watching a peculiar game show, where the losers had their heads shaved to remind them they had failed. It was pathetic, childish and—

The first shot startled Rajhid, brought him to his feet in an involuntary reflex, clutching the MAC-10's dismantled, useless pistol grip. He waited, thought perhaps someone had fumbled with a weapon, had a stupid accident—with Hezbollah, why not?—but then a blast of automatic fire rang through the building and he heard men's panicked voices shouting.

The police? A US Navy SEAL team, just for him?

Rajhid had no time to consider who might be attacking them. He called out to his comrades while he tried to reassemble the MAC-10, his fingers as thick and numb as sausages in his excitement.

Fear? Not yet.

As soon as he was finished with the gun, he had to get dressed. Rajhid could not go running through the streets of Ciudad del Este in his underwear, with a machine pistol. Police in Paraguay might be slow and foolish, but they would not miss a chance to get their faces in the newspapers.

The last part of his weapon finally snapped into place. More firing came from the second or third floor, below him, as Rajhid snatched up a magazine, then loaded and cocked the little SMG. Now all he needed was a pair of pants, his shoes and one of those baggy shirts that everybody seemed to wear in Paraguay, hiding a multitude of sins.

And once he'd dressed, Rajhid could figure out whether to join the fight or run and leave his hosts to save themselves.

CLEARING THE DOWNSTAIRS rooms required less than a minute. The office, mosque and two small bathrooms were the whole of it, and all unoccupied except for Hezbollah's late greeter in the lobby. The corpse was out of sight of anybody passing on the street, positioned beneath the desk, and they were set to take the game upstairs.

And upstairs it would be, specifically between the empty mosque and office space. The building had no elevator, meaning that anyone trying to flee the upper floors had to either fight his way past Bolan and Grimaldi, or go out the nearest window.

The Stony Man duo reached the second floor without encountering a problem, but it started to unravel there. The landing faced back toward Calle Victor Hugo Norte, three apartments on each side of a narrow hallway. Three doors open, three closed. Just as Bolan reached that landing, a bearded young man in a T-shirt and khaki pants, barefooted, stepped out of the second door down, to his left.

The terrorist saw them, saw their guns, and blinked once in surprise before he turned and lunged for the open doorway just behind him. Bolan beat him to it with a 3-round burst of 5.56 mm NATO rounds, punching the rag doll figure sideways, slamming him against the doorjamb on his way down to the floor.

The AUG's suppressor wasn't perfect, but it reduced the sound of gunfire to a kind of stutter-sneeze. Bolan moved forward, leaving his partner to cover the closed doors behind him while he cleared the first open apartment on his left. He stepped across the dead man on the threshold, checked the other rooms in nothing flat, and found them all unoccupied.

His next step was to double back and join Grimaldi for the two apartments he had bypassed, not surprised to find them both unlocked in what the occupants would have regarded as a safe environment. He barged in unannounced and uninvited, caught two more Hezbollah terrorists sitting on a sofa, eating pita sandwiches, and shot them both before they could react to the invasion of their home away from home.

Behind him, Bolan heard the muffled stutter of Grimaldi's SMG, ending another argument before it had a chance to start in earnest. Seconds later, the Stony Man pilot was back beside him in the hallway, nodding, turning toward the next door that stood open, on their right.

This time, they heard a shower running. Bolan went to find it, leaving Grimaldi to guard the open doorway and the last two apartments downrange. The bathroom wasn't hard to locate in a place that small, its door ajar, and Bolan eased his way inside. Behind a semi-opaque shower curtain, he saw two forms intertwined, both men, unless the women sprouted beards in Paraguay.

To each his own, in Bolan's view—but this was strictly business. He preferred to give an opponent a fighting chance, but in this case it was a no go.

Six rounds did it, ripping through the shower curtain to find flesh and bone, spilling two bodies on to the tiled floor. One was a man approaching middle age, the other younger, neither one concerned about embarrassment now that their time had suddenly run out.

He left the shower running—put it on Hezbollah's tab—and met up with Grimaldi in the corridor, to clear the last two apartments. Bolan would never know what had alerted one guy in the next apartment, to their right, but he was waiting with an AK-47, ripping off a hasty burst just as his door began to open under Bolan's touch.

The Russian rifle's 7.62 mm rounds were more than capable of piercing flimsy drywall, driving Bolan and Grimaldi to the floor. Instead of making it a siege, Bolan unclipped one of the frag grenades he'd fastened to his belt, removed its pin and pitched the bomb through the doorway, counting five seconds on its fuse. It blew on four, a foible common to that particular model, and he waited for the shrapnel storm to pass before he checked the apartment again and found his adversary facedown in a pool of gore.

No time to waste now, as they ran back to the stairs and stormed the third floor, ready for resistance from the Hezbollah terrorists remaining, meeting it almost at once. It was a tricky proposition, fighting for your life *and* watching out for three specific faces, knowing it was critical to capture one of them alive.

A challenge, right—but nothing unfamiliar to the Executioner.

CHAPTER TWO

Arlington, Virginia, Two Days Earlier

The punks were either soused or high on something, Hal Brognola guessed, noting their ruddy faces, sloppy walks and random slurring of their too-loud comments as they made obnoxious asses of themselves. They'd gotten an early start on getting wasted, since it wasn't half past ten yet, and the four of them were well en route to being comfortably numb.

Skinheads. He knew the low-life type from long experience. They'd failed in school and couldn't hold a job, assuming that they'd ever tried to find one, left their home or had been thrown out when Nazi tats and rants had riled their parents to the point of no return. Or maybe they'd been raised by homegrown fascists and had followed in their elders' goose steps.

Either way, Brognola saw them as a waste of space, and not at all what he'd expected to encounter at the Ballston Common Mall, on Wilson Boulevard. All members of the public were welcome, of course, to the four-level, 580,000-square-foot mini-city with its hundreds of shops, salons, cafés and other offerings, but most of those who patronized the mall upheld a certain standard of decorum.

Not these guys.

They had a dress code, sure, all four of them in jet-black bomber jackets decorated with the symbols of their rage, from swastikas and SS lightning bolts to Celtic crosses, Rebel flags and the distinctive blood drop crosses favored by the Ku Klux Klan. Beneath the jackets, they wore suspenders over black tees decorated with more neo-Nazi "art," tight jeans with metal-studded belts—a guy just couldn't always trust suspenders in a street fight—and red laces in their black boots.

It was a uniform of sorts that marked them as outsiders—or, in the alternative, *in*siders of a small, supposedly "elite" subculture most Americans were happy to ignore until it pushed into their faces and demanded equal time.

Like now.

Brognola had been hoping they would pass him, standing alone and minding his own business at the second-level railing, near the food court. As a rule, he didn't make a likely target for the random predators who scavenged urban landscapes. He was stocky, had an aging cop's face and an attitude toward strangers that made most think twice about disturbing him.

Not this time.

Maybe these four punks believed the line about safety in numbers. Or maybe they were just too wasted to care.

"Hey, Grandpa," one of them called out as they approached him. "Got a light?"

The big Fed figured silence wouldn't be the way to go this time. He turned to face them, saw them fanning out into a semicircle as he said, "No smoking in the mall."

"Ain't what I asked you, is it?"

Their elected spokesman was a burly specimen whose forehead bore the inked slogan "RAHOWA": *Racial Holy War.*

Brognola locked eyes with him as he answered, "No."

"So, do you got a light, or not?"

The Justice man scanned the other grinning, slack-jawed faces, then said, "No."

"Is that all you can say, man? 'No?'"

The second speaker would have been a redhead if he'd let it grow a little. As it was, the stubble only made his scalp look sunburned, serving as a background for the swastika tattoo on top of his shaved pate.

"I could say, 'Move along,'" Brognola offered.

That made two of them break out in laughter, while their leader and the almost-redhead eyed him with suspicion bleeding into fury. They were used to having people cringe before them, but it wasn't working out that way, this time.

"There's sumpin' wrong wid you," the leader said, and tapped his temple with an index finger. "Sumpin' wrong up here."

"Johns Hopkins, was it?" Brognola asked him. "Or maybe Georgetown? I'm surprised you found a med school that would let you in, with all that sloppy ink."

He was pushing the limit now, but punks like these had always ranked among his top pet peeves. Bullies were made for beating down, not coddling.

"Man, you gotta have a death wish," RAHOWA-face said. A thought surfaced inside his tiny mind. "Are you a Jew?"

"Are you a cretin?" Brognola replied. The four of them were close, but he still reckoned he could reach the Glock 23 on his hip before one of them punched him or landed a kick to his groin with a spit-polished boot. Bad news if it came down to that, but the big Fed had too much on his mind to suffer morons gladly.

"Man, you're askin' for it," Red Fuzz said. "I oughta—"

But he never finished, as a deep voice just behind him asked, "Is there a problem here?"

"I HAD IT COVERED," Brognola said. "They weren't going anywhere."

"I saw that," Bolan granted. "But I thought about the paperwork, the wasted time."

Brognola mulled that over, frowning, then agreed. "Who needs it?"

"Right."

They'd gone to Charley's Grilled Subs, once the four skinheads had gotten a glimpse of Bolan's graveyard eyes and figured out that two-on-four wasn't such inviting odds. He had a deli sub in front of him, with fries, while Hal was working on a Philly chicken hero.

"So, the mission," Bolan prompted.

"Right," Brognola said again. "I guess you've heard about the consulate in Jordan?"

"It's been hard to miss."

"Behind the politics, what hasn't been on CNN or Fox is the ID on those responsible."

"Already?" Bolan was impressed. "That's quick work."

"They left tracks—and two dead at the scene. The consulate's Marines got in a few licks."

"Semper fi," Bolan replied. "Who were they?"

"Members of a relatively new group," Brognola replied, chewing around the words. "It's called *Allah Qadum* in Arabic, or 'God's Hammer' to the likes of us. It split off from the AQAP roughly eighteen months ago."

Al-Qaeda in the Arabian Peninsula, that was, a splinter group itself, founded in January 2009 by defectors from the group that had masterminded 9/11 and assorted other horrors. One thing that predictably retarded global terrorism was the tendency of psychopaths to quarrel among themselves and storm out in a huff to form their own demented fragments of a parent group.

"So, it was organized?" Bolan asked. "All I've heard has been the stuff about that yokel burning the Koran."

"They saw an opening," Brognola answered, "thanks to Reverend Redneck. They'd have turned up somewhere, someday, but his sideshow gave them the jump start they needed. Nothing on par with the World Trade Centers, of course, but it put them on the map. They'll be looking to build on it, make a name for themselves and claim a seat at the table."

"What table?"

"Wherever the nuts meet and greet," Brognola replied.

"You said a couple of them didn't make it out."

"Correct. Jordan's General Security Directorate identified them from their rap sheets and drew up a list of known associates. CIA and Saudi intelligence put their two cents in, and some files turned up at Interpol. We now have sixteen names confirmed as God's Hammer members still at large."

"All present at the consulate?" Bolan asked.

"Hard to say, but probable. The whole bunch was in Jordan before the raid, and now they've scattered. Globally, we think."

"You *think*."

The big Fed took another bite of Philly chicken, chewed it, swallowed part of it and said, "You know how that goes. Whispers in the wind from NSA and anybody else who's listening. As of two days ago, we *know* three members of the gang are in Paraguay."

"That's some commute," Bolan observed.

"It's relatively safe," Brognola said. "We've had an extradition treaty with the government there since March 2001, but you know how that goes in South America. They talk tough on terrorism, and they crack down hard on anyone who threatens their control, but when it comes to foreign groups, they've got no statutes on the books. Their courts are as crooked as they come. We need chapter and verse to push an extradition through on narcotrafficking, much less something they view as foreign politics."

Bolan trimmed it to the bottom line. "They need retrieving, or elimination."

"Either one suits me, but here's the problem. When I say we have a fix on three, that means the other thirteen goons are in the wind. They could be anywhere from Marrakesh to Malibu by now, and burrowed deep. We figure their three pals in Paraguay will have some means of reaching out, but if they all go down without a chance to talk..."

Brognola left it hanging there.

Bolan saw the problem now, and it was not a pretty one.

"I'll take it," he told the big Fed. "But I need more intel."

Brognola slid a thumb drive in a paper sleeve across their little table. "That's got everything we know, so far, but we can run it down right now."

Bolan reached out and made the thumb drive disappear. "Okay," he said. "Before you start, though, if we're going global, I may need some backup."

"Anyone in mind?" Brognola asked.

"Just Jack."

Miami, Florida

THE CELL PHONE's buzzing caught Jack Grimaldi with a pint of Guinness at his lips, a plate of fish and chips in front of him, inside an Irish pub on South Miami Avenue. He recognized the number, took a sip and let it ring once more, then picked up.

"Hey, what's happening?" he asked.

"You busy?" Mack Bolan inquired.

"Just having lunch."

"I mean the next few days."

Grimaldi smiled. "I've got a window, if there's something going on."

"There is."

"Details?"

"We'd have to scramble it."

"Wait one," Grimaldi said. He had a special app to handle that, engaged with one keystroke while Bolan set up on his end.

"Okay," Grimaldi said. "Ready."

Bolan ran down the basic details, adding new twists to the foreign news that had been dominating every channel on the TV in Grimaldi's hotel room for the past week. The Stony Man pilot felt his pulse rate quicken. He took another sip of beer, then set down his glass.

"So, Paraguay," he said, when the Executioner was done.

"It's all we've got right now," Bolan replied.

"Someplace I've never been. Still Nazis down there, are they?"

"That was Stroessner. He was overthrown a while ago, but his party still runs things. They impeached a president in 2012 for not cracking down hard enough on the Left. Replaced him with a guy who spent ten years running a soccer club. The DEA claims he's connected to the drug trade."

"Sounds like they could use a visit," Grimaldi said.

"Only for the fugitives, this time around," Bolan reminded him.

"Too bad. Three guys, you said?"

"Hopefully giving us directions to the rest."

"You know me. I can be persuasive."

"So, you're in?"

"I wouldn't miss it. What's our estimated time of departure?"

"As soon as you can get up here to Arlington."

Grimaldi did the calculations in his head. There was drive time from the pub to Opa-locka Executive Airport, eleven miles north of downtown Miami, then the prep and clearance for takeoff. He guesstimated flight time from OEA to Arlington in his Piper Seneca, cruising speed 216 miles per hour, then the rituals of landing at Ronald Reagan National Airport.

"Six hours, minimum. I'll call you if they tie me up too long with paperwork."

"That's Reagan?"

"Right."

"I'll see you there," Bolan replied, and he was gone.

The Sarge had never been the chatty type, a trait Grimaldi had appreciated from the day they met. Their hookup had been strange, perhaps unique—a kidnapping, in fact, Grimaldi on the hostage end of it—but it had given the pilot a new life. Maybe *saved* his life, although the new one was a hectic roller-coaster ride of peril.

Fun, though, in a demented kind of way, once you had settled in and got into the spirit of the thing.

The bonus, in Grimaldi's case, was knowing that he sometimes made a difference. He'd gone from being part of the problem—a see-nothing, hear-nothing syndicate flyboy—to playing on the side of the angels.

No, scratch that. He would never be an angel, and the jobs he did for Stony Man, with or without Mack Bolan, sure as hell wouldn't strike most folks as angelic. He was still outside the law, but with a twist, pursuing bad guys who had been *above* the law so long, they thought they were invincible. He'd hated bullies from the time he was the shortest kid in kindergarten class, until he'd learned to take a punch and give back three or four for every one received.

Grimaldi thought about the next few days, unsure when he would have another chance to eat, and finished off the plate in front of him. He quaffed the beer and pushed his empty back. "Another?" the barkeep asked.

"Wish I could," Grimaldi told him, lifting off his bar stool. "But I have to fly."

Ronald Reagan National Airport

WAITING FOR JACK GRIMALDI, with nowhere else to go, Bolan picked out a reasonably isolated seat in Terminal A and settled in to review Hal Brognola's files. The thumb drive held a total of nineteen, one titled "AQ/AH," the remainder bearing what he took for Arabic surnames.

Bolan started with the file on God's Hammer, skimming over what he'd already learned from the big Fed about the group's roots and creation. It was a splinter of a splinter, descended from Osama bin Laden's al-Qaeda by way of the "subordinate" AQAP, active mainly in Yemen and Saudi Arabia. The parent organizations were dominated by Salafi Muslims—also called Wahhabis—who, in turn, comprised a subdivision of the Sunni sect. Bolan wasn't interested in Islam's doctrinal rifts, any more than he was by the multitude of self-styled Christian denominations, but he focused on Salafist jihadism preached by al-Qaeda and its descendants.

Bottom line: they were at war with Israel and the "decadent" West, especially that "Great Satan," Uncle Sam. Whatever they could do to hurt their enemies, from bombing navy ships in port to 9/11, Salafist jihadists were ready to go.

And if they died in that pursuit, well, hello Paradise: ripe fruit in shady gardens, bottomless goblets of wine with no hangovers, dark-eyed virgins galore to serve a martyr's every need.

Why not go out in one great blaze of glory for the cause?

God's Hammer had made its debut with the consulate attack in Jordan, and lost two fighters in the process. Stony Man or someone else had managed to identify the dead as a twenty-three-year-old Egyptian, Djer Badawi, and a nineteen-year-old Saudi, Sulaiman Waleed. Waleed had been a rookie, more or less, arrested once during a protest in Riyadh. Badawi was—make that *had been*— a veteran of the Muslim Brotherhood and al-Qaeda, suspected of participating in Alexandria's al-Qidiseen church bombing that killed twenty-one Coptic Christians in 2011. He'd been living off the grid since then, and clearly up to no good.

Those two were dead now, and no longer Bolan's problem. Moving through the other file as Brognola had numbered them, he came first to another Saudi, Saleh Kabeer, recognized as the founder and leader of God's Hammer.

He was thirty-seven years old, a Salafi jihadist from way back, the black sheep of a wealthy family who served the House of Saud without regrets. Kabeer had jumped the traces, following in bin Laden's footsteps as a rebel who rejected his inheritance and chose the path of war over a life of luxury.

Or so he said, at any rate. Brognola's dossier revealed that Saleh Kabeer had founded God's Hammer with a start-up contribution from his kinfolk, petro-dollars he had spent while posing as an enemy of any commerce with Crusaders from the West. Hypocrisy was nothing new, of course, and none of those who joined God's Hammer appeared to mind Kabeer's personal brand.

Kabeer's number two was a fellow Saudi, twenty-two-year-old Mohammed Sanea. He didn't share his leader's gold-plated background but came by his radicalism the old-fashioned way, after his father served three years in prison for his role in founding Saudi Arabia's National Society for Human Rights. Perhaps ironically, that hadn't turned him against his homeland's rigid Islamic monarchy, but rather against the "Western parasites" who propped it up with billions for oil and foreign aid. Suspected of leading terrorist raids from Yemen, Sanea had survived a US drone strike in 2013 and came back more rabid than ever.

Other known members of God's Hammer, still at large after the raid in Jordan, included four Palestinians, four Jordanians, two more Saudis, two Syrians, one Lebanese and one Egyptian. Bolan read their bios, noted their affiliation with various terrorist groups, drifting into al-Qaeda and on from there to God's Hammer as their views became more radical over time. All were relatively young men, ranging in age from nineteen to thirty. All but two

were named in outstanding warrants from their home-
lands or neighboring countries, circulated by Interpol
and Europol.

Sixteen mad dogs, and Bolan only knew where three
of them were hiding. He'd have to do better than that, and
quickly, before they could regroup and try to top their
first outing for mayhem and publicity.

Why not? He only had to search the whole damned
world.

"What are we flying south?" Grimaldi asked, once
he was on the ground at Reagan, with his Piper battened
down for the duration.

"Hal's got something waiting for us, subject to your
signing off on it," Bolan replied.

"Close by?"

"A couple hundred yards that way," Bolan said, pointing to the west.

"Let's check it out."

They walked across the tarmac to a hangar labeled
Bellair Charters, where an Eclipse 500 microjet sat waiting for them. "Not bad," Grimaldi offered as they did a
walk-around. "A service ceiling of forty-one thousand
feet, maximum range of 1,295 miles and a top speed of
425 miles per hour. That's five refueling stops before we
land in Paraguay. I'm thinking Dallas, Oaxaca, Mexico,
Panama City over the Gulf, Canaima, Venezuela, Alta
Floresta, Brazil, then on to Asunción. A lot of stops, but
it's the best this little bird can do."

"How long?" Bolan asked.

"Air time, about eleven hours. Ground time, messing
with the locals?" Grimaldi considered it and shook his
head. "Your guess would be as good as mine."

"No time to waste, then," Bolan said. "The sooner we're airborne, the better."

"Roger that. I'll start the preflight check right now, then have a chat with the tower."

Bolan left Grimaldi to it. He wasn't happy with the time lag between takeoff and their final touchdown in Paraguay. If something spooked the people he was hunting in the meantime, he could miss them altogether and be back to square one, hoping Stony Man could run them down again.

And if they couldn't, he'd be waiting for the next attack, like everybody else.

But that was unacceptable. Failure was not an option for the Executioner.

The plague of terrorism was as old as humankind. It could not be eradicated, only held at bay, until such time as fundamental change in human nature was achieved. So far, in Bolan's lifetime, there had been no sign of that occurring. Planet Earth still needed soldiers standing watch against the predators who populated so-called "civilized" society, taking advantage of the weak and hopeless for their own ends, masked by politics, religion, pick your poison.

In his idle hours, few as they might be, Bolan sometimes philosophized about a world without atrocities, devoid of greed and cruelty, hatred, discrimination and suspicion. He would never live to see it—no one would, in fact—because the human animal was deeply and irrevocably flawed.

Men craved what they could not afford, what they had no right to possess. When frustrated in their pursuit of *more*, they turned on those presumably obstructing them. Some humans learned to channel greed and hatred into lucrative careers in various fields. Others sated their greed through commerce, raping the environment with utter disregard for future generations. Altruists, when they appeared, were such a novelty that they were usually murdered, canonized as saints or both.

The bottom line: there were no angels, and no demons. Every man and woman on the planet was an individual, resisting or surrendering to baser instincts as they passed through life, taking it one day at a time. Some gave free rein to their desires, and in the process jeopardized communities, whole nations, or the world at large.

When those predators stood beyond the reach of ordinary law, they had to be curbed by extraordinary force.

Enter the Executioner, commissioned to continue with a job he'd started on his own, without official sanction, to repay a private debt of blood. He kept on fighting now because he could, because somebody *had to* if "polite" society was going to survive.

That meant confronting human monsters where they lived and preyed on others weaker than themselves. It meant destroying them, scorching the earth to stall— where he could not prevent—another monster rising in their place.

The war, he realized, could not be won. It was a holding action, not some grand crusade.

Bolan would occupy the firing line as long as he was able. After that...

He hoped that someone would rise to grab the torch.

CHAPTER THREE

Ciudad del Este, Paraguay

Bolan had reached the fourth floor and still had not seen any of the God's Hammer fugitives among the men he and Grimaldi had put down so far. This was the last floor left to check, and he'd begun to worry that they might have slipped the net—or, at the very least, gone shopping, out to get a meal, whatever, and eluded him by sheer coincidence.

Not good.

Before they rushed the final set of apartments, Bolan huddled with Grimaldi on the stairwell. Just above and to their left, he heard the last defenders talking excitedly and priming their weapons, maybe trying to decide if they should rush the stairs or dig in for a last-ditch fight.

"It's getting dicey now," he told Grimaldi, almost whispering. "The guys we're after could be here, but if they're not—"

The Stony Man pilot saw where he was going and finished for him. "Then we need to bag somebody who can tell us when they left and where they went."

"Right," Bolan said. "I'd like to take one down but leave him breathing so we can question him, but don't take any chances. Still take care of Number One."

Grimaldi flashed a grin. "Which one of us is Number One?"

"Ready?" Bolan asked him.

"Set."

Bolan eased up and pitched the frag grenade that he'd been holding while they talked, a blind toss down the narrow hallway. Four-point-something seconds later it exploded, filling the corridor with smoke and dust.

One guy was down and out, sprawled in the middle of the hallway, leaking from at least a dozen shrapnel wounds. A couple others staggered through the battle mist, approaching Bolan in a daze, but neither of their faces rang a bell from Brognola's portfolio of God's Hammer fugitives. The Executioner dropped both of them with one round each and moved on, searching.

First door on his left, ajar. He ducked and nudged it open, ready for a burst of autofire, but it was vacant, no one hiding underneath the bed or in the tiny bathroom. Doubling back, he heard Grimaldi's muffled SMG responding to a challenge from the Hezbollah gunners and went to join him on the firing line.

Grimaldi had already cleared the rooms directly opposite, then run into a roadblock from the second flat in line, off to the right. At least one terroriat was battened down in there, firing short bursts from a Kalashnikov without putting much effort into aiming. So far, he had strafed the ceiling and the walls to either side, while Grimaldi lay prone out in the hallway, waiting for a shot.

Bolan got there ahead of him, his different perspective granting him an early crack at the defender. Three rounds from the Steyr chewed his adversary's face off—not a face he recognized—and dumped him back across the threshold of the last room he would ever occupy.

Grimaldi bolted to his feet and cleared the apartment,

while Bolan took the next one on his left. He saw no further movement in the hallway, no signs of continuing resistance, but they'd have to go the whole route, checking every room and closet, just in case.

Unless…

There was no one in the apartment, but on a whim, he checked the window, the first one he'd seen standing open yet, despite the building's air-conditioning. A fire escape was bolted to the wall outside, and down below, three men were running toward the far end of an alley lined with garbage bins. One of them paused long enough to glance back at the room he'd lately vacated, and Bolan made his face.

Salman Farsoun, one of the three he'd come to find in Ciudad del Este.

"Jack!" he shouted, through the empty rooms. "Outside! They're bailing!"

The Stony Man pilot was in the doorway, following, when Bolan clambered through the window and began his steep rush down the fire escape.

ABDULLAH RAJHID WAS SLOWING, almost at the alley's mouth with cars and foot traffic beyond, when Salman Farsoun overtook him, blurting out, "I've seen them!"

"Seen who?" Rajhid asked him without stopping, without looking backward.

"The Crusaders! One of them, at least."

"Then he's seen you," Rajhid replied. "Come on!"

Walid Khamis was already ahead of them, shoving his Micro Uzi underneath his baggy shirt. Rajhid did likewise with his MAC-10, hoping Farsoun could do something with the larger MP-5 K submachine gun he carried.

The sounds of battle from the building they'd abandoned were already drawing notice. Rajhid did not fancy jogging down the boulevard with military weapons on display, alerting passersby to summon the police.

"He was a white man," Farsoun said, still going on about the fellow he'd seen or had imagined. "An American, perhaps."

Rahjid would never fully understand these Palestinians. Although himself a Saudi, he was well aware of how the Arab residents of Palestine had suffered since the state of Israel was created by outsiders from the West. Indeed, that had been the spark that lit the fuse on Rahjid's own jihad, but there was still something peculiar about soldiers such as Khamis and Farsoun. They suffered from excitability, erratic moods, and Rajhid found them easily distracted at important moments of an operation.

Now, for instance, when his mind was focused on escape, Farsoun wanted to talk about some man he'd seen—but why? To what result?

"Come on!" Rajhid repeated. "We can talk about it later."

"But—"

"Enough! Now hide that gun or leave it here!"

Farsoun lifted his shirt and shoved the MP-5 K underneath one armpit, lowering his arm to keep the weapon clamped against his side. Rajhid hoped he could keep it there, but had no plans to stay behind and help Farsoun if he got careless, drawing notice to himself.

The sidewalk they emerged on to was crowded, some people already slowing, peering down the alley toward the sounds of battle echoing along its length. Rajhid pushed through and past them. He might have warned

Khamis to slow his pace a bit, attempted to act more normal, but he didn't want the strangers passing by to put the two of them together.

One less thing for them to tell the police when they finally arrived.

And the police could turn up any moment, Rajhid realized. Then there could be gunfire, explosions, smoke and flames, for all he knew. The residents of Ciudad del Este were well acquainted with crime, but not with pitched battles fought in their midst.

Putting distance between himself and the scene, Rajhid spared a thought for whoever had raided the complex. Unlike Farsoun, he'd seen none of the raiders, therefore had no clue if they were locals or some kind of special unit from outside. The charm of Paraguay, for freedom fighters on the run, lay in its curious interpretation of what constituted terrorism. Any opposition to the ruling party was suppressed, but what a man did elsewhere—most particularly if his actions were directed against Jews and their supporters—might be overlooked, especially if cash changed hands.

But if the raid had been conducted by Crusaders, as Farsoun surmised, that would be something else.

Bin Laden had been slaughtered a US Navy SEAL team, at his lair in Pakistan, without a by-your-leave to the legitimate authorities. How many other heroes had been slain by rockets from a clear blue sky, triggered by hunters sitting in a bunker somewhere, half a world away?

Watching the traffic pass, alert for military or police vehicles, Rajhid wondered how the damned Crusaders could have found him here.

No matter.

For the moment, all he had to focus on was getting out alive.

THE ALLEY STANK, but that was par for any urban landscape in the tropics, where the seasons ranged from hot and damp to hot and soaking wet. The blacktop under Bolan's feet was old, but still felt tacky from the heat, as if it had been freshly laid. He was halfway to the alley's intersection with the street when Grimaldi dropped from the fire escape and started after him.

The runners he had glimpsed were gone, but they had turned left when they reached the street and Bolan went from there, tucking the AUG back underneath his raincoat, pausing long enough to let Grimaldi overtake him on the sidewalk.

"Farsoun was the one I recognized," he said. "That makes the others Khamis and Rajhid. Two wearing white shirts, one in red, all three in khaki trousers."

"Packing?" Grimaldi asked, while his eyes swept both sides of the street.

"Farsoun had something like an Ingram or a Micro Uzi. It was hard to tell. Assume they're loaded."

"There!" Grimaldi said, pointing as Bolan's eyes locked on to a red shirt, retreating through the flow of window shoppers. Even as he spoke, the man in the red shirt glanced backward, seeming to meet Bolan's gaze.

"Farsoun," he said. "Let's go."

Before they'd covered half a block, he saw the other two, moving ahead of Farsoun on the same side of the street. Rajhid and Khamis wasted no time looking back, perhaps afraid of what was gaining on them, maybe just intent on getting clear and finding someplace new to hide. Whatever, Bolan had them spotted now, and he was bent on stopping them before they had a chance to disappear.

That thought had barely formed when one of them, wearing a white shirt, separated from the others, darting into traffic like a *kamikaze* bent on suicide, ducking and dodging as he ran to reach the far side of the street.

"I'm on him," Grimaldi said, launching from the curb into a stream of steel and chrome, ignoring angry bleats from auto horns.

Instead of watching the pilot's progress, Bolan pursued the targets dressed in red and white. They weren't exactly running yet, but they were picking up the pace, anxious to clear the neighborhood before it swarmed with uniforms. Bolan had much the same idea himself, but couldn't bail before he'd caught at least one of the fugitives.

Or done his best to catch them, anyway.

In a scene like this, he knew there was a chance he could lose both of them, or else be forced to take them down without a chance to ask the vital questions. Given that choice, Bolan would prefer dead terrorists to killers still at large and plotting their next move.

Ahead of him, the runners reached a cross street; one of them said something to the other, then they broke in opposite directions. One guy peeled away to Bolan's left and out of sight around the corner, while his comrade bolted to the right, crossing against the light and nearly getting flattened by a taxi just before he reached the other curb.

There was no way to take the farthest runner down without endangering civilians and revealing he was armed. Bolan turned left and started running hard after the red shirt as its owner put on speed.

GRIMALDI WASN'T BIG, but he was fast. A mad dash through traffic with horns blaring at him, brakes screeching, had gotten his heart pumping. The shoulder-slung Spectre M4 slapped his ribs as he ran, until the Stony Man pilot clamped his right arm against it to stop the drumbeat. Every footfall sent a jolt along his spine and urged him to run faster.

Up ahead, his target—leaner, younger, desperate—had gained a lead on him and wasn't slowing. The guy had glanced back once, treating Grimaldi to a glimpse of a familiar bearded face, then started running as if his life depended on it.

Which, in fact, it did.

Crossing the street in mid-block took them to another alley and more stinking garbage bins, rats the size of puppies scurrying where trash had overflowed or simply been discarded carelessly. The ground beneath their feet was asphalt, not concrete, almost spongy in the heat with soft rain pattering. Grimaldi knew that they were eastbound, headed for another street crowded with traffic and pedestrians, cars parked at crazy angles, people shopping under awnings that, for some reason he couldn't grasp, were mostly blue.

It was the last place he would have chosen for a firefight.

If there was going to be gunplay—and Grimaldi didn't doubt it for a second—he would rather keep it in the alley, where he didn't have to fret about civilians wandering into the line of fire. The alley's distant mouth was problematic, open to the street for any shots downrange that missed their mark, but it was better than a dose of *Wild Bunch* action on a teeming thoroughfare.

The runner had to have thought so, too, because he

stopped abruptly, jerked some kind of stubby automatic weapon from his waistband, and cut loose at his pursuer from thirty yards. Grimaldi dodged behind a large garbage bin to his left, heard slugs plowing through blacktop and a few more rattling off the far end of the bin.

Whatever his intended mark was carrying, it had a rapid rate of fire—one of the MACs, perhaps, or one of the homegrown knock-offs. Whatever, it could slice and dice a man in nothing flat, the down side being that it burned through magazines like there was no tomorrow.

And if the Stony Man pilot's intended target blew his load on random fire, there wouldn't be.

At least, for him.

Grimaldi risked a peek around the bin, and his enemy unleashed another burst, cut short as he ran out of ammunition. Switching magazines took time—not much, but possibly enough—and Grimaldi broke toward the spot where he had seen his man duck out of sight, behind another rusty bin marked with gang graffiti.

It was going to be close, but if his luck held…

He was halfway to his destination when the wiry runner popped back into view, his weapon leveled from the hip. Grimaldi fired without a break in stride, a short burst meant to wound, but that was tricky from a stationary post, much less while sprinting. He saw bullets strike the target's shirt, crimson erupting through the white fabric, and then his guy was going down, wasting his fresh mag on a slash of open sky above the alley.

Grimaldi reached him, kicked his little SMG aside and crouched beside the dying terrorist. The pilot spoke English, Italian and a little Spanish, so he went with English first.

"You're dying," he informed the fallen gunman. "Do

your soul a favor while you can. Tell me where I can find your buddies from the raid in Jordan."

The shooter's eyes were fading in and out of focus with the pulse of blood from open lips. Grimaldi wasn't sure the guy could speak at all, but something came out, sounding like *"Elif air ab tizak!"* The way he smirked, despite his pain, told Grimaldi it hadn't been a compliment.

And then, he died.

ABDULLAH RAJHID WAS WINDED, but he could not stop to catch his breath. Two men had chased him from the four-story apartment building, along with Khamis and Farsoun. One of them had pursued Farsoun when he broke ranks and fled across the street, a panicked move that nonetheless had helped Rajhid by splitting up their enemies. He'd tried to do the same again—and save himself—by sending Khamis east while he turned west at the next intersection, but the ploy had failed.

He was alone now, with an enemy behind him, closing in.

The MAC-10 underneath his belt was chafing, gouging Rajhid, but he could not pull it out in public, running down the sidewalk with the weapon in his hand. That would be desperate, a last resort, and only useful if he had a chance to kill his adversary with the first rounds from his small machine pistol.

If he was forced to use the gun with witnesses around, it did not matter who else fell, as long as Rajhid dropped his man and ended the insane pursuit. Beyond that, if his past experience was any guide, a blaze of gunfire on a busy street would shock and terrorize most workaday pedestrians and buy Rajhid enough time to escape on foot.

Where would he go?

There was another place in Ciudad del Este, operated by Hezbollah, though his brethren might not be pleased to see him after what had just occurred at their so-called secure facility. Police were probably swarming around the shooting scene by now, exposing things that Rajhid's hosts would not appreciate.

It could be death, returning to their company—but at the moment, in this foreign land, he had no other choice.

Kill first, he thought. Then run and hide.

But first, if possible, he had to spot a likely murder site.

Not murder, he corrected. Self-defense.

He needed cover. Not a lot, but ample for a brief exchange of fire in case his first shots failed to do the trick. A drawn-out duel would be the death of him, no matter what his adversary's fate. With cell phones all around him, someone—*many* someones—would alert police, bringing them down on top of him with sirens whoop-whoop-whooping like demented banshees.

That would be the end. A martyr's death, of course, but not the one Rajhid envisioned for himself.

He still had plans for the *jihad*.

The cross street he had chosen was a kind of outdoor market, with stalls under awnings positioned outside stores. Its barely orchestrated chaos made him feel at home, reminding him of marketplaces where his mother used to shop, where he had run and played in childhood, still oblivious to all the perils of the world. Rajhid could pick out any stall and duck behind it for a moment, turn and—

Yes! the voice inside his head ordered. Stop wasting time!

MACK BOLAN SAW the changeup coming, read his target's body language when the runner nearly glanced behind his shoulder, then resisted at the final instant. Breaking to the right meant running into traffic, no percentage there, but there were stalls and stores along the whole block to his left.

And left it was, a pivot in midstride, and Rajhid of the red shirt dropped from sight. Bolan slowed but didn't halt his forward motion, just in case the Saudi had a bluff in mind, stalling pursuit with fear of gunfire, while he wriggled clear behind the outdoor stalls. It might have fooled somebody else, if that was what he had in mind, but not the Executioner.

Most definitely not this day, with so much riding on the line.

Bolan closed in at walking speed, ready to peel off left or right, depending on what happened in the next few seconds.

When it came, however, Bolan *was* surprised.

It started with a squeal. The woman selling used books from the stall where Rajhid had concealed himself let out the cry, as Rajhid sprang erect and whipped an arm around her throat, clutching her as a human shield. His weapon—a MAC-10 or MAC-11, unmistakable—was pressed against her head, its stubby muzzle in her ear. At that range, if Rajhid fired, he would blind himself with brain and bone fragments, but that would be no consolation to the woman he'd have killed.

Bolan already had the Steyr at his shoulder, half of Rajhid's face framed in the reticle of his integrated telescopic sight. Rajhid was stuck there, obviously knowing that the only way to hide his face completely was to lose sight of his enemy.

"Put down the gun and you can walk away from this," Bolan said, lying through his teeth.

"Put down *your* gun," Rajhid replied, "and you can—"

Bolan's bullet drilled Rajhid's forehead just above his right eye. The 5.56 mm bullet left a tidy entrance wound, then tumbled through the man's brain, yawing after it cleared the bony barrier of his frontal bone and found soft tissue. Dead before the impact registered, Rajhid slumped over backward, still clutching his female hostage as he fell.

Bolan was on the pair of them in nothing flat, released the woman from Rajhid's dead grasp and plucked the subgun from his other hand. No questions would be answered here, but Bolan did his best under the circumstances, patting Rajhid's several pockets, locating a compact satellite phone first and then a regular cell phone. He claimed both, then kept digging until he found a bulging wallet, while a group of cautious rubberneckers started edging closer.

Time to go.

Rising, he tucked the Steyr out of sight beneath his raincoat, left the stall with no attempt to hide his face and walked away. An alley beckoned to his left, and Bolan ducked in there, then sprinted down past its stinking garbage cans to reach another cross street, operating from a street map of the city he had memorized beforehand.

How long before police arrived to check out Rajhid's corpse and start interrogating witnesses? The apartment-building battleground should distract most of them for a while. With any luck, enough time for him to regroup with Grimaldi and clear the scene.

When he was on the next street over, strolling with the flow, Bolan fished out his cell phone and pressed the button for Grimaldi's number. Two rings in, he heard his voice.

"I blew it," the Stony Man pilot confessed, without preliminaries. "Got the shot, but came up empty-handed."

"Nearly the same for me," Bolan replied, "but I've got two phones and a wallet."

"Could be helpful," Grimaldi said.

"Fingers crossed. I'll meet you at the car in five."

CHAPTER FOUR

Walid Khamis sat and watched the Hezbollah fighters conferring in the dining room, just out of earshot from the sofa where they'd ordered him to sit and keep his mouth shut. They were angry, obviously, seeking ways to blame him for the raid on their apartment building, but he did not intend to stoke that anger by admitting the attack might well have been, in fact, his fault.

Not his specifically, of course, but all of theirs, his comrades and himself. He sat and wondered if the others, Rajhid and Farsoun, were even still alive.

Upon arrival in the city, when the Hezbollah team had grudgingly accepted them, Khamis and his companions had been warned against leaving the four-story apartment building. If they managed to forget that simple rule, or were forced out somehow and got lost, they'd been provided with an alternative address, the house in which he now sat, waiting for these strangers to decide his fate.

There was a chance, he understood, that they might kill him. Hezbollah was ruthless with its enemies, and he might qualify as one if they believed he was responsible for the attack on Calle Victor Hugo Norte, costing them that property and any men who had been killed or nabbed by the police because of it. They risked the wrath of God's Hammer if they executed him, but Hezbollah was vastly larger than his own small group of fighters, famous globally for decades, and they feared no one.

His only hope, Khamis believed, was to play stupid, claim that he had no idea the raiders could have come for him and his compatriots specifically. The more he thought about it, Khamis almost managed to convince himself. Who could have traced their path to Paraguay and mounted an attack there, after all?

A phone rang in the dining room. One of the Hezbollah fighters answered, listened and answered in Spanish. Khamis had no clue what he had said, but when the call was ended, his interrogators whispered urgently among themselves, glancing frequently in his direction, then approached him as a group, their faces dour.

"Your friends are dead," their spokesman told him bluntly.

"Both of them?" Khamis thought he could feel the planet tilting underneath him.

"Both. Shot down a mile apart. You separated?"

"To escape," Khamis acknowledged. "Yes."

"And you alone survived." There was suspicion in the man's gruff tone.

"If you say so." A shameful tremor shook his voice. He had been disarmed upon arrival and felt vulnerable now, an easy target.

"We have had no trouble at the safe house for the past eight years," his interrogator said. "You arrived mere days ago, and now we have a dozen soldiers dead, police demanding answers. It's peculiar, you'd agree."

"I would not," Khamis answered. "You're all fugitives from the Israelis and Crusaders, just as I am. Who's to say they did not come for you, over the rockets that you send from Gaza?"

His hosts—captors?—exchanged dubious glances, two of them shaking their heads. Their mouthpiece said, "The timing is suggestive. We have no faith in coincidence."

Khamis stiffened his spine and squared his shoulders. It was time to bluff, he thought. What did he have to lose?

"All right," he said. "If you believe I am responsible for this somehow, then I shall leave you. Give my weapons back, and you will see no more of me. Whatever happens next, find someone else to blame."

The Hezbollah man smiled at that, a hungry jackal's smile.

"It's not so easy," he replied. "Before we rid ourselves of you, we must decide whether you are, in fact, responsible for this attack. If someone wants you, it may be to our advantage to accommodate them. Possibly, we might receive some compensation for our losses."

Praying that they could not see him trembling, Khamis said, "So, you would ransom me? A soldier of the same cause you avow? I thought the men of Hezbollah were freedom fighters, not a pack of gangsters."

"You'd be wise to say no more," the leader warned him. "Even if we sell you, there's no reason why we shouldn't take a few fingers and toes."

BOLAN AND GRIMALDI chowed down at an American fast-food restaurant, a familiar stop these days no matter where on Earth you were. Over hamburgers and fries with coffee, Bolan gutted Rajhid's wallet, while Grimaldi did the same with one he'd lifted from Salman Farsoun. Walid Khamis was in the wind.

Between the two of them, the fallen God's Hammer members had been carrying a hundred and fifty thousand Paraguayan guaranís—some thirty-five US dollars—in cash, two bogus passports and a notebook, Farsoun's, filled with Arabic notations Bolan couldn't translate. He set the currency aside, secured the notebook in his pocket and placed the other items on the empty seat beside him, where he planned to leave them when they left the restaurant.

That left the telephones, two cells and Rajhid's satellite phone. Each of them took a cell phone first, scrolling through their memories in search of any recent numbers called by either of the two dead terrorists.

"Nothing on this the past ten days," Grimaldi said.

"I've got one local call," Bolan replied. "Prefix sixty-one. Rajhid called it three days ago."

"Around the time they'd have checked into Hezbollah Arms," Grimaldi stated.

"We can try for an address from Stony Man," Bolan suggested, reaching for the small sat phone. Three calls had been logged in memory and not erased, a bonehead move. He set the phone beside Grimaldi's plastic food tray. "Do the numbers ring a bell?"

The Stony Man pilot studied them. "The 249 is a country code, so forty-one is the city and the rest a local number. Off the top, I couldn't tell you where it is. Sorry."

Bolan got out his smartphone, thankful that the restaurant offered free Wi-Fi. He went online to check the foreign phone codes, found what he was looking fo, and told Grimaldi, "Two forty-nine is Sudan. The city code's Kassala."

"Never heard of it."

"More homework for the Farm. I'll send the numbers through."

He switched to email on the smartphone, typed an address that would eventually allow the message to reach

Stony Man Farm in Virginia without pinpointing his or Stony Man's location and sent two phone numbers with a request for a speedy response. It was a relatively easy job for Aaron Kurtzman's cyber-team, hopefully landing some pointers for Bolan within the half hour.

"When we get the local number—" Grimaldi began.

"We check it out."

"Hoping Khamis is there, assuming that he even knows where *there* is."

"Hoping," Bolan granted. "If he's not around, smart money says we'll find another Hezbollah hangout."

"Small favors." Grimaldi was working on his last few fries. He washed them down with coffee, pushing back his tray. "Ready when you are, *kemo sabe*."

Zermatt, Switzerland

SALEH KABEER WAS dining when Mohammed Sanea interrupted, bringing him a sat phone.

"My apologies," Sanea said. "A call from Paraguay."

Kabeer frowned at his second in command. "Rajhid?"

Sanea shook his head. "One of the Hezbollah men. Ashraf Tannous, he says."

The frown became a scowl. Kabeer set down his fork and took the phone, waving Sanea toward the nearest exit from the dining room.

"Greetings."

"And greeting be unto you," the caller replied. "I hope I have not reached you at an inconvenient time."

Kabeer glanced at his cooling dinner, likely ruined by the interruption. "Not at all," he lied.

"We have a problem," the man said. "Is this line secure?"

"It is, if you are."

"Very good. I'm sorry to report that there has been… an incident."

"Explain." Kabeer was not the most patient of men, nor the most courteous.

"Crusaders have attacked a safe house here. It's possible they came for your men."

"Possible?"

The caller's shrug was nearly audible. "Your three fled from the building. They were followed. Two of them are dead now."

"Followed." He was sounding like an echo chamber. "Do you mean *pursued*?"

"It seems so."

"You say two are dead," Kabeer stated.

"We have the third one here, Walid Khamis. He claims it was coincidence."

"You disagree?"

"The evidence—" the caller began.

"I understand. Is he available to speak with me?"

"One moment."

It took longer, but Kabeer tried not to grind his teeth. When Khamis came on the line at last, his tone was cautious, worried.

"Sir, have they explained what happened?"

"Not in any great detail. We've lost two friends, I understand?"

"Yes, sir. I can't explain it, but—"

"Another time, perhaps," Kabeer said, cutting off the man's inept apology. "When we can speak more privately."

"Of course, sir…if there is another time."

"Why should there not be?"

"They…um…are considering a ransom."

"Are they?"

"I've discouraged it, of course, but—"

"Pass me back to Tannous, if you'd be so kind."

"Yes, sir."

Another moment's silence, then Tannous came on the line again. "You've finished with your man, then?"

Kabeer ignored the question, asking, "What is this about a ransom?"

He had spoiled Tannous's lead-up to the pitch. The Hezbollah cell leader took time to clear his throat, then said, "Housing your men has cost us more than we anticipated. Twelve men dead, and our best safe house lost for good. I feel we should be compensated."

"*You* feel?" Kabeer challenged. "Have you discussed this plan with your superiors?"

"They have received a tabulation of the damages," Tannous replied, rather evasively.

"And their response?"

"I'm waiting for it now."

"Do you imply that my men are responsible for the attack on yours? And if so, what do you present as evidence?"

"They were pursued by two Crusaders from the scene. Why them, if they were not the targets?"

"Ask the two Crusaders," Kabeer told him.

"I would, and gladly, if we had them here."

"So, you don't know who sent them? Whether they're Americans, Israelis? Nothing?"

"At the moment—"

"I thought not. But since you seek to profit from a tragedy we share, here is my offer—nothing."

"Nothing?"

"Tell Walid our prayers are with him. We shall miss him—and we shall remember you."

Smiling at last, Kabeer cut off the call and turned back to his veal.

Barrio San Blas, Ciudad del Este

THE CALL CAME in twenty minutes, not a record for the Farm, but close. Kurtzman—called "Bear" by anyone who knew him well—read off two addresses, the first on Avenida San José in Ciudad del Este, the other in Kassala, halfway round the world, in far-eastern Sudan.

"That's near a teaching hospital," Kurtzman added. "Also near the Mareb River, if that helps."

"It will, when we get there," Bolan replied.

"It's not the best place to go hunting, but you know that, right?"

"We do," Bolan agreed.

Sudan's latest civil war had dragged on for more than two decades, finally ending—at least, on paper—in 2005. Before the ink was dry on that treaty, slave traders went back to business as usual, capturing at least two-hundred-thousand victims in the intervening years, while mayhem in Darfur killed at least three-hundred-thousand people, displacing nearly three million more. Some of that was religious warfare, Muslims versus Christians, and conversion from Islam to Christianity ranked as a capital crime in Sudan. A recent State Department report found that in the Darfur slaughter, all parties to the conflict committed serious crimes.

Nothing much had changed since then. At least, not for the better.

"Well, take care," Kurtzman said, at a sudden loss for words.

"I always do," Bolan replied.

The computer wizard was laughing when he cut the link.

"So, what's the word?" Grimaldi asked him.

"We're good to go on both ends," Bolan said. "Addresses, anyway."

"And what's the game plan if we don't find Khamis at the new place? Do we stick around and hunt for him?"

Bolan had already considered that and shook his head. "If he hasn't gone back to the Hezbollah team, it means he's on his own and likely lost in Ciudad del Este. Or he could've caught the first bus out of town, maybe across the Río Paraná to Foz do Iguaçu. From there, who knows where?"

Foz do Iguaçu lay just across the river, linked by a Friendship Bridge constructed to promote traffic between Paraguay and Brazil. Another crossing, the San Roque González de Santa Cruz Bridge, carried traffic back and forth between Ciudad del Este and Posadas, capital of Argentina's Misiones province. Either way, there'd be no way to track Walid Khamis once he slipped out of town.

Welcome to the wonderful Triple Frontier.

"The good news," Bolan said, "is that he's stranded here, at least for now. If we can find the other remnants of his crew and deal with them, he's neutralized."

"Until he makes his way back home and finds *another* crew," Grimaldi pointed out.

"It's not ideal, I grant you," Bolan answered. "But the time we'd waste looking for him across three countries gives his thirteen pals a chance to plan their next performance."

"Right, a trade-off. So we'd better hit it."

Outside, the rain had stopped, and steam was rising from the pavement. To Bolan, glancing up and down the street, it seemed as if fires were burning underneath the city, looking for a place to break through and devour everyone above.

"YOUR FRIENDS DON'T want you back, it seems," Ashraf Tannous told Walid Khamis.

"You expected them to pay for me?" Khamis was smiling, but it strained the muscles in his face and did nothing to ease the sickly churning in his stomach.

Tannous shrugged, seeming disinterested. "It was worth a try," he said. "My problem, now, is what to do with you."

"Release me," Khamis offered. "Then you have no problem."

"On the contrary. I doubt you'd last two days in Paraguay alone, much less in Argentina or Brazil. You don't speak Spanish, don't speak Portuguese, can barely manage simple English. How long until you make a mistake and find yourself in custody? From there, it's but a short step back to us, when you begin to squeal."

"I'm not a rat," Khamis said indignantly.

"Not a rat *so far*," Tannous corrected him. "Police in Paraguay…well, let us say they are not known for sensitivity, especially to foreigners."

"Are they worse than the Saudis?" Khamis challenged him. "Worse than the Egyptians? Worse than the Syrian?"

"After the bloodiness this afternoon, they will be hunting Arabs to arrest and question. You, alone, don't stand a chance against them."

"So, show me a way out of the city, then," Khamis replied.

"I have already lost a dozen men because of you and your two friends. You think I'd risk another? Even one?"

"What, then?" Khamis asked Tannous, hating how his dry throat made his voice crack.

"You disappear," Tannous replied. "If any of your comrades ask—which seems unlikely, you'll admit—I simply say that we released you, at your own request, to make your way…wherever."

"Kabeer will not believe it."

"Have you not been listening? Your friend Kabeer told me to deal with you as I see fit.

"All of Israel wants me dead," Tannous reminded him, smiling, "along with half of the United States, at least, and much of Britain. The Saudis have sentenced me to death *in absentia*. Warrants are out for my arrest in Syria and Jordan. I assure you, little man, that Saleh Kabeer is the least of my worries."

As Tannous spoke, he reached around behind his back and drew a pistol from its place beneath his shirttail. Khamis recognized the Beretta 92 issued to Paraguayan military officers as a standard sidearm, then noticed its extended, threaded muzzle, added to accept a sound suppressor.

"I'm sorry that you ever came here," Tannous said. "More sorry for my brothers than for you, of course, but still. You struck a blow at the Crusaders. It's unfortunate that you've become a liability."

Walid Khamis was tired of worrying about what happened next. Now that his fate was sealed, he simply wanted to get on with it and minimize the small talk. Paradise awaited him, he still felt sure. Tannous was simply standing in his way.

"So, kill me, then," he blurted, as Tannous affixed a sound suppressor to his Beretta. One of his men had produced it from a pocket, all the time watching Khamis for his reaction, seeming disappointed when he did not weep and wail.

"You're anxious now?" Tannous inquired. "Ready to see the virgins waiting for you? Or would you prefer boys, if I may ask?"

"Bastard!" Khamis spit back at him.

"Alas, my mother is deceased, but she would not have joined in any such activity were she still living. Now, your jackal of a father, on the other hand—"

Khamis lunged for him, hands formed into claws, but someone struck him from behind, and suddenly the lights went out.

"IT DOESN'T LOOK like much," Grimaldi said, as they rolled past the target.

"No, it wouldn't," Bolan said. "Low profile. Trying to fit in."

"And Bear was clear about the address?"

"Crystal," Bolan said. "He's never steered me wrong."

"Okay."

It was still daylight as they drove down Avenida San José, but dusk was closing in on Ciudad del Este after one hellacious afternoon. Bolan knew crime was rampant all along the Triple Frontier, but he had no idea what the average daily murder rate might be for any of the district's top three border cities. The number was totally irrelevant, but he and Grimaldi had bumped the day's statistics.

And they were about to give the stats another nudge.

The rain had passed but might return at any time. Both warriors left on their raincoats, concealment for the weapons hanging from their shoulder slings, pistols in armpit leather, frag grenades attached to belts. Even in Ciudad del Este, those accoutrements would raise eyebrows and have observers reaching for their cell phones to alert police.

Their Bluetooth headsets, on the other hand, were normal.

On the drive across town, Grimaldi had scanned the neighborhood on Google Earth, getting the layout and an aerial of the Hezbollah safe house. It was on the small side, maybe four bedrooms, although he couldn't judge the floor plan from a snapshot of the roof, taken from outer space. The last snap hadn't captured any dogs roaming the fenced backyard, which faced a narrow alley at the rear. There'd been no guards outside, either, and Bolan wasn't sure exactly what to think of that.

It could go either way, he knew, after their hit on Calle Victor Hugo Norte. If the Hezbollah hardmen were hurt and spooked badly enough, they might have fled the city, but he didn't think so. It was more likely, to Bolan's mind, that they would go to ground at their alternate hideout, pull the blinds and disconnect the phones, hoping the storm blew past them and moved on.

If he was wrong, this second stop-off was a waste of time. They should be airborne, winging out of Paraguay and toward their next meeting with God's Hammer, on the far side of the world.

But Bolan wasn't often wrong. He had a feel for what his enemies were thinking, how they'd play it in a given situation. Even dealing with fanatics hyped on hatred and religion, he could get inside most predators' minds and guess what to expect, at least in generalities.

Because at bottom, where it mattered, they were all the same.

"You want the front or back?" Bolan asked.

"Front," Grimaldi said. "I know enough Spanish to confuse them and get a foot in the door."

"As long as they don't chop it off," Bolan said.

"No problemo, señor."

"Okay, you convinced me."

The back door could go either way, once Grimaldi dropped in around in front. The men they wanted could come boiling out the back or plaster Grimaldi with everything they had to keep him out. If it went down that way, Bolan would be a rude surprise for them, another drop-in they were not expecting.

Watching curtained windows as he made his move, he steeled himself for anything.

CHAPTER FIVE

Jack Grimaldi felt like Avon calling, but with nothing anyone inside the target house would want to buy. The treatment he prescribed wouldn't improve their health or make them more attractive, but at least, if he applied it properly, the world would be a better place when he was done.

And would he still be living in it?

Doorbells hadn't caught on yet, it seemed, in Ciudad del Este, though the door did have a peephole set at about eye level for a person five foot four or five. Whoever answered to his knocking wouldn't see the Spectre M4 held against Grimaldi's hip, ready to rise and shine the moment that the door was opened, but they'd have a fish-eyed view of the Stony Man pilot's face underneath a faded baseball cap.

Just for the hell of it, he smiled.

Footsteps approached the door. Grimaldi willed himself to stay relaxed, at least to all outward appearances. A shadow blocked the peephole and a man's voice called out to him through the door, *"Quién es?"*

They were speaking Spanish. Great. Grimaldi didn't know how long the Hezbollah team had been in Paraguay or how much of the native language they had learned, but he could only bluff it out. Dropping his voice a notch to make the doorman strain his ears, he answered back.

"Es mi amigo en su casa hoy?"

Grimaldi had no friends in town, and if he had, they wouldn't have been here, but what the hell.

"Que estás diciendo?"

Good question. What *was* he saying, standing there and waiting for a storm of bullets to rip through the door at any second? Broadening his smile, he tried again, pure gibberish this time.

"Mi perro es loco ahora por dias."

The doorman wasn't loving it. *"Usted tiene la casa equivocada. Vete!"*

But Grimaldi didn't have the wrong house, and he wasn't going anywhere.

"Mi elefante está enfermo," he said, almost whispering, forcing the doorman to lean in closer to hear him.

"Que?"

Instead of answering that time, Grimaldi raised his SMG and fired a short burst through the door, approximately were the greeter's torso ought to be, eyes slitted against any blowback from the flimsy paneling. A swift kick to the lock forced the door open, and it caught the Hezbollah gunner inside as he was falling, shoving him away to clear the threshold.

A hallway stretched in front of Grimaldi, rooms branching off to either side, the home's back door facing the pilot from the far end of the corridor. In Dixie, once upon a time, they called homes with that simple layout shotgun houses, meaning you could fire a weapon through the front door, down the hall, into the yard out back, and never hit an intervening wall.

Somewhere inside the house, from some room to his left, a man called out a question. This one spoke in Arabic, not trusting Spanish, and Grimaldi didn't bother answering. He ducked into the first room on his right and found a parlor, unoccupied, a TV set playing without an audience. Contestants on a game show looked excited, but Grimaldi didn't have a clue what they were doing.

Two male voices called down the hallway now, first curious, then shouting when they saw their buddy stretched out in the foyer, marinating in a pool of blood. More voices answered from the back, all Arabic, and Grimaldi heard automatic weapons being primed.

The doorman he had taken down was not Walid Khamis. As for the rest, he'd have to meet the lot of them head-on and see what he could see. Grimaldi smiled ferociously and went to meet his enemies.

ASHRAF TANNOUS HAD watched while others rolled Walid Khamis up in a plastic tarp, secured at each end by black zip ties. Perhaps, he thought, the worthless slug would suffocate in there while they transported him to a disposal site, and save Tannous a bullet. They would have to check him, though, and not risk leaving him to struggle free once they had left

Another problem, courtesy of the strangers whom he had been ordered to accept as guests, providing shelter until it was safe for them to leave. Now, they were never leaving Paraguay, and neither were a dozen of his soldiers who had died in vain, protecting them.

Stupid.

The men in charge of Hezbollah should never have agreed to hide the upstarts from God's Hammer, but they did not consult Tannous on such decisions, even when the order put his life at risk. He would be happy when the last of them was gone, and wondered if he ought to leave a message with the corpse, something to lead police away from Hezbollah, or would that only make things worse?

A knocking on the door distracted him. He heard Adel Asaad answer the summons, using the Spanish he had learned to send away whoever it might be. Tannous leaned into the hallway, listening, and saw Asaad bending as if to press his ear against the door. In profile, the man looked confused, then angry at whatever he was hearing, all of it inaudible beyond the threshold.

Asaad ordered the pest to go away. Tannous could understand that much, but something else was said, causing Asaad to stoop once more and ask a question. When a burst of automatic fire ripped into him, causing Tannous to jump, the shots were nearly silent but for rattling sounds as they punched through the cheap front door.

Tannous backpedaled, nearly tripping over Khamis in his rolled tarp, cursing as he heard the front door to the house being smashed open. There were no shouts to identify police, but what did that mean, in a town like Ciudad del Este, where the police were a lawless bunch?

Nothing.

Tannous could hear his soldiers rallying, responding to the sudden threat. He stood immobile for an instant, looming over Khamis, then bent and probed the bundle with his free hand, searching for the interloper's head.

A muffled protest told him when he'd found it, and Tannous stepped back a pace, then fired two muted shots into the plastic where his finger marks were visible. Another second, and the dead man's blood spilled out, pooling at first, then seeping into cracks between the wooden floor's thin slats.

At least that job was done, and he could leave disposal to whoever managed to survive the firefight now in progress, echoing throughout the house. Whoever wanted him could have the worthless dog. Tannous had to think about survival now, and that meant getting out before he wound up with a bullet in his own head.

Job one was to obtain a better weapon. He'd already fired two of his pistol's fifteen rounds and was not carrying an extra magazine. More firepower improved his chances of escaping, and the instrument was already at hand.

Stepping around the leaking bundle on the floor, Tannous retrieved an AK-47 from a nearby coffee table. The assault rifles were plentiful in Paraguay, despite laws restricting civilian ownership. They were traded for drugs at the border, no cash changing hands, or sold by rebel groups who needed money more than surplus arms. Tannous's rifle was a vintage weapon but in good shape, loaded with a 40-round curved magazine that had another taped beside it, in reverse, for quick reloading in a fight.

He jacked a round into the chamber, swallowed hard and braced himself to join the fight—just as another home invader smashed in the back door.

BOLAN HAD MISSED Grimaldi's entry to the house but heard it loud and clear when the defenders opened up on him in there. He waited for a heartbeat, just in case some of them tried to rush the back door, then he gave the door a flying kick beside the dead bolt and pushed through.

Downrange, the front door stood wide open with a body wedged behind it. There was no sign of Grimaldi, but his work was recognizable. Movement to Bolan's left directed his attention to a kitchen, where two bearded men had been distracted from the chore of chopping vegetables and dropping them into a pot. Both of the Hezbollah hardmen held knives, but neither seemed to have a gun.

Bolan shot them, anyway, one muffled 5.56 mm round apiece, then scanned the kitchen to make sure he hadn't overlooked a lurker waiting for the chance to jump him once his back was turned.

How many rooms were left to clear? Oddly, the house seemed smaller on the inside than it had when he was on the street, the very opposite of what he usually found on entering an unfamiliar structure. When he checked the central hallway once again, Bolan knew why: there was a second corridor, crossing the first halfway between the home's two doors, with more rooms leading off it from either side.

More to explore. More traps waiting to close around him, if he didn't watch his step.

More places for Walid Khamis to hide himself.

Shooting on the street side of the house had lagged for just a moment, but it started up again now, drawing Bolan toward the fight. He still had no idea how many Hezbollah gunners were in the house, how many more might be arriving from some errand or in answer to a hurried cell phone call once Grimaldi had breached the front door, but the racket they were making now would surely prompt at least one neighbor to alert police.

There was no time to waste.

Bolan had only two rules that he followed without deviation in his endless war. First, he would always minimize the risk to innocent civilians before he made a move or pulled a trigger. Second, he would not kill a cop. He viewed police in general as soldiers of the same side, earning danger money in pursuit of criminals.

If cops arrived, he had two choices: slip away some-how, or go to jail.

And jail, inevitably, would mean death.

Hearing the clock tick in his head, he left the kitchen, edged along the hallway toward the sounds of combat, closing on the next two doors in line. One ought to be a dining room, judging by proximity to the kitchen, while the other would be up for grabs.

The door to Bolan's right flew open as he neared it, someone coming late to join the party, with a toilet and a dripping shower in the background. It was not Walid Khamis, which made the new arrival Hezbollah. He had a pistol in his hand, a towel around his waist and an expres-sion on his face that might have been excitement, maybe fear. Whichever, Bolan shot him through his naked chest before the man had an opportunity to attack him.

Four down, including Grimaldi's kill in the entryway, but from the sound of it, there were enough defenders left to hold the house if they could pull themselves together and decide on a strategy.

His job was to make sure they died before they had that chance.

ASHRAF TANNOUS SPENT a moment in the open doorway, wondering if he should fight or flee. He was a leader, with a certain standard to uphold, but that was only use-ful if he lived to fight another day.

The neighborhood would surely be aroused by now. The police were not loved there, were rarely called, and never to a simple family disturbance, but he knew that someone would alert them to a full-scale battle going on. Arrest meant prison, once they found Khamis and matched the bullets from his body to Tannous's pistol.

There was no death penalty in Paraguay, but he would rather die than spend his life inside a stinking prison cell.

With that in mind, Tannous began to plan his exit from the house. The room where he had killed Khamis was windowless—the very reason he had chosen it—so he would have to find another exit. That meant moving *toward* the sounds of gunfire and away from safety for the moment, until he could break off to the left or right, choosing a door and slipping through it, hopefully unseen.

Get on with it, a harsh voice in his mind commanded, spurring Tannous into motion. Three of his men passed by his doorway, one of them—Maroun Rahal—pausing to stare at him and ask, "Are you all right, Ashraf?"

"Fine," he replied. "I'm right behind you."

With a jerky nod, Rahal moved on, seemingly anxious for his chance to face the unknown enemy.

Young fools. At Rahal's age, Tannous had felt the same, but he had quickly learned to bide his time, strike without warning and retreat, keeping survival foremost in his mind. Let others wear the vests with high explosives packed in scrap metal and cow dung, hastening their flight to Paradise. Tannous was happy to remain on Earth and plot his moves against the enemy from safety, letting others do his killing for him—and the dying, too.

What famous general in history was not the same?

He stepped into the hallway, saw Rahal and his companions jogging off to meet whatever fate awaited them, and followed at a cautious distance. When they reached the central, east-west corridor, Rahal and company turned left. Tannous had picked the opposite direction as his best path to escape, and he would hold to that unless something prevented him from using it.

"There is no shame in living," Tannous muttered to himself. In fact, it was his duty to their sacred cause.

An explosion rocked the house as Tannous neared the central hallway. A hand grenade, he thought, and that was bad, because his men had none, even assuming they were fools enough to set one off indoors, where it could kill or wound their comrades. That told Tannous that his enemies had come prepared for anything and did not plan on taking prisoners.

No problem there.

Surrendering had never crossed his mind.

GRIMALDI PUMPED THREE rounds into a gunner who had surprised him, springing from a doorway to his left with a Kalashnikov that almost looked too big for him. The guy was just a kid, maybe nineteen, but his AK and the expression on his face marked him as dangerous, until the Stony Man pilot blew his face apart and left him on the threadbare carpet, leaking brains.

What was it that the "cool" youth sometimes said? *Live fast, die young and leave a beautiful corpse.* The Hezbollah gunner had bagged two out of three.

Grimaldi put him out of mind and tried to estimate how many rounds were left inside the Spectre's casket magazine. It was a closed-bolt weapon, meaning that the last round fired would leave the bolt locked open, but Grimaldi liked to plan ahead and eliminate surprises any time he could.

Because, one day, a rude surprise could get him killed.

He hadn't found Walid Khamis so far, had no idea whether the scumbag they were looking for was even in the house, but taking out another nest of Hezbollah still counted as a fair day's work. It wasn't strictly kosher—hell, it violated both the Paraguayan and the US constitutions—but the modern world had reached a point where evil often seemed untouchable, corrupting governments from top to bottom. When the slow machinery of justice jammed and then broke down, a clear-eyed, able-bodied man could make a difference.

Bolan had showed Grimaldi how to do that. It was in his blood now. There was no retirement plan, no thought of turning back.

Grimaldi left the gunner where he'd fallen, pausing first to pluck the magazine from his Kalashnikov and flinging it away. He'd barely straightened when bullets started snapping through the air around him, hasty shots from downrange, poorly aimed but getting better as the shooters compensated.

With a curse, Grimaldi ducked into the doorway that his late adversary had appeared from, quickly checking out the room and making sure he had it to himself. The storm of autofire outside was picking up, and he knew it would leave him trapped, cut off, unless he did something about it in a hurry.

Reaching underneath his raincoat with his left hand, he retrieved one of the frag grenades clipped to his belt, pulled its pin and moved back toward the doorway in a crouch. A left-hand pitch wasn't his strongest play, but it would have to do in this case, since he couldn't stick his head into the hallway and expect to keep it on his shoulders.

Grimaldi made the blind pitch, felt—imagined?— the heat of a near miss on his knuckles as he whipped his hand back under cover. In their rush to reach him, his opponents didn't recognize their danger. By the time one of them barked a warning to the rest, it was too late.

The close-range detonation stung Grimaldi's ears. He ducked as shrapnel ripped into the walls around him, highlighting the house's cheap construction. Some of it apparently took out electric wiring, since the room where Grimaldi sat huddled suddenly went dark. The hallway had its lights on, though, but dimmer, as if one or more of its successive ceiling fixtures had been shattered.

Move it, Grimaldi thought. Get it done.

He burst out of the dark cave, Spectre at the ready, slamming short bursts into enemies who'd made it through the blast of his grenade. Some of them bled from wounds, others were simply dazed, all vulnerable to the close-range Parabellum rounds that ripped their flesh. A couple of the hardmen got off shots in self-defense, one bullet tugging at Grimaldi's sleeve, but they were down and out before the slide locked open on his SMG.

Time to reload and go in search of other prey.

BOLAN MOVED THROUGH dust and battle haze, no smoke alarms announcing danger from a fire. After the blast from a grenade—hopefully one of Grimaldi's—the gunfire had slacked off remarkably, down to a stray shot here and there. He couldn't tell yet whether that meant victory or just his enemies regrouping, but the time to push forward was now.

As if on cue, a figure turned the corner just ahead of Bolan, yet another unfamiliar bearded face above a T-shirt and a folding-stock Kalashnikov, a handgun tucked into a pair of low-slung jeans. Another Hezbollah hardman, not Bolan's target from God's Hammer, and there was no point taking any chances with him, trying to interrogate him when he had that crazed look in his eyes.

They fired almost together, Bolan slightly quicker

off the mark and certainly more accurate. His 5.56 mm rounds impacted in a cluster that he could have covered with his hand, maybe three fingers, while the 7.62 mm bullets his adversary's piece spewed out went high and wide, etching a zigzag slash across the wall to Bolan's right. Falling, the shooter shivered once, twice, then lay still.

The Executioner moved on, turned left to probe a hallway that he hadn't checked and cleared two empty rooms in nothing flat, before he saw the third door standing open. This one was an inside room, with no windows, and a man-sized bundle in a blue tarp occupied the center of the room, black zip ties fastening each end. The near end of the blue burrito had a leak, drooling fresh blood on to the rug.

The Randall Model 18 knife occupied an armpit rig on Bolan's left side, hanging with its pommel downward, toward his hip. He drew it, knelt to feel around the bloody end of the blue bundle, then began to slice the tarp with care, cutting a flap he could peel back and bare the face within—or what was left of it.

Five seconds later, he looked into the bulging eyes of Walid Khamis, no longer a threat to anyone unless he stayed there, rotting, and eventually spread disease. The major pathogens he carried—hatred and fanaticism—had departed from the living world with his last breath, leaving an empty, useless husk behind.

Bolan reached out to Jack Grimaldi via Bluetooth, telling him, "I've found our guy. He's out of it."

"Where are you?" the pilot inquired.

"Side hallway, north side, second on your right. It's standing open."

"With you in a second."

That was an exaggeration, but he made it inside ten, with no more sounds of killing as Grimaldi circled through the house. Bolan allowed himself to hope that it was finished for the here and now, at least.

They stood together, looking down into Khamis's shocked dead face.

"Guess he pissed them off," Grimaldi said.

"Looks like it." Bolan wished they could have grilled Khamis, but doubted whether he'd have broken without drugs to which they had no access. Short on time and opportunity, they'd missed their chance.

"Sudan, then," Grimaldi stated.

"Right."

"One thing. We're gonna need a plane with longer range."

Bolan nodded, hearing the first *ping-pang* of sirens in the middle distance.

"Right," he said. "I'll make a call."

CHAPTER SIX

Zermatt, Switzerland

The last phone call from Paraguay was no surprise to Saleh Kabeer. He had been wise enough to hedge his bets, acquiring an informant at a mosque in Ciudad del Este that solicited donations for the Palestinian Islamic Jihad, arranging for a call if, for whatever reason, his three men in Paraguay were lost and Kabeer's link to Hezbollah was broken. A strategic cash transfer from one Swiss account to another had sealed the bargain, and now it had paid dividends.

The loss of three men from his meager force—twenty percent of the survivors from their debut raid in Jordan—was grim news, naturally, but God's Hammer could still survive it, soldier on and gather new recruits in droves after their next event earned them publicity around the world. The worst part for Kabeer, right now, was wondering exactly who to blame for the demise of Rajhid, Khamis and Farsoun.

His mind immediately focused on America, that nest of vipers that had meddled in the Middle East since 1947, first among the nations of the world to buttress Israel, sponsors of a Syrian coup d'état in 1949, deposers of Iran's prime minister in 1951, collaborators with the British in the 1956 Suez crisis, looters of oil, invaders of Lebanon and Iraq. The list of crimes went on, but most Americans were so naive, their first response to any pushback from the region was a plaintive wail: "Why do they hate us?"

Saleh Kabeer knew the answer to that question. He was an expert on the subject, doubtless qualified for an exalted Ph.D. if he had spent his life in classrooms, rather than the front lines of his people's struggle to be free of Western interference and oppression.

So, America had killed his men in Paraguay, retaliating for their strike against the Zarqa consulate. But who *specifically* had carried out the executions? Which among the countless agencies devoted to intelligence, homeland security and all the rest of it had hunted down the three? How were they traced to Ciudad del Este and, beyond that, to the safe houses maintained by Hezbollah?

One possibility—the obvious—would be a Hezbollah informer. Spies and traitors were a daily fact of life for any revolutionary. Choosing comrades was more difficult than picking out targets or weapons, every step and spoken word a risk for those who fought against Western aggression. Some joined revolutionary movements with the goal of undermining them, while others started out sincere, then lost their fervor and surrendered to temptations.

He understood the impulse but did not excuse it. If and when Kabeer identified the individuals responsible for selling out his men, he would gain access to them somehow, question them and find out who they served. Only when he was satisfied, when he had all the facts required, would Kabeer mete out retribution for their crime against God's Hammer and their insult to him. They would die screaming.

And once the sponsors of the raids in Paraguay had been identified, what then?

Kabeer was not entirely sure, yet, how he would reach out and touch specific enemies in Washington, reducing their rich lives to ashes, but at the moment he had more immediate priorities. The remnants of his little army had to be warned without delay. He was not looking forward to that task, but it was inescapable.

Frowning in thought, Kabeer reached out for his sat phone.

Guarani International Airport, Ciudad del Este

THE PLANE SWAP took some time, slowing them. No stranger to delays in war, Mack Bolan had developed stoic patience, but he was aware of fleeting time and felt its sharp teeth gnawing at the corners of his mind.

The new plane, when it got there, was a Hawker 400 twin-engine corporate jet, formerly owned by a leader of Mexico's Sinaloa Cartel. The boss had hired the wrong pilot, a ringer who diverted him to Miami on a hop from Mexico to the Bahamas, landing both the boss and his high-flying toy in DEA hands. Maybe he missed it, from his cell in a supermax, but it belonged to Bolan and Grimaldi now.

The jet was forty-eight-feet long, with a forty-five-foot wingspan and seating for nine passengers. It cruised at 510 miles per hour, with a service ceiling of forty-five-thousand feet, and had been custom built with oversize fuel tanks, granting a nonstop range of thirty-five-hundred miles. That still meant pit stops on their long flight to East Africa, but Grimaldi had worked it out.

They would be in the air twelve hours, plus six more

on the ground, refueling, checking in with Customs at their several stops along the way, waiting for clearance to depart, and so on. Anything could happen in three-quarters of a day, now that they'd made their first move against God's Hammer and potentially sent tremors racing off across the outfit's spider web. Forewarned *was* forearmed, whether his targets chose to flee Sudan or stand and fight.

Grimaldi joined him on completion of the preflight checkup.

"Everything shipshape?" Bolan inquired.

"We're good to go," the pilot said. "This cartel guy spared no expense."

"Wet bar?"

"Hot tub," Grimaldi answered, grinning. "You can catch a transatlantic soak. I promise not to peek."

"I'll pass," Bolan said. "It always makes my fingers pruny."

"That can be a problem," the pilot agreed.

"I touched base with the Farm. They've got a couple guys who can equip us in Sudan."

"They're solid?"

"Nothing's really solid where we're going, but they have connections to the Company. They're vulnerable if they try to pull a double-cross."

"Too late to help us, though."

"It's all a gamble," Bolan said, stating the obvious.

Grimaldi knew that, but he liked to vent sometimes, like anybody else. It never interfered with his performance on a mission, and he'd never disappointed Bolan in a crunch.

"You think the Hammer has official cover in Sudan?" Grimaldi asked.

"The Farm didn't come up with anything on that," Bolan replied. "Officially, they're an Islamic state under Sharia law, but it's hit or miss. They still have slavery. South Sudan split off in 2011, and its warlords have been skirmishing with Ethiopia for border turf since then."

"Sounds like Somalia," Grimaldi commented.

"They have their share of pirates, too, but mostly smuggling arms to South Sudan. They haven't pulled a major hijacking at sea, so far."

"Small favors, eh?"

"How long until we're cleared for takeoff?" Bolan asked.

"Slow day," Grimaldi said. "We're good to go in twenty, if we're squared away."

"Sooner the better," Bolan said, and followed him aboard the jet.

Robert F. Kennedy Department of Justice Building, Washington, DC

THE PRESIDENT WAS calling, and Brognola couldn't let it go to voice mail. Sitting at his desk, a late-lunch hero sandwich spread in front of him—sausage and peppers, screw the doctors just this once—he recognized the red light blinking on the nearest of his two phones. He reached out to snare the handset on its second ring, tucking a bite of sandwich into one cheek as he answered.

"Yes, sir."

"Hal, how are you?"

"Hanging in there, sir."

"I know the feeling. Congress, right? Don't get me started."

"Yes, sir."

"So, I wanted to check in with you about that thing. The one we talked about."

Cagey. In Washington, even with those you trusted to perform the dirtiest of dirty work, those who ascended to the heights of power knew enough to watch their words, aware that anything you said might be recorded for posterity by someone who could turn against you later, muddying your legacy or even sending you to prison.

"Yes, sir. I've got my best asset on top of it."

"Any results, so far?"

"Yes, sir. The word's just in. I would have called you with a confirmation in the next half hour or so."

"Well, since I've got you now…"

"Of the original sixteen, three have been neutralized," Brognola said.

"If I may ask…"

"Yes, sir. In Paraguay."

"That's hitting close to home."

"We think it was a hideout, rather than a staging area, but there was no time to discuss it with the principals."

"Of course. I understand. As for the others…"

"There's a lead, sir, to East Africa. Sudan, specifically."

"Uh-huh. Well, if they have to be somewhere, I'd rather have them over there than in our own backyard."

"Yes, sir. There is a chance, with transit time from South America, that we could miss them on the other end."

"You could have gone all day without telling me that, Hal."

"Yes, sir. Sorry, sir. I know you value straight intelligence over Pollyanna kind."

"Rose-colored glasses never got me anything but blurry vision. Still…"

Brognola took the opportunity to swallow his last bite of sausage, cleared his throat, and sent another "yes, sir" down the line.

"About the three down south, if we could give the public something…"

"Sir, I'm bound to say that would be premature, at this point. News like that goes global in a heartbeat. If there's any chance at all the others haven't heard about their pals yet, it would be a serious mistake to tip them off, in my opinion."

"And if they already know?"

"They can't know who's behind it, sir. That's definite. I'd rather have them paranoid right now, jumping at shadows, than convinced we're on to them. A statement now, from us, might even spur them into further action."

Silence on the other end, as the big Fed's caller digested that. "Okay," he said at last. "I see that, and I wouldn't want to be responsible for something else, God knows. It would be nice to have some points on our side of the scoreboard, though."

"We have the points, sir. We're just saving the announcement till the final victory's confirmed."

"How confident are you of that, Hal? On a scale of one to ten?"

"Well, sir…"

"Scratch that. Dumb question, never mind. I'm talking like a senator."

"I wouldn't say that, sir."

Most senators, Brognola had decided, talked to please their base, and for the kick of showing off on Fox or CNN. This was a leader strapped for answers, in a corner, with the country clamoring for justice. Sure, any announcement of a victory against the terrorists responsible for killing Americans would be politicized, as well, but Brognola believed his caller—unlike others he could name—was more concerned with duty than the latest Gallup poll.

"You'll call me, then?"

"Most definitely, sir."

"All right. Thanks for your time."

And he was gone. Brognola turned back to his sandwich, found he'd lost his appetite, and dropped its remnants in his wastebasket.

Kassala, Sudan

NOUR SARHAN ROLLED OVER, gasping, finished with the prostitute beside him. She was young and pleasing to the eye, but no one Sarhan cared to share a conversation with on any subject other than her price per hour for the service she had rendered with a semblance of enthusiasm.

Pay for play. Where women were concerned, he had no interest in anything beyond the obvious, the physical.

Sarhan had paid for this one in advance, no awkward arguments after the fact. She'd named a price—or, rather, her pimp had named the price—and that was business easily disposed of in advance. Now all she had to do was dress and leave.

"We're finished," Sarhan told her. "You may go."

She seemed about to ask him something, for a small extra gratuity perhaps, but Sarhan's frowning face discouraged her. She scrambled out of bed, collecting items of apparel from the bedroom floor. When she was dressed, a relatively simple process in the costume she affected, she moved toward the doorway without looking back.

Kinan Asker stood waiting for her on the other side, his face deadpan. He stood back to let her pass, then entered and closed the door behind him.

"I'm glad you're done," he said, one hand extended with a sat phone in it as he neared the bed. "Kabeer is calling."

Sarhan snatched the phone and thumbed a button, taking it off Hold. "Saleh," he said, "it's good to hear from you. Please, tell me that you have advanced the schedule."

"You know we cannot change the target date," Kabeer replied, his voice as gruff as ever, even from twenty-six hundred miles away. "The enemy must come to us. We need them all assembled in one place."

"Of course. I only thought—"

"I'm calling with a warning," Kabeer said, cutting him off.

"Warning?"

"You—all of us—may soon be facing danger. Our associates in Paraguay have been eradicated."

"What?" The news struck Sarhan like a swift punch to the gut. He jackknifed out of bed, stood naked, with his back to Asker. "When? Who did this thing?"

"The last of them was lost within the hour," Kabeer said. "And many of their hosts fell with them, I should mention, if you happen to be speaking with their comrades."

Sarhan had a sudden urge to spit. Screw the mewling rats of Hezbollah. He'd left them in the first place because they were soft, all turning into politicians now, instead of warriors. He was not concerned about retaliation from those weaklings, but with vengeance for his friends.

"You must be on alert, these next few days," Kabeer told. "If necessary, use the exit route we talked about."

Over the nearby border to Eritrea, and on from there to Yemen or Somalia, depending on the circumstances.

"I remember," Sarhan said.

"Because we don't know who may be responsible—"

"I'll be alert to everyone and everything," Sarhan replied.

"And I will be in touch about the next event."

"I shall be waiting," Sarhan said, and cut the link.

Roberts International Airport, Monrovia, Liberia

JACK GRIMALDI LIKED long flights. Winging across the wide Atlantic was the perfect way to disconnect from Planet Earth and all its problems, put your mind on autopilot for a while and bask in simple freedom from the draw of gravity. As long as he had fuel, fair visibility and a beacon to his next LZ, the long jaunts liberated him as nothing else could ever do.

The down side: when he landed, all the same old problems waited for him, some compounded by events that had occurred while he was soaring through the clouds.

As airports in Africa went, Monrovia's was fair. It had been built in 1942 and christened Roberts Field, after Liberia's first president, used as a base for air strikes against Rommel in North Africa and U-boats in the North Atlantic. After the war, it was revamped to serve Air France, Pan Am and Delta, later ranked as an emergency alternative landing site for NASA's space shuttles. Damaged at the turn of the last century, during one of Liberia's periodic civil wars, the main terminal still needed major renovations, but progress had always been slow in this part of the world.

Grimaldi had the Hawker fueled and ready by the time

Bolan returned from dealing with the officers at Customs. English was Liberia's official language, so they had no failure to communicate. The trick would be to speed up the minutiae of paperwork, when no one on the airport's staff had an incentive to work faster than a snail's pace. Bolan had done well, based on Grimaldi's personal experience in Africa, and he was smiling as he reached the plane.

"How much?" Grimaldi asked.

"Two hundred bucks, Liberian," Bolan replied.

"That's what…two dollars in the States?"

"Two and some change."

"Terrific. Cheap at half the price." Grimaldi glanced at Bolan's empty hands. "No eats?"

"Nothing I'd trust," Bolan replied.

"Good thing we stocked up in Belém."

Val de Cans International was something else. They'd purchased food from three airport cafés, trusting the Hawker's fridge and microwave to see them, though.

"How's pizza sound, once we get airborne?"

"Suits me," Bolan answered. "When can we take off?"

Grimaldi glanced along the empty runway. This early in the morning, he could easily have used the runway as a bowling alley with no risk to life or limb.

"Soon as we're ready," he told Bolan, "since we're covered on the fees."

"All good to go," Bolan replied.

"Okay. Next stop, Khartoum."

Over Nigeria, at 40,000 Feet

THE PIZZA WASN'T BAD, considering. It had a certain tang to it, some spice the chef had added in Belém, which

Bolan didn't recognize, but it was fine. He ate three slices, put the rest in the fridge in case they wanted it before touchdown, and picked a seat behind the cockpit, leaving Grimaldi alone at the controls for now.

World maps, he'd found, often diminished Africa. The Mercator projection was probably worst, making Greenland seem three times the size of Australia, when in fact, the very opposite was true. Flying over Africa, you realized it was the second largest continent on Earth, nearly twelve million square miles of jungle and desert, savannah and mountains, sprawling from one horizon to the next in all directions: vast, inscrutable and beautiful.

Of the many hot spots on the continent, Sudan ranked right up there. It wasn't all chaotic like Somalia, next door, but its radical Islamic stance made trouble with most of its neighbors, one time or another, compounded by endemic human rights violations, institution of Sharia law despite a constitutional pledge supporting freedom of religion, strict media censorship, and near-genocide in Darfur. The good news was a rapidly growing economy, founded on oil, complicated by seventy native languages.

And somewhere in the midst of all that, more targets Bolan had to find, interrogate if that were possible, and then eliminate.

Unlike the job in Paraguay, he had no names to match against Brognola's dossier on God's Hammer, no idea how many of the thirteen members still alive were hiding in Sudan. He doubted any of the team had traveled solo to a place so far from home, but it could still range from a minimum of two or three to all thirteen.

That was too much to hope for, he decided, catching the remainder in one place and taking out the Hammer, root and branch; too easy for the universe to smile on him that way. Bolan would take what he could get and go from there, doing his best.

"About three hours," Grimaldi announced over the intercom. "In case you want to get some sleep."

Instead, Bolan went forward, settling into the copilot's seat. "I'm too keyed up," he told Grimaldi.

"About this outfitter we're meeting in Kassala…"

"Alek Nimeiry," Bolan said. "He's got a garage on the west side of town, near the Kassala Teaching Hospital and the Mareb River, which locals call the Gash."

"I hope he's not expecting us."

"No way. I've got a password for him. He can check it with the Company if he gets hinky on us."

"Starting rough," Grimaldi said.

"Starting *and* finishing, I'd bet. The usual."

Grimaldi didn't ask what they would do next if the birds had flown when they arrived. He had to have known that Bolan wouldn't have an answer for him, that they'd have to put their trust in Stony Man to strike another trail, dig up a name or address somewhere in the world, before God's Hammer decided it was safe to make another grandstand play.

He knew the heat had to be on high in Washington, with politics piled high and deep on top of anger at the killing of five Americans abroad. Opponents loved to twist the knife, find blame where none was evident and use it to support themselves come next election day. Bolan did not engage in those games, and he was not advancing anyone's agenda but his own.

Identify the targets. Isolate them. Take them out.

A recipe for slaughter in Sudan.

CHAPTER SEVEN

Khartoum International Airport, Sudan

"Nothing much to look at is it?" Grimaldi said.

He was right: one runway, asphalt, with security restricted to a simple chain-link fence, beside a terminal that had seen better days. It looked like something from the Seventies, and while a multilingual billboard boasted plans for new construction, it was fading from exposure to the weather, with no sign that any work had been attempted. Military planes shared space with jets bearing the logos of assorted African and Middle Eastern airlines.

From its appearance, Bolan thought that terrorists could overrun the airport easily. Maybe they'd never thought that it was worth the trouble.

They were about 250 miles from their target, Kassala, located due east of Khartoum. Eight hours and change if they'd been driving, fifty minutes with Grimaldi in the Hawker's cockpit.

They were almost there, and Bolan still had no idea what they would find.

"I'll go take care of Customs," he told Grimaldi, and headed for the terminal.

It wasn't quite so bad inside. The place had benefited from a face-lift sometime during recent months, but there was only so much decorators could accomplish when it came to hiding age. The morning light through tinted windows showed where cleaners had slacked off while buffing vinyl floors, and the employees working ticket counters had a weary look about them, even with the standard-issue smiles clamped doggedly in place.

Customs was worse. Two scowling officers in uniforms that wouldn't pass inspection at a small-town cop shop in the States examined Bolan as he stepped up to their station, almost willing him to give them grief. Maybe they still resented Sudan being tagged as a state sponsor of global terrorism, back in 1993, or held a grudge from US bombing raids in '98. Tension had eased since then, with Sudan listed as a "cooperative partner" against al-Qaeda in 2010, but the State Department still hadn't removed the country from its roll of states to watch where terror was concerned. Four gunmen convicted of killing two US Embassy staffers in 2008 had been sentenced to death, then escaped from the counrty's "maximum-security" prison, with only one of them captured at last report.

Bolan presented two passports, both of them genuine in form, although they bore false names. Bolan's identified him as one Matthew Cooper from New York; Grimaldi's listed him as James Burrell from Florida. If anyone took time to check, both home addresses were legit—up to a point—and calls would be accepted at their listed phone numbers. Both IDs had clean credit histories, bills paid on time and they had other documents to back them up: state driver's license, Social Security, the whole nine yards—all courtesy of Stony Man.

The Customs men took fifteen minutes poring over both passports, exchanging them to search for glitches, finding none. While that was underway, they asked the usual questions: why was Bolan visiting Sudan, how long did he intend to stay, where would he be residing while within the country.

Bolan told them he was on vacation, booked for a big-game safari. They could check the company and find a reservation for Matt Cooper in its files, if they were so inclined. Sudan was big on letting wealthy foreigners slaughter its wildlife—leopards, lions, hippos, elephants, giraffe, whatever—so the tale was plausible and had a twist of irony that Bolan could appreciate.

The big game he had come to find was human, the most dangerous of all. He hoped to put them all on the endangered species list.

The Customs men considered shaking down his plane, then finally decided it was too much work. They stamped both passports, let him go and glowered all the time that he remained within their line of sight.

Another hurdled cleared.

Next stop: a little slice of Hell on Earth.

Kassala, Sudan

NOUR SARHAN HAD pondered ways to make himself secure while waiting for the call to action from Kabeer in Switzerland. It was a strange world these days, soldiers scattered to the corners of the world in hiding, when he'd grown up huddled in the refugee camps where his people had been relegated, first in Egypt, later in the desert wastes of Jordan. In Sudan, at least, he had a roof over his head instead of canvas, indoor plumbing rather than a foul latrine and no guards peering at him every time he made a move.

Sarhan could have remained there, could have given

up the cause and lost himself in Sudan, with its 597 identified ethnic groups. Seventy percent of the country's population was Arab, close enough to his own Egyptian, and Arabic was the dominant tongue among four hundred clashing languages and dialects. He could pass, change his name…and do what?

That was the rub. Sarhan had never learned a trade, unless you claimed guerrilla warfare as an occupation. He had never graduated from a school of any kind, though he could read and write in Arabic, to some extent. His life had been devoted to revenge against oppressors. After twenty-seven years, fighting was all he knew or cared to know.

But how to keep himself secure until he had a chance to fight again?

He was strapped for personnel, with only two members of God's Hammer in town, besides himself, but he had hired street urchins to maintain surveillance on Kassala's four top weapons dealers for the next three days. Bahjat Libdeh—Jordanian, but still reliable—was at the local airport, watching all incoming flights from Nova and Sudan Airways, as well as private planes landing with foreigners aboard. Kinan Asker, their Syrian, was at the border crossing from Eritrea, watching for anyone suspicious on that side.

It was the best Sarhan could do with the resources presently in hand. As for defense, if enemies were spotted, he preferred a swift preemptive strike. They had a small but potent arsenal, and local thugs who would kill anyone desired for the grand sum of twenty Sudanese pounds—about $3.50 US. Sarhan's bankroll could cover that, and then some, with enough left over for plane tickets when Kabeer summoned his team to battle once again.

Waiting was what he hated most. There'd been no place for him to watch and wait. Kassala's railway station had been closed for years, most of the track that once served daily trains now lost to scavengers. He could go out and sit beside the highway stretching from Khartoum to Port Sudan, but what would be the point in that?

And so he waited, with nothing to distract him since Sudan banned liquor outright, and the bootleg stuff—*Aragi*—could be dangerous, from both a health perspective and the risk of being noticed by police. Drugs fell under the same ban, and while one could always find hashish around Kassala, this was not the time for Sarhan to expand his consciousness with cannabis.

He had to remain alert, prepared to rally both his comrades and their motley crew of mercenaries at a moment's notice, if potential enemies were seen. From that point, Sarhan would direct more strenuous surveillance, taking part himself, and then decide if violence was justified. In that case, he would err on caution's side and kill the strangers, hope that he had got it right, and leave police to tidy up the mess. If only—

The vibration of his cell phone startled him. Sarhan peered at its screen and recognized the caller as Bahjat Libdeh, his airport spy. He took the call and listened for a moment, feeling his blood pressure soar.

Kassala, Sudan

THE AIRPORT, SMALLER than the last, looked even more run down. Customs was no more difficult than in Khartoum, with only a single officer on duty here, though he took time to check their bags for contraband. When nothing surfaced, he applied the proper stamps and waved them on their way.

The airport's only car rental agency was small, apparently consisting of a youth in his late teens or early twenties, operating from a kiosk smaller than the kissing booth at county fairs back home. Bolan and Grimaldi both presented driver's licenses and waited for them to be photocopied, and for "Matt Cooper's" Visa platinum card to be swiped, and left the booth with keys to an Audi A4 compact executive sedan featuring permanent four-wheel drive.

Their first stop, from the airport, was Alek Nimeiry's auto body shop, located on a street whose signage neither Bolan nor Grimaldi could translate. They found the place regardless, parked outside and entered, to be greeted by a roly-poly man of fifty-something, with a shock of snow-white hair. He read their faces and approached them speaking English.

"Gentlemen, how may I serve you?"

"We were told you carry special tools," Bolan replied.

"Sometimes," Nimeiry said. "They are expensive."

"Money is no object," Bolan said. It wasn't his; why count the cost?

"In that case…"

The collection, when they saw it in Nimeiry's back-room storage area, was small but adequate. They both picked AKMS autorifles, chambered in 7.62 mm, with folding metal stocks, and backed those up with Chinese QSW-06 semiauto pistols in 9 mm Parabellum, both with factory standard sound suppressors attached. On his own initiative, Bolan added an RPG-7 shoulder-fired launcher, with a mixed bag of high explosives, fragmentation and thermobaric warheads to choose from. Finally, he took two dozen Russian RGD-5 frag grenades packed with one-hundred-ten grams of TNT, their casings scored to produce three-hundred-fifty shrapnel pieces on detonation, with a killing radius of eighty feet.

The price was high, but Bolan covered it with money squeezed from thugs whenever he spent time enough in one place to go hunting on his own, in his spare time. Money didn't know where it had come from, didn't care where it was going. As for Bolan, he could not have said whether the cash he spent this day had been contributed at gunpoint by a pimp, a drug dealer, a loan shark or the owners of a stolen car chop shop. It was all the same to him, going to serve a common cause.

They stuffed the weapons, extra magazines and ammunition into Army OD duffel bags for transport to the Audi parked outside. Alek Nimeiry showed them to the door, all smiles, and wished them luck on their safari. Neither he nor his new customers paid any notice to a teenager examining a set of chrome rims in the shop's showroom, or noticed his eyes trailing them out to the street.

When they were safely out of earshot, the youth pulled a borrowed cell phone from his pocket, dialed the only number programmed into memory and spoke for fifteen seconds, listened briefly and then happily agreed to trail the white men on his old motorcycle.

MANDOUR MAYARDIT was careful as he left the car shop, trailing the two Americans. He mimed continuing his cell phone call, speaking Arabic to dead air in the hope that neither one of them would understand what he was saying or regard his sudden exit from the shop as threatening. His battered motorcycle stood waiting for him, chained to a lamppost, as the white men loaded their purchases into an Audi with rental stickers and climbed into the car.

Mayardit pocketed his phone and quickly got his bike unfastened from the post, brought it to life with only two jumps on the kick-starter, and checked both ways before proceeding into traffic, trailing the Audi. His caution was rewarded when a gray Mercedes-Benz Vaneo stopped short just in front of him, its driver barking out to him, "Which way?"

Mayardit pointed, answering, "The Audi, there," and watched the compact van screech off without regard to any other vehicles around it.

This was better than he had expected. When the Arabs hired him, they had vaguely told him "help" would come if he reported foreigners obtaining guns from old Alek Nimeiry's shop, but he had not expected them to come so quickly. Mayardit had been prepared to trail the buyers, checking in by phone, until someone caught up with him, but this was different, as if the van was tracking them already when he called.

Excited now, Mayardit revved his bike and followed the Mercedes. This was more fun than he'd had in weeks, and he was getting paid for it besides, ten pounds for his report, another ten if those he spotted were the foreigners whom his employers sought.

Mayardit had smelled the fear on them, despite their smiles and cocky attitudes, as they'd described the nature of his job. The three Arabs were worried, and when they'd assigned him to Alek Nimeiry's shop, Mayardit knew they thought the foreigners had come to kill them. Why else would they have him stationed at an auto body shop notorious for selling weapons on the side?

With that in mind, Mayardit had prepared himself for trouble. Normally, when working hustles on his own behalf, he carried a short dagger for defense against street gangs. For a job like this, however, he'd retrieved his Webley Break-Top Revolver, an ancient British relic he had tested only once, to make sure it would fire without exploding in his hand. His hoard of ammunition came to fifteen rounds, six of them loaded in the pistol's cylinder right now.

Mayardit had the Webley tucked beneath his long, baggy shirt. It was uncomfortable back there, gouging him as he hunched forward on the motorcycle, but he could bear it for the thrill of being in on something new, exciting, dangerous.

And there *was* danger here. He knew it from the way the men in the Mercedes sped through traffic, swerving as if there could be no consequence to striking other vehicles, as long as they eventually overtook the Audi that was still a block or so ahead of them. Mayardit did not know what they would do when they caught up with the Americans, but he intended to be present, watching— and perhaps earn extra pay if he assisted in their capture.

What did he care about foreigners? Life in his homeland was already bad enough without intruders meddling and making things worse. That went for the Arabs who'd hired him, as well. Their actions told Mayardit that they had something to hide—but they were paying him to help them. That was business, which took priority over his personal feelings.

Unless, at some point, Mayardit could sell them out, as well.

"WE'VE GOT A TAIL," Grimaldi said.

Bolan checked his wing mirror, then half turned to scan the crowded street behind them. "The Mercedes van?" he asked.

"That's it," Grimaldi said. "And there's a motorcycle tailing them. I think I saw it parked outside Nimeiry's place."

Bolan considered that. "He would've had to speed-dial reinforcements while we walked out to the car. And if the bike was already in place—"

"Somebody staking out the local dealers," Grimaldi finished his thought. "They knew trouble was coming."

"*Someone* knew," Bolan corrected him. "We can't connect it to the Hammer positively, yet."

"Coincidence?" Grimaldi smiled. "One thing I know for sure. They're not cops."

Sudan's National Police drove an assortment of vehicles, some donated from foreign countries, but they all bore insignia and emergency lights, some with the added touch of camouflage paint jobs. A Mercedes was out of line, from what Bolan knew of the national economy, and that meant private money had gone into hunting them— or *someone*—in Kassala.

"Take for granted that it's us," he told Grimaldi. "We need someplace relatively safe to deal with them."

"When you say 'relatively'…"

"Minimal exposure for civilians."

"Right. You know it's rush hour?"

"Just do your best," Bolan replied.

Reaching behind his seat, he found the zipper on a duffel bag and tugged it open, pulled one of the AKMS carbines from inside and set it on his lap. A second stretch retrieved a curved 30-round magazine loaded with steel-core ammunition capable of penetrating six millimeters of steel plate at 328 yards or drilling through standard body armor from one hundred feet.

It was enough to stop a van, sure—even a Mercedes-Benz—if Bolan got a clean shot in the teeming traffic, without jeopardizing any innocents.

And that would be the trick.

He left it to his partner, who was tops at flying *and* at driving. Some men had the knack of handling machines, while others never managed it. Grimaldi was a natural.

They'd studied street maps of Kassala in advance and knew where they were headed, north to reach the address Stony Man had matched to Abdullah Rajhid's sat phone, back in Ciudad del Este. Now that they were being followed, though, it meant they couldn't head directly for the target, telegraphing their intentions to the enemy. And if the tail meant something else…

Bolan still didn't know how many members of God's Hammer were hiding in Kassala, but he counted four men in the trailing van, at least. Its tinted window interfered with a precise head count, but that was close enough in terms of mounting a defense. Toss in the biker who was following the Mercedes, and that made five for sure.

It was far from the worst odds he had ever faced, but five men—all presumably well armed—would take some killing. Bolan didn't want to undertake that kind of action on a crowded city street, if he could help it, with the high potential for stray rounds turning simple cleanup into a god-awful massacre.

"The river?" he suggested, making it a question so he didn't cramp Grimaldi's style.

"Worth trying," the Stony Man pilot agreed, and Bolan realized they were already headed in that direction, from their last left turn.

He double-checked the carbine in his lap and settled back to wait.

"GET AFTER THEM!" Kinan Asker snapped at his driver, one of the young locals Sarhan had recruited for surveillance of potential enemies arriving in Kassala. Asker knew his name but could not think of it just now.

"You want me to run over people?" the driver asked.

"I don't care!" Asker replied. "Just catch them!"

With a bleat of crazy glee, the driver Asker stomped on the accelerator and their van surged forward, sideswiping an ancient blue sedan and forcing it into a street-side market stall. Asker heard people screaming, shouting curses after them, as they sped on, chasing the Audi with two men inside.

The *right* men?

He had spotted them at Customs, in the airport terminal, two out-of-place white men whose faces were expressionless while dealing with the solitary officer who stamped their passports. He had followed them and watched while they arranged a rental car, using his cell phone to contact Sarhan, receiving orders to stay with them and report what happened next. Asker had left the terminal ahead of them, sat watching in the van with three of Sarhan's locals, while the new arrivals drove through crowded streets to reach an auto body shop. Worried that they would be too obvious, sitting outside, he'd told his driver to circle the block—four circuits, twice reversing their direction to be clever—when Sarhan had called to say his spotter at a local weapons dealer's place of business had two white men buying guns.

God be praised, the address was identical.

Their last mad rush around the block had missed the strangers, but Sarhan's lookout had just been preparing to chase after them. He'd pointed out the Audi, two blocks down and gaining distance, and the chase was on.

"The kid is still behind us," one of Sarhan's shooters said from the backseat. Asker had not bothered listening when Sarhan gave their names.

"His problem," Asker said, his mind focused on the chase. He did not know the boy and had no interest in him, only hoping that the young fool did not interfere in Asker's dealing with the foreigners.

I am a foreigner myself, he thought, but shrugged it off. White men were different. They had no business in Sudan or anyplace where Islam was the law.

"They've spotted us," his driver announced, just as the Audi swerved around a truck in the street, accelerating.

"Just catch up to them," Asker replied. "I need a clear shot."

He had already pulled his short AKS-74U carbine from the paper bag between his feet, and had no need to double-check and verify that a live round was in the chamber. Asker never made mistakes like that. It was the first sign of an amateur playing at war and asking to be killed. The little weapon weighed six pounds and measured only nineteen inches with its metal stock folded, but it retained the full firepower of its larger parent model, spitting 5.45 mm rounds at a cyclic rate of seven-hundred rounds per minute. The eight-inch barrel reduced its effective range to some four-hundred yards, but Asker planned to be much closer when he sent these white men to their hell.

His driver, Zeinab, he now remembered, was shifting, milking every ounce of speed he could from the Vaneo's engine. He was Asker hunched forward with his hands like claws around the steering wheel.

"Get ready," he told Asker. "You can take them any minute now!"

CHAPTER EIGHT

"Heads up," Grimaldi said. "We're about to have incoming."

Bolan had seen the van's shotgun rider lean out of his window, looking awkward as he tried to aim his piece left-handed. Grimaldi was ready for him when it came, a short juke to the right, dodging men in their long *jalabiyas* and women in colorful *thoub*, making them scatter like chickens. He managed to miss them all, which was no small achievement, and sent the first rattling burst from their enemy's gun high and wide, strafing shop fronts and forcing pedestrians to dive to the sun-bleached sidewalk.

They'd almost made it to the river—Gash or Mareb, take your pick, with roughly another block or two to go. Bolan had swiveled in his seat, bringing up his AKMS carbine, thankful that the Audi's right-hand drive gave him a better angle firing backward than the shooter in the Mercedes Vaneo had.

That wouldn't matter in the least to Bolan if his opposition scored a lucky hit.

Behind the Benz, he glimpsed a youngster on a motorcycle, keeping pace, now visible, then tucked behind the van and out of sight. Bolan had seen a bike outside Alek Nimeiry's shop, but they were everywhere around Kassala, most showing their age, nothing remarkable about them until they turned up in the middle of a running firefight through downtown.

So, make it *five* shooters whom he and Grimaldi might have to deal with, if the biker weighed in on the other side. He wasn't the youngest foe Bolan had ever faced, but pushing it, and it wasn't his choice if someone with a full life still in front of him decided it was better thrown away, trying to kill a total stranger.

If the kid was old enough to play, he had to be old enough to pay.

"I see the river, Sarge."

It lay in front of them, a muddy brown, maybe two hundred fifty yards across to reach the other side, with waste ground stretching out another couple hundred yards between a road that paralleled the river and its eastern bank. The soil looked solid there, with scrub brush spiking from it.

"Can you drive on that?" Bolan asked.

"The Audi's got four-wheel drive," Grimaldi replied. "It's worth a try."

If they got stuck somehow, it could be fatal, but Grimaldi had his full, implicit trust. He'd plucked Bolan from more hot LZs than the Executioner could count, never complaining, never flinching under fire. On wings or wheels, he got it done.

But if that waste ground turned out to be shifting sand…

The Mercedes Vaneo spit another burst of AK fire. Bolan cut loose with his own assault rifle and saw the chase car's left headlight explode. It was too low and too far to his right, as Grimaldi dodged to avoid incoming bullets, spoiling Bolan's aim.

"Sorry!" he offered from the driver's seat.

"No sweat," Bolan replied, and fired another short burst at the van, strafing its narrow grille this time, maybe the radiator. The volley wouldn't stop the Mercedes immediately, but an overheated engine could slow them in the short run, before it locked up tight.

A good plan, if they had been running down an open desert highway. As it was, though, they had reached the last paved road before the riverbank, crossing from east to west, while north-south drivers blared their horns, shook fists and shouted curses in the Audi's wake.

Road rage. Damn right.

The van was crossing now, pursuing them, and Bolan saw the biker trailing it, decelerating as he saw where the fight was headed. Bolan hoped he would be smart, turn back and live to see another day, but that wasn't his call.

He had four men to kill, at least, before they finished him.

A bloody beach party.

"WE HAVE HIM NOW!" Zeinab crowed, slamming one fist on the steering wheel in triumph.

Not so fast, Asker thought, but he kept it to himself. His men needed encouragement right now, not warnings that would put them off and slow their reactions in the crunch.

A truck nearly clipped them as they crossed the final stretch of blacktop separating traffic from the riverbank. Its horn blasted a futile warning as its brakes locked, and the trailer jackknifed, spilling several hundred green-and-yellow melons on the pavement, where they shattered to reveal their pink insides.

Zeinab gave another hoot, blaring the van's horn as a riposte to the truck's, then they jumped the curb and came down on to desert hardpan, following the Audi's plume of dust toward the river's edge. Asker squeezed off another short burst, wasted, but it made him feel a little better to make noise and keep his quarry running, even when the hot brass blew back in his face.

As Asker drew his rifle back, he caught a glimpse of movement in his wing mirror. The crazy kid was still behind them on his motorcycle, hunched over the handlebars and grimacing as cars swerved to avoid him on the road. He nearly lost it when he left the pavement, airborne for an instant, then lost traction on the loose dirt as he landed, but he kept the bike upright, himself on board, and powered after the Mercedes.

Asker wished God's Hammer had five, ten thousand warriors with that spirit. They could topple governments, make history and wipe the stain of Israel from the map for all time.

But before he let his mind traipse into fantasy, he had to overtake the two men in the Audi. Capture them alive if possible, and take them back to Nour Sarhan for questioning. Failing in that, they had to be eliminated as a message to whoever sent them, teaching infidels *again* that they had no right meddling in affairs beyond their understanding.

Asker's war was not a matter of convenience, or politics or greed. It was a holy conflict—a *jihad*. He had no fear of losing, since no earthly army could defeat the one and only God, but he, a lowly individual, might fail and die before the final victory was won.

If so, he was determined that his sacrifice had to count for something.

If today was Kinan Asker's day to die, then he would face it like a man.

The Audi was outrunning them, it seemed, veering away to Asker's right, northward, running along the open riverbank. Fuming, he slapped Zeinab's left arm and shouted, "After them! You're letting them escape!"

"Hang on!" the driver snarled in answer, cranking hard right on the steering wheel to follow the sedan.

Asker felt the Vaneo's tires slipping, saw loose dirt flying up on his side as Zeinab negotiated the sharp turn. An image flashed in Asker's mind: the warning label pasted inside each sun visor set above the windshield, cautioning against abrupt turns in top-heavy vehicles. Too late, he tried to warn Zeinab, and then their vehicle was tipping over on to his side, crashing onto the hardpan with a thorny bush thrusting through Asker's open window, stabbing at his face.

BOLAN SAW THE van roll over in his wing mirror, obscured by the Audi's drifting cloud of dust. Grimaldi had to have seen it at the same time, as he hit the brakes, but cautiously, avoiding a nasty skid or spill. Behind the van, the trailing teenager had also stopped, sitting aside his bike in profile, well back from the action, watching it unfold.

"Be careful of the kid," Grimaldi cautioned, before going EVA, taking his AKMS with him.

Bolan didn't need that warning. He had been in combat zones where children were combatants, raised on revolution or resistance from the time their brains could hold a thought, ready to kill or die for causes that their parents and their older siblings had espoused. The biker didn't have a weapon showing, but that didn't mean he was unarmed—or that he wouldn't phone for reinforcements to assist the shooters in the capsized van.

And they were on the move now, all of them apparently recovering in something close to record time. It hadn't been a bad crash, as rollovers went, more dust than anything, though it would take a crane or several dozen helping hands to right the van again.

The Mercedes Vaneo was a five-door model. Two front doors opened traditionally, for the driver and the front-seat passenger. Behind those doors, on either side, two rolling doors granted access to the van's backseat. The fifth "door," as designers chose to call it, was a hatch that rose vertically to expose the cargo deck in back. Five exits, but the Merc was lying on its left-hand side, precluding use of two.

The shooters kept their wits and did the smart thing, bailing through the hatchback, so the van's bulk screened them from their adversaries in the Audi. Bolan couldn't see them bailing out from where he stood, in settling dust by the sedan, but guessed they wouldn't waste much time before they rallied to defend themselves.

"You make it four?" he called to Grimaldi, across the car that separated them.

"That's all I saw, except the kid," Grimaldi answered.

"So circle them?"

"Suits me. And watch—"

"The kid. I know."

Bolan would watch the kid, all right. So far, he was a spectator, standing apart, outside decent pistol range but well within the reach of AKMS rounds at something like two hundred yards. He'd have a clear view of the action that was coming, down the open riverbank, but couldn't make out faces from that distance, unless he was carrying binoculars somewhere beneath the baggy shirt he wore.

Not that it mattered, since he might have been up close to Bolan and Grimaldi, at the auto body shop. If so, he hadn't made a move against them then. Only a spotter, Bolan guessed, but he'd stuck with the chase from there, and now had stopped to watch its end, however that went down.

Bolan circled to his right, toward the roof of the Vaneo as it lay on its left side, covered with settling dust. He heard its engine running, even now, and guessed the shooters huddled by its tailgate would be sucking down exhaust fumes with the dust that swirled around them.

Good.

Whatever clouded their perception, slowed them in any way, helped Bolan. Closing in with cautious strides, not rushing it to make himself a hasty target, he ignored a line of cars stopped on the frontage road, drivers and passengers engrossed by the enfolding drama on the riverbank. Even in wild Sudan, it wasn't every day they saw a firefight in the flesh.

Someone would be phoning the police, he knew, whether the biker called for help or not.

No time to waste.

THE TIPPING VAN had shaken Kinan Asker. When the spiny bush had come through his window, pushing at his face, it shoved his sunglasses aside and gouged a bloody track along the left side of his nose. A second later, Zeinab had tumbled from the driver's seat—to Asker's right, originally, now *above* him—landing heavily on top of him, grinding Asker's AKS carbine into his ribs.

When Asker had caught his breath, he'd snarled at Zeinab, "Move! Get off of me!"

"I'm trying," Zeinab had replied, and managed finally to scramble clear, into the backseat, after further bruising Asker with his elbows, knees and feet. Asker crawled after him, aware of passing time and his helplessness as long as he was trapped inside the van. Their enemies could riddle it with bullets, set the vehicle on fire, and those within when it exploded would die screaming.

It wasn't a death that Asker craved.

From the backseat, he saw that someone had already opened the Vaneo's hatchback, exiting that way instead of through the right side's rolling door, now pointed toward the sky. Taking the high route would have made them sitting targets as they poised to drop and run around behind the van—a gift to men who might be moving in to kill them, even now.

Asker had lost sight of the Audi when his van rolled, shaken as he was, nothing but dust immediately visible beyond the van's windshield. Emerging from the rear hatch with his team intact—one bloody nose, some minor scrapes and cuts—he seized the opportunity to look around the van and found the car they had been chasing fifty yards in front of them, immobile, both doors standing open like an elephant's ears where its two occupants had stepped out.

They were advancing now, on foot, both armed with variations of Kalashnikov rifles. He registered grim faces that he recognized from the airport, thinking how odd and *wrong* it seemed that they had turned into the hunters, while Asker became the prey.

He was not helpless, though. His side had four guns, to the white men's two, and they had cover, while his enemies were out on open ground. Killing them should be easy.

His eyes strayed to the spotter on his dusty motorcycle, then moved on, back toward the road where Asker's van had nearly been broadsided by the melon truck.

Up there, he saw cars stopped, some people gawking, others stooped over the pavement, grabbing melons for themselves.

Bastards, he thought. If they had stopped to watch him die and make a picnic of it, Asker planned to disappoint them.

"You and you," he told the backseat gunners, unfamiliar names deserting him in his excitement, "watch around the right here. Take the Westerners when you have a clear shot. Try to wound one of them if you can."

"Wound?" one of them asked, incredulous.

"To hold for questioning."

"Hold where?" the other asked. "We have no car to carry away a prisoner."

"Do as you're told!" Asker gritted back at them. "Kill only as a last resort." Then, to Zeinab, he said, "You come with me, around the left, to meet the other one."

It was a poor plan, Asker realized, but it was all he had.

One final chance to carry out his orders before he lost everything.

BOLAN HAD COVERED nearly half the distance from the Audi to the Mercedes van when the shooting started. The incoming rounds were low at first, and not well aimed. He dropped and rolled across the hardpan, wound up prone and facing the van, peering along the barrel of his AKMS carbine.

Was it an illusion, or had they been firing low deliberately, trying to disable him and Grimaldi without inflicting fatal wounds? There might have been some logic to it, if they'd had a vehicle to carry off a wounded prisoner, but as it was, he wrote it off to shaken gunners wasting rounds before they aimed.

Bolan saw a head poke out around the van. Squeezing off a 3-round burst, he watched the head explode and pitch back out of sight, one adversary down and out for starters. Whether that would slow the others was anybody's guess, but Bolan hoped so, rising suddenly and sprinting forward, as he heard staccato gunfire from the far side of the van. Grimaldi had engaged the enemy, as well, and they were going at it, his friend's 7.62 mm rounds distinct and separate from lighter-caliber answering fire, some 5.45 mm and what sounded like a Parabellum submachine gun.

Bolan wished his partner luck and focused on his own objective, closing on the capsized van. He saw the nearly headless body of his first mark being hauled back out of sight, before another rifleman popped out, firing before he got a fix on anyone or anything. Bolan dropped flat again, firing before he hit the ground this time, catching his would-be killer with a rising burst that gutted him and dropped him on his backside.

In a heartbeat Bolan was up and running toward the sounds of gunfire, recognizing his second kill as Kinan Asker, one more of the God's Hammer crew. The faceless body dragged aside short moments earlier could have been anyone.

And that left two.

Bolan had nearly reached the corner where he'd have to turn and face his enemies, when more firing erupted just beyond his line of sight. That had to be Grimaldi closing in, dueling with the survivors, drawing automatic fire in answer to his own.

The Executioner took full advantage of the moment, scuttling forward in a half crouch, ready with his AKMS carbine. Both of the remaining shooters had their backs to him, firing around what used to be the gray van's right-rear bumper, when a slug caught one of them and spun him on his heels, blood spraying from a wound high in his chest. The falling gunman just had time to notice Bolan, before the Executioner's carbine stuttered, chopping ragged vents across his chest, then tracking on to ventilate his comrade from behind.

The last man standing never knew what hit him, as the bullets punctured vital organs, slamming him face-first against the van's body. He slumped, legs folding, sagging toward the open hatchback, but a dead man couldn't resist the pull of gravity. He slithered down to earth, muscles relaxing for the last time as he left a trail of blood behind.

Another second, and Grimaldi peeked around the van's undercarriage, counting bodies. "I don't know these two," he observed.

"We've got one from the hot sheet over here," Bolan advised.

"Okay. We'd better split," Grimaldi said, his gaze drifting to his left. "Unless you want the kid."

Bolan glanced back in time to see the biker peeling out, hunched low over his handlebars and revving hell-for-leather out of there, away from all that death. It would have been a long shot for the carbine at a moving target, but still feasible.

He let it go.

"They know we're here now," he stated. "We'd better get a move on."

"Right," Grimaldi said, and joined him on the run back to their vehicle.

MANDOUR MAYARDIT WAS running for his life. Not literally, since it seemed no one was chasing him, but he had panicked in the final moments of the firefight by the riverside and totally disgraced himself, abandoning the others as they died.

He would not get his full pay for the mission now, and that was fine.

At least he was escaping with his skin intact.

He had pursued the Audi and the van in search of some excitement, thinking in some abstract way that he might join the fight if necessary, and impress his sponsors with some act of heroism done on their behalf. Nothing in his imagination had prepared him for the absolute reversal of what seemed to be a sure thing, with the marks killed or captured by a hunting party twice their strength.

The motorcycle was rattling, and he slowed a little for the straining engine's sake, when he had put the best part of a mile between himself and the massacre sight. It was important to seem normal now, and not attract attention, since a hundred witnesses or more had seen him fleeing from the riverbank in broad daylight.

Mayardit pulled into an alley, parked beside an industrial garbage bin older than he was and sat astride his motorcycle, trembling. Life was cheap in Sudan, where beggars died on the streets every day and were picked up like trash. Most of the noteworthy mayhem occurred in South Sudan, but Kassala had its share of muggings, robberies and such, sometimes ending in murder.

Still, this was the first time Mayardit had witnessed bloody death himself, and it had chilled him.

He heard sirens rising from the west, no doubt responding to a rash of calls about the shooting. Thankfully, most law enforcement officers were lazy and incompetent, unlikely to pursue vague eyewitness descriptions of a boy riding a motorcycle in a city jammed with two-wheel transport of all kinds. The odds were good that he would never be identified—but that did not mean Mayardit was safe.

He still had one more duty to perform. It wasn't something he'd been paid for, strictly speaking, but a debt of honor that was weighing on his shoulders. Or, if you preferred, call it a way to free himself from future contact with the man who had employed him for a simple job of watching that had turned into a nightmare.

Just forget it, said a small voice in his head. They'll never find you.

But they *might*, and Mayardit did not want that threat hanging over him. He had to be rid of them, once and for all.

He pulled the cell phone he'd been given from a pocket of his khaki trousers, opened it and pressed a button to contact the only number programmed in its memory. The man who'd hired him had furnished the phone, with orders to call him if Mayardit saw any foreigners shopping at Alek Nimeiry's supposedly secret gun shop. Mayardit had done that job, and now he wished fervently that he'd let it go at that.

Why bother to report the killings he had witnessed?

To alert the stranger who'd employed him and to sever their connection for all time, with an assurance that Mayardit could be trusted with a secret. Possibly, he thought, it just might be enough to save his life.

CHAPTER NINE

"How many people do you think were watching us back there?" Grimaldi asked.

Bolan pictured the cars stopped on the river frontage road, bicyclists slowing, pedestrians crouching to see the show. "A hundred, anyway," he said. "It could be twice that."

"How many of them do you think had cell phones?"

"Seven out of every ten," Bolan replied, plucking his answer from an online guidebook he had skimmed in transit. Sudan ranked thirty-eighth in the world for cellular coverage, with some twenty-eight million registered phones.

"Okay," Grimaldi said, "so seventy, eighty phones on the highway back there, minimum. How many were snapping pictures of our little hoedown?"

That could be a major problem, Bolan realized, not only for completion of their mission in Kassala, but for clearing out of Sudan once they'd finished. Bolan didn't know where they were going next, as yet, but any flight out of the country meant returning to Khartoum, more wasted time there on the ground while members of the National Police—not brilliant, certainly, but not the dumbest in the world—broadcast a slew of photos snapped by rubberneckers at the crime scene.

"How hard would it be to leave the country from Kassala?" Bolan asked his wingman.

Grimaldi considered it while he proceeded toward their final destination in the city. "There's no problem with the plane," he said. "It's fueled, ready to go. We're fifteen miles or so from crossing over to Eritrea. Their capital's Asmara, say a hundred miles due east of here. They have an international airport, two asphalt runways that can take the Hawker."

"So you've thought about it," Bolan said, smiling.

"That's why I get the big bucks, Sarge. The down side is, we have to file a flight plan when we leave Kassala, and their airport isn't international. Officially, leaving the country means we fly out of Khartoum."

"And *un*officially?"

Grimaldi shrugged. "Feed them some bullshit here and make a run for it. Make a one-eighty, heading east instead of west. We'd cross the border in under five minutes from takeoff. Fifteen minutes later, tops, we're in Asmara."

"But…"

Another shrug, while Grimaldi swerved to avoid a driver coming head-on in their lane, something that seemed to be a common practice in Sudan. "There's still the flight plan that I mentioned, but I'm thinking we could get around it."

"How?"

"Check out a map. Khartoum is due west of Kassala, which is due west of Asmara, give or take a few miles. On Asmara's radar, eastbound flights could be arriving from Sudan, Nigeria, wherever. They don't care, as long as you arrive with proper paperwork."

"We're back to the flight plan."

"Correct. But who's to say some clerk in Khartoum didn't mess it up somehow? It's simple, write the wrong name down, whatever. I've been brushing up on my geography," the pilot said. "You know about the tension between Sudan and Eritrea."

"I do," Bolan replied.

The two countries had squabbled since the 1980s, with Eritrea complaining that Sudan supported rebels trying to topple Eritrea's government. Diplomatic contact had been severed for a dozen years, and its tepid resumption in 2005 left many old grudges unsettled.

"So, we blame Khartoum for any mix-up on the flight plan, maybe lay a few bucks on whoever's asking questions, and we should be good to go."

"Should be," Bolan echoed.

"There are no guarantees, of course," Grimaldi said. "But overall, I'd say it's looking better than Khartoum."

Bolan had nothing to counter that assessment.

"Okay, that's the plan," he said. "Now, all we need is our next destination from Asmara."

The next step wouldn't happen if they were detained there, maybe busted by a Customs officer who didn't share the widespread prejudice against Sudan, or who reacted badly to a bribe offer. A phone call to Khartoum would land them in hot water, and if photos of their skirmish with God's Hammer were on the wire, it just might send them back for trial.

The end of everything.

Bolan put that bleak picture out of mind, focusing on the here and now. Before he left Sudan, he had to see if any other fugitives from God's Hammer were in town and take them out, while hopefully obtaining pointers to the other scattered terrorists.

Simple.

The only thing he stood to lose was life itself.

"Repeat that, if you please." Nour Sarhan barely contained his urge to shout and curse.

"Your men are dead," the caller answered, with a tremor in his voice. "I followed them and watched them die."

It was the young spotter he had employed to watch Alek Nimeiry's combination auto body shop and private arsenal. Kinan Asker had trailed two white men from the airport to that very spot, and then pursued them as they left. Since then, there had been no contact with Asker, and Sarhan's nerves felt as if they had been flayed.

Now, this.

"How can you be sure they are—"

"Dead?" the caller interrupted him. "Because I saw their brains blown out! A hundred other people watched it happen. The police are with them now."

"And where are you?" Sarhan inquired, trying to keep it casual.

"It makes no difference," the voice replied. Sarhan tried to recall a face, but he had hired two dozen locals for surveillance and pursuit, too many to recall.

"We will not meet again," the youth said. "After I hang up, I will destroy this phone. Your secrets will be safe with me, unless you try to find me."

So, a threat. Sarhan tried an appeal to greed. "But the remainder of your payment—"

"Keep it. I've already spent the rest on gas, doing your work. Now—"

"Wait! Don't hang up!"

"I know you're tracing this," the young man said.

"You flatter me. I have no such technology at my disposal."

"So *you* say."

"One question, then, before you go? A short one."

Silence, then, "What is it?"

"You have seen the men who killed mine. Closely?"

"Yes."

"Can you describe them?"

"That's a second question."

"Even so."

"Two white men, as I told you, probably Americans. One taller than the other. Both looked fit. They wore billed caps and sunglasses. No beards."

"And what about their car?"

"Ask the police. I'm going now."

The line went dead. Sarhan resisted an impulse to fling his phone across the room.

He had to focus, before it was too late.

Somehow, these two Crusaders had traveled to Sudan from Paraguay, and knew which city they should search for Sarhan and his two compatriots—*one*, now that they had liquidated Asker. Sarhan had no clue how they had managed that. It was irrelevant. The fact was, they were in Kassala and had killed four of his men, including one member of God's Hammer. Should Sarhan feel safe where he'd been hiding for the past few days, since the attack in Jordan?

It seemed impossible that the Crusaders might know where he was. And yet...

His best move was to leave, find other quarters for himself and Bahjat Libdeh at the very least. The rest could take care of themselves. They had been nothing more than hirelings from the start, no one he cared about beyond their momentary usefulness.

Thankful that he had not destroyed his phone, Sarhan punched in a number for Libdeh and waited while it rang through at the other end.

THE KASSALA TEACHING HOSPITAL was Bolan's landmark, not too impressive with its rough concrete facade, two stories tall and pale gray, with a beige front door, although it seemed to be a point of pride on every city map Bolan had seen. Their target address was another half mile north and east, set on a rectangular plot of land surrounded on all sides by thorny acacia trees.

"Can't see much from out here," Grimaldi said on their first pass.

Advancing dusk helped foil the purpose of their drive-by, casting long shadows between the trees rimming the property. Bolan glimpsed two cars standing near a single-story house made out of something that resembled adobe. Lights were on inside the house, but there was no one visible outside.

"We need eyes on," Bolan said.

"Right."

It wasn't often that Stony Man intel was inaccurate, but anything was possible. Bolan didn't plan to blast a house he'd never seen before, unless he first confirmed some of the men he wanted were inside. He had twelve faces filed away in mind, the last surviving members of God's Hammer who'd been identified so far, and if he couldn't verify at least one of those fugitives in residence at the address they'd found, he meant to pull the plug on this attack.

And then, what? Nothing.

If he lost the contact address, there was no Plan B.

It defied logic that Kinan Asker would wind up in Kassala on his own, after the consular attack in Jordan, but that conviction wasn't getting Bolan anywhere. If other God's Hammer members were in town, hiding at some other address, he had no way of tracking them. And if they'd been where he was now but fled after the riverside firefight, they might as well be smoke, tattered and blown away on desert winds.

"Looks like a place to stash the car, up here," Grimaldi said.

More waste ground to their right, on the pilot's side of the Audi, with a scattering of thick, top-heavy baobab trees and more acacias. There was no curb or sidewalk, no streetlights, where Grimaldi pulled off the pavement, cut the Audi's lights and waited while they listened to the ticking of its engine cooling down.

They sat that way for close to fifteen minutes, Bolan watching through a pair of small binoculars while young men ferried bags and boxes to the waiting cars. "They're bugging out," he said, and then, "We've got one. Bahjat Libdeh in the doorway."

"Rock and roll," Grimaldi replied.

Bolan switched off the Audi's dome light before he opened his door. They were already dressed for battle, more or less, but there were still refinements to be made. Both men plugged a compact Bluetooth headpiece into one ear, granting hands-free communication once they separated for the strike. They slipped on bandoliers of extra magazines for their assault rifles and verified that every gun they carried had a full magazine, with a live round in the firing chamber.

Finally, Bolan hefted the RPG-7, fifteen pounds without a rocket in its launching tube, its canvas strap dangling. He chose a PG-7VL HEAT projectile—short for high-explosive anti-tank, designed to penetrate five hundred millimeters of rolled homogenous armor—and loaded it, adding twelve inches to the launcher's length and six pounds to its weight. For backup, he picked two slender OG-7V fragmentation rounds, tipping the scales at four pounds each, slipped them into a canvas pouch designed to carry them, and slung the pouch over his left shoulder.

"Ready," he told Grimaldi.

At a nod from his partner, they left their shadowed lair to cross the street.

"I DON'T SEE why we're leaving," Bahjat Libdeh said.

Idiot, Nour Sarhan thought, but said, "We have lost Kinan. Security dictates that we must go."

"But no one knows we're here," Libdeh protested.

"No one?" Sarhan shot a glance toward two young mercenaries lugging boxes from the room where he and Libdeh stood, taking them to the vehicles outside. "We have five of those men remaining, if you have forgotten," he told Libdeh. "And the spotters, still out there some-where, with our cell phones."

"Untraceable," Libdeh replied. "Cheap throwaways."

Sarhan nodded, as if suddenly infused with wisdom. "All right, then," he said. "You stay behind and wait to see whoever turns up next. But as for me, I'm leaving with the men and weapons. Good luck with your vigil."

"I didn't say I was not coming with you," Libdeh whined. "It simply seems…extreme."

"Tell that to Kinan and the three who died with him."

"You win, Nour," Libdeh conceded. Then he asked, "Where are we going?"

"To Khartoum," Sarhan replied. "There are more people there. We'll find a place to stay while the Crusaders run around Kassala, chasing ghosts."

"But we were ordered to avoid the capital after arriving. Saleh chose Kassala for security."

"And does it feel secure to you, Bahjat?"

"Well…"

"I thought not. Are your things prepared?"

"Already in the car," Libdeh stated, sour-faced.

"Good. We're nearly ready, then."

"And what about the hired men?" Libdeh asked him. "Since they worry you, why take them with us to a new place that we have not found yet? Won't they still be dangerous?"

Sarhan glanced toward the doorway, verified they were alone, then dropped his voice and said, "They would, if they were still alive."

Libdeh stood blinking at him. Almost whispering, he asked, "You mean to kill them?"

"When they've finished serving as our beasts of burden," Sarhan answered, smiling. "What else are they good for, now?"

"But there are five of them."

"Surprise is critical. They are expecting payment, yes? They shall receive it, only not as they anticipate."

He had already attached a sound suppressor to his Helwan Super semiautomatic pistol, an Egyptian licensed copy of the famed Beretta Model 92. It presently held sixteen Parabellum rounds, more than enough in Sarhan's estimation for five lackeys who would be expecting cash rather than bullets in their heads.

"Are they not armed, as well?"

"That's why I need your help," Sarhan replied. "You have your weapon?"

Libdeh touched his shirt, above one hip, as if he had to check. "I do."

"And do you have a silencer?"

His shoulders slumping, Libdeh shook his head.

"No matter," Sarhan said, holding his temper. "We are fairly isolated here. The shots won't carry far beyond these walls. I will begin it. You be ready if they prove more capable than I expect."

"Yes," Libdeh answered, with a jerky little nod.

"And wipe that grim look off your face, before you give the game away."

Libdeh tried to invert his frown. The new expression made him look as if he had to use the restroom urgently.

Was he this bad at Zarqa? Sarhan wondered. Busy with his own tasks when they struck the consulate, he had not monitored the other members of the team during the fight. Those who emerged alive had been adequate. He took that for granted. But now he wondered whether that judgment had been mistaken.

Was Bahjat Libdeh a weakling, masquerading as a warrior? Should Sarhan eliminate him with the hirelings and be done with it? That would mean leaving half their gear behind, since he could only drive one car, but if Libdeh was unraveling, it might be preferable to continuing with an unstable comrade.

No. That call belonged to Saleh Kabeer, and Sarhan did not feel like phoning him to ask whether Kabeer would mind losing another soldier on this day when one had already been slain.

He heard the local flunkies coming back, talking among themselves. He called them to the parlor where he stood with Libdeh, waiting until all of them were present. Reaching casually for the pistol wedged beneath his belt in back, he said, "Just one thing before we—"

With a crash of thunder, something struck the house, exploded, and immediately filled the room with smoke.

GRIMALDI WAITED FOR the RPG blast, crouching in darkness near the north side of the house while Bolan took the south, or front. He didn't see the rocket fly, streaming its tail of fire, but there was no doubt when it struck, a clap of thunder rolling out beneath a clear and starry sky.

There was a broad glass sliding door on his side of the dwelling, light behind it, even though the drapes were closed. He saw them ripple with the shock wave from the blast, approaching swiftly with his AKMS at the ready, finger on the trigger, even though they taught you otherwise in boot camp. Why waste half a second when it meant the difference between surviving and a cold hole in the ground?

Grimaldi reached the sliding door and tried it, crouching lower just in case someone was waiting on the other side. It moved, rolling along its tracks without a hitch, and he allowed himself a feral grin before he slipped inside, letting his carbine's muzzle part the drapes ahead of him.

It was supposed to be a rec room, he supposed, though it contained no evidence of any games: no billiard table, table tennis, barely any furniture at all. Wires dangled listlessly from one wall, where faded paint revealed the outline of a flat-screen television hanging, once upon a time.

"Clear," Grimaldi advised himself from force of habit, not quite whispering. He headed for a doorway opposite

the sliding glass behind him, where he heard men's frightened, angry voices, separated from him by a wall or two.

Grimaldi had the face shots of their targets memorized, had pictured Bahjat Libdeh with his patchy beard
as soon as Bolan spoke the killer's name. If there were
other members of God's Hammer inside the house, he'd
know them, too, as soon as he laid eyes on them.

And he was hoping that he saw them first.

Grimaldi edged into the hall, turned toward the voices,
then picked up his pace as gunfire echoed through the
house. Was Bolan inside now, or were the occupants firing at phantoms? Either way, the noise marked their position for Grimaldi as he closed in, going for the kill, just
as a second detonation shook the house.

As soon as Bolan sent the HEAT round on its way, he had
unsheathed one of the fragmentation rockets slung across
his back and loaded it into the hot RPG-7. Grimaldi would
be on the move now, coming in the back, and Bolan didn't
want to jeopardize him with the second 40 mm round,
so timing would be critical.

He counted off five seconds from the first blast, which
had left a smoking hole in the beige adobe-like front wall.
It could have taken down the door for Bolan, but he'd
counted on the HEAT round turning plaster, concrete, or
whatever the supporting walls were made of, into shrapnel. Now, he meant to follow up with the real thing.

The OG-7 antipersonnel rounds had a relatively small
kill radius, around twenty-five feet. Bolan couldn't be
sure that anybody was inside the room his first warhead
had penetrated, but he had rockets to burn and meant to
use them well.

He sighted on the hole his first round had created in

the front wall, saw flames leaping in the room beyond, and sent his follow-up directly through the bull's-eye. This time, when the 40 mm round exploded, there was less visible fire, more smoke and dust with jagged bits of steel flying in all directions, seeking flesh to mangle, bones to break.

Bolan laid down his launcher, shucked the dangling pouch and ran toward the house with his AKMS on full-auto. He guessed the front door wasn't locked, considering its recent traffic back and forth to cars, and felt his guess confirmed as the knob turned under his hand.

He shouldered through into an entryway just off the smoky room where his two rockets had exploded, to his left. He checked that open doorway, squinting through the smoke screen, and saw no one sprawled on the floor. The rounds hadn't been wasted, though. Bolan had simply rung the doorbell to announce that he was dropping in.

Someone was shouting from another room, making him wish they had an operative floor plan of the house. There'd been no time, and nowhere he could think of where the plans might have been cached. Kassala was the kind of town where people holding land built what they wanted, how they wanted it, and greased inspectors with a payoff if the neighbors didn't like it. He supposed there was some kind of building code downtown, all evidence to the contrary, but outside the city's crowded business district it was clearly each man for himself.

Bolan hesitated for a heartbeat at the junction of a central hallway, then turned left, trailing the sound of voices. He had no idea what they were saying, but the mood was obvious—startled, frightened, pissed off. One voice was talking loud over the others, trying to bring order out of chaos and not being successful.

He had the likely source of all that chaos marked, and was approaching yet another open doorway when a young man bolted through it, bailing out and shouting back over his shoulder as he left the room. He wasn't one of those from Brognola's rogues' gallery of fugitives from God's Hammer, but he had a pistol in his right hand, finger on the trigger.

His first sight of Bolan, dressed in battle gear, cut off whatever the young man was saying in midsyllable. He blinked once, then began to raise his pistol, fairly quick with his reaction time, all things considered.

But not quick enough.

A 3-round burst from Bolan's carbine took him in the chest and blew him backward, through the doorway he'd just cleared, dropping his body back inside the room, as if he had been reeled in by a bungee cord.

And that was when all hell broke loose.

CHAPTER TEN

Bahjat Libdeh had no idea what had gone wrong. One moment, he was standing in the parlor of their safe house, building up his nerve to join Nour Sarhan in gunning down the five young locals they had hired to help them with surveillance and disposal of their enemies. He was concerned about the odds, of course, but thought Sarhan would be the focus of attention when he started firing, freeing Libdeh to unload from his position in a corner of the room.

A cross fire. Take them down in seconds flat, before the targets could react.

Not safe, exactly, but it was a decent plan.

Libdeh was reaching for his pistol, wishing there'd been time to fetch a sound suppressor, when the world exploded. Shaken by the blast, though physically uninjured, he had looked to see how Sarhan would react. Were they still going to kill the others, or had that plan been discarded?

"Get your weapons," Sarhan told the five who had been marked for death without their knowledge. Frightened and disoriented, they began to sluggishly obey. Sarhan, meanwhile, was edging toward the nearest exit from the parlor. His eyes locked with Libdeh's for a moment, then he turned and bolted from the room.

Where was he going? Maybe to the small room he had turned into an office.

Libdeh did not plan to follow him.

The hirelings had guns in hand now, saw that Sarhan had deserted them, and turned to Libdeh with expressions ranging from raw fear to fury. Thinking of himself, Libdeh produced his pistol, brandished it above his head, and told them, "The Crusaders are upon us! Find and kill them now!"

When no one budged, he pointed toward the front part of the house, where the explosions had occurred. "There! Go!" he ordered, watching as they muttered, then moved off to battle with an enemy they'd never seen, bearing their motley collection of pistols and full-auto weapons.

The moment that their backs were turned, Libdeh slipped through another exit from the parlor. This one took him through the kitchen to another doorway and a corridor beyond. He cleared the door—and stopped short when confronted by a stranger in a baseball cap, weapons hanging all over him, a short Kalashnikov pointing at Libdeh's chest.

"I know you," the intruder said. "Lay down your gun."

Libdeh could not decide if he should fight, flee or surrender. Was that truly even possible, under the circumstances? His mind vomited images of torture by Israelis or some other client state of the Crusaders, maybe even at Guantanamo, where it was said that the jailers recognized no law. How would he hold up as the pain increased? What secrets would he spill?

Libdeh lifted his sidearm, and the stranger fired a burst from fifteen feet.

The pain was everything.

The agony within Libdeh's chest was absolute. He felt nothing when his shoulders struck the wall behind him, and he slithered down into a seated posture. When he tried again to raise his pistol, there was nothing in his hand.

"Payback's a bitch," his killer said, kneeling in front of him before the world went black.

BOLAN SAW NOUR SARHAN from a distance, halfway down the corridor in front of him, emerging from a room to Bolan's right and turning left immediately, jogging toward another doorway on the hall's left side. Even in profile he was recognizable, his hawk nose prominent beneath the thick eyebrows shown in photographs from Hal Brognola's file on God's Hammer. The pistol in his hand was muzzle-heavy with the fat extension of a sound suppressor.

Bolan did not call out for Sarhan to surrender, knowing the odds of getting him to drop his gun and come along without a fight were nil. He had the AKMS at his shoulder, aiming low to cut the runner's legs from under him, when suddenly a group of armed young men burst through another doorway to his right, blocking his aim.

They all saw Bolan, recognized an enemy and stopped dead in the hallway, obviously thinking his Kalashnikov was aimed at them. He couldn't fault them much on their reaction time—only a second, maybe two, before one of them opened fire and all the rest joined in, spraying the corridor with bullets.

But if their reaction time was decent, Bolan's was superb. He'd dropped and rolled before he finished counting heads downrange, forgetting Sarhan for the moment as he scrambled to survive. The storm of fire from pistols and at least one submachine gun passed above him, ammunition wasted as the bullets meant for Bolan ripped through walls, some going high and wild into the ceiling overhead, where a fluorescent light exploded, raining glass, phosphor and toxic mercury.

Bolan began returning fire before the jumpy shooters could correct their aim, working from left to right along their ragged skirmish line. He pumped three 5.56 mm rounds into the nearest target—young man, clean-shaven, armed with what appeared to be an old Beretta M12 SMG—and put him down. Falling, the youth triggered one last spray of Parabellum slugs into the ceiling, bringing down more plaster and a rat that landed on its feet, considered options in a heartbeat and escaped past Bolan, squealing all the way.

Second on Bolan's hit parade, a chubby, bearded guy dressed all in black like something from a movie, trying to look sinister and coming up short. His pistol was a knock-off of the venerable Colt 1911, loud and dangerous, but jumping in his hands as if it wanted to escape. When Bolan shot him in the chest, the man in black seemed to deflate, collapsing where he stood.

The third shooter in line saw what was imminent, tried to turn and run, but wasn't fast enough. A single slug from Bolan's carbine drilled a tidy hole between his shoulder blades and burst out through his chest in front, taking enough of his heart with it that he dropped facedown on to the carpet, shuddered once, then moved no more.

The two surviving shooters both had Bolan covered, but he didn't give them time to take advantage of their opportunity. He stitched them left to right, then back again, and watched them fall into a tangled heap together, one's head resting on the other's shoulder as if seeking consolation from his friend.

Sarhan had vanished from the corridor, but Bolan

knew which door he'd chosen, fleeing from the firefight. As to where it led, the only way to find out was by following his quarry.

Bolan half expected more shooters to spring from somewhere, coming after him, but none appeared. Silence had settled on the not-so-safe house, with its smell of gunpowder and death. Now he was racing time, before police arrived or Nour Sarhan vanished into the desert night.

The Executioner reached the door he sought, found it ajar and listened for a moment to the shuffling, thrashing sounds that emanated from the unseen room beyond. If Sarhan planned to ambush him, he wasn't being very subtle. Pushing through the doorway, Bolan caught his man lighting a twist of paper, dropping it into a metal trash can filled with jumbled documents.

Bolan leaped forward, slammed his carbine's pistol grip into the base of Sarhan's skull, and dropped him senseless to the floor. His next step tipped the wastebasket, spilling its contents just as they caught fire. He stamped out the flames, scooped up the papers and fanned the air with them until the last of them stopped smoking, then dropped them together on the small desk to his right.

Behind him, Grimaldi said, "Good job, Sarge. My guy didn't make it."

Grimaldi counted fifteen documents in all, or maybe it was fifteen pages of a single document. Counting was one thing, but he couldn't read a word on any of the pages, written all in Arabic. It struck him as peculiar, not for the first time, numbers used throughout the world— your basic *1, 2, 3,* etcetera—were labeled "Arabic," and yet he thought the written language looked as if someone had dipped a beetle's legs in ink, then let it run around the paper aimlessly.

"Make any sense to you?" he asked, knowing the answer in advance.

"I'll scan them when we're clear," Bolan replied, "and email them to Stony Man."

"Speaking of getting clear…"

"I know."

They heard no sirens yet, which was a good sign, but for all Grimaldi knew, Sarhan or Libdeh might have called for local reinforcements when their buddy Asker bit the big one. Getting out, sooner than later, ought to be the priority right now.

"Is he coming with us?"

"That's the plan," Bolan replied. "I doubt he'll tell us anything, but trying's why we came."

"We'd better get a move on, then."

Bolan folded the documents in thirds and stuffed them into his left hip pocket, then knelt next to Sarhan and started going through his pockets, tossing cash, a handkerchief, a folding knife. He kept the snoozing shooter's wallet, satisfied himself that Sarhan had no other weapons hidden on his person, then said, "Help me get him up."

Grimaldi took one side, Bolan the other, hoisting Sarhan's deadweight from the floor until they had his buttocks resting on the near edge of the little desk. Instead of letting him fall back, Bolan crouched, tucked his left shoulder into Sarhan's gut, then rose, lifting their captive in a classic fireman's carry. Almost as an afterthought, he took his AKMS from the desktop, holding it in his right hand, his left securing Sarhan's dangling legs.

The walk back to their rented Audi took a bit more time than crossing to the wooded property on their approach. They had to let three cars pass, one taking its own sweet time, but finally they stood behind the Audi, Bolan passing off his carbine to Grimaldi, digging in his pocket for the key fob, opening the trunk.

Sarhan wasn't a large man. Folded properly, he fit inside the trunk just fine. Bolan removed his belt, used it to bind his arms behind his back and keep him out of mischief if he woke up on the drive, then dropped the lid.

"Here's hoping," Grimaldi said, as he slid into the driver's seat.

"Here's hoping," Bolan echoed, but Grimaldi couldn't hear hope in his tone.

Stony Man Farm, Virginia

"BARB? WE'VE GOT something from Striker coming through."

"Be there shortly," mission controller Barbara Price said, already up and moving as she answered Aaron Kurtzman via intercom.

She found Kurtzman in his wheelchair, seated next to former UCLA cybernetics professor Huntington Wethers, peering at a string of documents reduced to thumbnail size on a laptop monitor in front of them. She leaned in closer, saw that they were all in Arabic, and asked, "Translation?"

"Working on it," Wethers said. "Handwritten documents this dense require—"

"Some time," she finished for him. "Right. Was there a note with these?"

"Just basic," Kurtzman said. He tapped a key and brought up Bolan's terse email. It read: "Translate ASAP."

"A man of few words," Wethers said, before he minimized the email.

"How's the translation going?"

"The program should have the first page coming up in thirty, maybe forty seconds."

"Can we see it?" Price prodded him.

"Patience, please."

"I'll take that as a 'no.'"

"The page will not display until translation is complete, of course."

"Of course. So, how long *now*?"

Wethers shot Kurtzman a sidelong glance. "I warned you not to call her yet," he said.

"You what?" Price felt the heat rise in her cheeks.

"And here we are," he said, ignoring her. "The first page."

Another key-tap, and the monitor displayed an English version of the first page scanned and translated. Price skimmed it, frowning. "What the hell is this? A letter home?"

"It may have been intended as a correspondence of some kind," Wethers replied. "The first-person description of events suggests as much. But we should not rule out the possibility that it's a journal of some kind, perhaps a diary."

"Because?" she prompted.

"For a start, the salutation."

"I don't see one," Price replied.

"Exactly. One assumes a letter should bear some form of address. If not a name or nickname, then a title used in greeting, such as Father, Mother, Sir, To Whom It May Concern."

"I get it."

"This, as you can see, described events beginning—Ah! Here comes the second page."

And so it went, page after page. The writer—whoever he was—related events from the night of the consulate raid in Jordan to his arrival in Sudan, and the move from Khartoum to Kassala.

"It's a confession," Price said.

"Or, more properly, a manifesto," Wethers countered.

"Like the Unabomber?"

"Or any number of other fanatics. Not destined, I suspect, for publication at this point."

"You got that right." She felt frustration settle on her shoulders. "Anyway, it's all old news. If Striker has these, he's removed the players in Sudan. It's useless if it doesn't give a lead to where the rest are hiding out."

"One page to go," Wethers reminded her. "And coming up in five...four..."

The page appeared, and Price read through it, feeling the dull pulse of a headache beginning at her temples. As she reached the end, she muttered, "Dammit! Nothing."

Wethers blinked at her. "Excuse me? It's right there." He pointed at the monitor.

"Right *where*?"

"The reference to comrades waiting at the Roof of Arabia."

"Okay, enlighten me."

"The Roof of Arabia," he answered, smiling, "is a common nickname for Yemen."

Kassala, Sudan

NOUR SARHAN HAD no idea where he was. Wherever the Crusaders had delivered him and bound him to a metal folding chair, it seemed to be an old abandoned factory of some kind, with equipment that he did not recognize standing around him, rusted and forgotten. The generic smell of mildew and rat droppings offered nothing in the way of clues, nor did it matter.

They had brought him here to torture him while asking questions. Nothing else made sense. Unless they wanted information from Sarhan, why was he still alive?

He sat—no choice—and cursed himself for being slow, clumsy and stupid. Why had he allowed his enemies to capture him, and in the process to obtain the manifesto he had started writing in his exile to Sudan?

Granted, the writing was not his idea. Saleh Kabeer, in his infinite wisdom, had chosen Sarhan as the organization's official recording secretary and historian. His orders had been simple: to prepare the first draft of a document explaining why the group was formed, what it had done so far and what it planned to do in the pursuit of justice for Muslims living under the thumb of so-called "superpowers" from the heathen West. Kabeer should logically have done that job himself, but leadership demanded too much of his time, as he explained.

In fact, Sarhan had seen his leader's handwriting and knew that it was childish, barely legible. His thoughts, at least on paper, were unfocused and obscure, as difficult to follow as a looping snail's track on a garden path, the product of a spotty education. Sarhan, by contrast, had been second in his class at Cairo's Helwan University, studying Arab literature with an eye toward teaching at the college level, when he had been drawn into the movement by a young man's passion to oppose injustice.

Which, it seemed, had brought him here, to face an agonizing death.

So far, neither of the Crusaders had laid hands on him, aside from clubbing him unconscious at the safe house and transporting him to the appointed place of his interrogation. Neither of them had so much as spoken to him yet, leaving Sarhan to watch them from his corner of the vaulted room while they stood out of earshot, tapping keys on a laptop, scrutinizing whatever appeared before them on its monitor.

Trying to translate what he'd written out in Arabic, perhaps?

Sarhan had tried to free himself. He thought the bonds restraining him might be electric cords, something his captors had discovered cast off in the onetime factory. In any case, they were unyielding, and he lacked the strength to break them. He was well and truly trapped.

A scuff of shoes on concrete made Sarhan open his eyes. The white men were approaching now, no readable expression on their faces other than a vague disgust at being in his company. And how did they imagine Sarhan felt, looking at them?

The taller of the pair spoke to him in English. "So, it's Yemen next, I guess."

Sarhan tried to conceal the sudden churning in his stomach. He could feign incomprehension, make believe he did not speak their language, but to what end? Thinking quickly, trying to ignore the throbbing headache he'd awakened with from being bludgeoned, Sarhan tried to reconstruct what he'd last written in the document demanded by Kabeer.

He had not mentioned Yemen by its proper name, that much he knew, but they had worked it out from the allusion to its nickname. Stupid! As to a precise location, there was nothing. He was sure of that. It all came down to his resilience now, his pain threshold and what he could endure without breaking.

"You're smart Crusaders, eh?" he said, sneering at them. "All right, go search the desert, then."

"You want to tell us where to look?" the tall one asked. "To make it easy on yourself?"

"Infidels!" he spit at them. "Go on and do your worst."

The thinner man smiled and said, "If you insist."

Kassala Airport

THEY HAD DECIDED on Grimaldi's scheme, filing a flight plan for Khartoum, with no intent of going there. Bolan had watched for extra cops and soldiers at the airport terminal, but saw nothing that smacked of an emergency manhunt. With any luck, the scene where they had snatched Nour Sarhan would keep investigators busy overnight, sifting for clues in the rubble and coming up empty.

It hadn't been that hard to crack Sarhan, a shot of amobarbitol in lieu of something more extreme. Grimaldi had the drug on hand, anticipating problems if they had to question any of the people they were hunting. Bottom line, it was a barbiturate derivative with sedative-hypnotic properties, long used by the CIA and other covert agencies to loosen tongues when time was of the essence and an operative couldn't trust pain to produce helpful intelligence.

They'd be flying into Aden from Asmara International, assuming that they got that far and weren't arrested on arrival. Sarhan had identified three of his cronies lying low in Lahij, north of Aden but with easy access to the airport and the sea, in case of an emergency.

They would be hunting a Jordanian, Tareq Talhouni, and two Saudis, Khalid Kamel and Yusuf Zuabi. As to where they were, precisely, in the smallish city of some twenty thousand souls, Sarhan had no idea.

It was something to work on when they got there. Bolan had the brains at Stony Man working that problem, combing undigested intel from the NSA, searching emails, captured cell phone chatter—anything at all, in fact, that might direct them to their targets.

Bolan had considered greasing palms to get them out and on their way in a timely fashion, but Grimaldi had advised against it. As he noted, you could never tell when some petty official might go rogue and try to throw his weight around, if something struck him as an insult to his dubious integrity. Better to simply run for it, in Grimaldi's opinion, and to trust the Hawker's speed.

Five minutes remained until they reached the border, maybe less. No sweat.

If someone in Kassala put out an alarm to the Eritrean authorities—unlikely, Bolan thought, given the countries' history—they'd have to deal with that upon arrival. Clearance from the tower in Asmara would release them for another hour's flight to Aden, some four hundred fifty miles to the southeast.

Grimaldi filed their flight plan via radio, in conversation with the tower, and got clearance for a takeoff to Khartoum in twenty minutes. He was smiling when he gave Bolan the thumbs-up signal, showing they were good to go. What happened when they jumped the rails and headed east, instead of west…well, that was up for grabs.

The good news: Bolan had a copy of their flight plan on his laptop and was fiddling with it as they taxied toward the runway. By the time they landed, it would show Asmara as their destination all along. He hoped that would be good enough.

If not, Bolan still had an hour, give or take, to come up with plan C.

CHAPTER ELEVEN

Zermatt, Switzerland

Saleh Kabeer tried his sat phone again, speed-dialing Nour Sarhan's number and waiting through eight, nine, ten distant rings, before he gave up for the fifth time. A sour taste in his mouth made him wish he could drink alcohol, to wash it away, but this was no time for falling out of favor with God.

Sarhan was gone, he thought, along with Asker and Libdeh. The rule was to immediately answer any sat-phone calls, to keep apprised of news and any changes in their plan that might be necessary. Breaking contact was forbidden, except in the direst emergency—and even then, there was a coded, automated message ready to be sent before the final curtain fell.

So, they were dead. Kabeer had lost one-third of his Zarqa survivors within the past thirty-six hours, and he still had no idea specifically who was responsible.

Americans, of course, which meant the CIA, the NSA, Homeland Security or any of a dozen other agencies that worked in competition or collaborated as the mood took them. To stop the bleeding, though—and to assure a margin of success for his dramatic sequel to the consulate attack—Kabeer needed to know *which* agency, *how* it had found his scattered men and *where* the hunters would strike next.

All answers that eluded him and made Kabeer's pulse throb until his ears rang. He felt like a man confronting enemies inside a pitch-black room, unarmed, swinging his fists at empty air and striking no one.

His next window of opportunity would open briefly, in the coming week. This time, he would not have to chase his targets: they were coming his way, to an epic meeting in Geneva, about one-hundred-fifty miles by car from where he sat in his hotel room, with a clear view of the Matterhorn and Monte Rosa through his windows facing northward. The surviving remnants of his team should join him two days prior to the attack, and they would all descend together with a day to spare, taking their time on unfamiliar mountain roads to reach their places on what the Crusaders liked to call D-Day.

That was, if any of his men were still alive.

Impotent rage consumed Kabeer. Instead of strengthening him, as a rush of fury often did in battle, this sensation left him feeling weak and drained, almost…ashamed. He had burned bridges when he left al-Qaeda, certain that he could improve upon its leader's sluggish tactics and produce important victories. Perhaps he'd let his ego get the better of him, but the goal was still within his grasp.

His focus was on world leaders traveling from half a dozen of the planet's richest Christian nations to Geneva, where they would enjoy the very best cuisine while plotting how to run, manipulate and loot the vast "Third World." If Saleh Kabeer could take them out, his place in history would be assured.

If he could do that *and* escape to fight another day, it would be proof that God smiled on him.

There were worse things than death, of course. Being ignored was one of them; humiliation, even worse. Throughout his years as a guerrilla fighter, first with Hamas in Gaza, then with al-Qaeda, he had always felt devalued, being told to watch and wait his turn while older men either dismissed his plans or—worse yet—claimed full credit for themselves when Kabeer's schemes succeeded. Finally, it was too much. He had stormed out to find his own path, joined by a handful of visionaries loyal to him, and their first effort, to Kabeer's mind, had been an unqualified success.

If they could carry off the second strike, even depleted as they were, it hardly mattered whether he survived or not. Success meant Kabeer's enemies would marvel at his courage and audacity for years to come. The so-called allies who had cheated or ignored him would be stunned, and then humiliated when his manifesto reached the farthest corners of the Earth.

Kabeer could watch all that from Paradise, content with his reward.

But first, he had more bloody work to do.

Asmara International Airport, Eritrea

AS IT TURNED OUT, they had no problem with the altered flight plan, after all. An officer from Customs, middle-aged and lost inside a uniform too large for him, had shown up on the tarmac after they touched down, spoken to Grimaldi for a quarter of an hour and appeared to swallow everything the pilot told him. Bungled paperwork was common in Khartoum, he granted; some might say it was routine. In confidence, the officer shared his belief that most Sudanese air traffic controllers were hired on the basis of family ties or friendship, rather than any skill or training they possessed. Of course, the same could not be said about Eritrea!

Grimaldi had agreed, nodding and smiling sympathetically. Their parting handshake, with five one hundred nakfa changing hands, sealed the deal. Grimaldi figured it just might be the best forty-eight dollars he had ever spent.

"All set," he told Bolan, when the Customs officer had wandered off, no interest in what they might be carrying aboard the Hawker, since the jet was only passing through.

"You called it," Bolan said.

"It's an acquired skill," Grimaldi replied. "So, Aden, here we come."

"And Lahij," Bolan added.

"Right. I searched it while we were airborne, and I have to say it doesn't sound like much."

"I thought about bypassing it and heading straight on to Zermatt," Bolan said. "If I had to guess, I'd say Kabeer's more likely to be hiding out in Switzerland than Yemen, but I could be wrong."

"And we don't want to leave loose ends."

"That, too."

"If Kabeer *is* in Switzerland, and he's been talking to his other buddies like the ones in Paraguay, smart money says he knows the net is closing on him. He could split and leave us nothing."

"Always possible," Bolan agreed. "Less likely if

there's something in the neighborhood to keep him there a while."

"Such as?"

"I did some searches while in the air, myself," Bolan replied. "Turns out Geneva has a summit meeting scheduled for next week. Big names booked at the Grand Hotel Kempinski on the lake."

Grimaldi had to ask. "How big?"

"Our President, Britain's prime minister, the chancellor of Germany. World leaders."

"A tempting target."

"Could be irresistible," Bolan said.

"Even with security up the wazoo."

"When is enough enough?" Bolan asked, in reply. "It only takes a few committed shooters. Or, let's say, a van from catering that's dropping off plastique."

"The Swiss are good at this," Grimaldi said. "But if they don't know they've got God's Hammer in their own backyard…" He let it trail away, unhappy with the general direction that his thought was taking.

"Better off to nip it in the bud."

"When does the meeting start?" he asked.

"Monday," Bolan replied. "The bigwigs should be flying in on Sunday."

"So, we have to finish up in Aden—sorry, Lahij—and then do Switzerland, all in the next three days."

"If that," Bolan replied. "Kabeer might not like waiting until Monday."

"Right. No pressure, then."

"But miles to go before we sleep."

Grimaldi smiled, said, "He's a poet now. Come on. We're burning daylight."

Lahij, Yemen

"I THANK YOU for the warning," Tareq Talhouni said. "We shall be alert to any threat."

"And if you think it wise to leave ahead of schedule…"

"I don't believe that will be necessary, sir."

"Remember, we are counting on you," Saleh Kabeer replied.

"We shall not disappoint you, sir. Blessings be upon you."

"And upon you," Kabeer replied, and he was gone, the sat phone going silent in Talhouni's hand.

The news was bad: three dead in Paraguay and three more in Sudan. Worse yet, Kassala was a ninety-minute flight from Aden via jet, with another twenty-minute drive from there to Lahij. For all Talhouni knew, a team of killers could be on Yemeni soil already, searching for him and his comrades.

Let them come, he thought, and smiled.

Unlike Kabeer or any of their comrades who had died within the past two days, Talhouni was prepared. It was dumb luck that they had caught the clumsy spy snooping around their safe house, but they had him. That was all that mattered. He would spill whatever secrets he possessed before Talhouni let him die, including the identity and number of the enemies he should expect.

Talhouni sat hunched forward on a sagging, threadbare couch, his knees pressed against the near edge of a table where he had distributed the items taken from their spy. A well-worn nylon wallet held a laminated card identifying him as Naseem Damari, an officer of the Yemeni Criminal Investigative Department. No rank appeared on the ID, suggesting he was no one of importance, but the information he possessed could still be useful.

Next to the wallet lay the spy's sidearm, a standard-issue Makarov pistol with eight 9 mm rounds slotted into its box magazine. The weapon's bluing had been worn away over the years, from being tucked away in pockets, under belts and into holsters. Whether it had ever killed a man or not, Talhouni could not guess, nor did he care.

Beside the pistol there were other useless items: a cheap cell phone with its battery removed to frustrate traces; a small wad of Yemeni rial banknotes secured with a rusty paper clip; a few coins; a handkerchief someone had taken time to iron, though it was wilted now; a small spring-activated knife; and a red plastic whistle.

The final item struck Talhouni as pathetic. Who had this Naseem Damari planned to summon with his child's toy if all else failed? Who did he think would come to rescue him if he was captured?

No one.

Damari was alone and had not learned the address of their safe house when they scooped him up the night before. He had been drifting through the local marketplace, pestering weapons dealers with "casual" questions about al-Qaeda and Yemen Islamic Jihad, obviously seeking leads to the guerrillas who had blacked out all of Yemen in June 2014, with a mortar attack on the country's main power plant and transmission towers. In the process, he had mentioned God's Hammer, and had thereby sealed his fate.

Word got around. Naseem Damari was as good as dead.

But first, he would reveal whatever secrets he possessed.

Talhouni's two companions had been working on the spy in shifts, not maiming him, but softening him up, persuading him that silence would not serve him well. He had resisted so far, rather bravely, but this night they would remove him to a special place Talhouni had procured for more advanced interrogation.

The spy would speak, or he would scream until his throat burst, and he drowned in his own blood.

Above the Red Sea

SOME SCHOLARS SAID the Red Sea took its name from seasonal blooms of ruddy-colored bacteria nicknamed "sea sawdust," sometimes found drifting on the surface in long, ropy strings. Others claimed the sea derived its name from the classical Greek word for *south*, just as the Black Sea's name meant *north* in ancient times.

Mack Bolan didn't know who named the sea, or why, but he was headed south-southwest at thirty-seven thousand feet, hurtling toward his next date with the enemy at five hundred miles per hour. Laptop open on a folding table large enough to hold a three-course dinner, he was brushing up on Yemen, planning their first hours on the ground.

First thing, there would be no sneaking around in search of weapons once they landed. Yemen ranked second worldwide, after the United States, for the number of guns in civilian hands. Public dealers were required to hold a license, but beyond that, anything was permissible, with open-air shops displaying everything from World War-era pistols to assault rifles, RPGs, mortars and light antiaircraft weapons. A glutted market kept prices down, letting the poorest man feel macho with a pistol on his hip or rifle slung across his back.

The trick, for Bolan and Grimaldi, would be arming up without drawing undue attention to themselves, before they took on God's Hammer. They had agreed to pose as shoppers for a group of men seeking "adventure" in the general vicinity, leaving the nature of their purpose vague enough to titillate suppliers with prospective future sales, discouraging reports to the authorities that would prevent those sales from going through. If a cop or two turned up before they'd filled their shopping list, Bolan hoped bribery would do the trick.

Nour Sarhan had not been able to provide an address for his three comrades in Lahij, but he had a sat-phone number, which in turn let Stony Man's team track the phone itself when it was turned on and in use. It had been operational for two minutes and thirty-seven seconds, earlier that morning, and they had an address now that might, or might not, lead them to their targets.

Baby steps.

"Ten minutes," Grimaldi's voice came to Bolan through the Hawker's speakers. "Wakey-wakey."

As if there'd been any time for sleeping on the short flight from Asmara down to Aden. Bolan closed his laptop, slipped it back into its bag and folded up the table he'd been using.

This time, their flight plan was legit, which didn't guarantee a hassle-free arrival. Still, their paperwork would pass inspection, even if it came to checking through the embassy, and their vague cover story—assessing investment opportunities for an unnamed major American retail chain—shouldn't logically raise any eyebrows.

What Customs didn't know wouldn't hurt them.

But it was about to land on God's Hammer like a ton of bricks.

Aden International Airport

THERE CAME A time in most protracted journeys when the traveler had to stop and double-check the local time, perhaps even the date. Mack Bolan hadn't reached that point, exactly, in his globe-girdling pursuit of God's Hammer, but he felt it drawing closer as he scanned the terminal at Aden International, reflecting that all Middle Eastern airports had begun to look the same.

Aden International was not identical to Asmara International before it, or Kassala's airport before that. There was a certain *sameness*, though, in the single runway, the terminal built small by Western standards and the relatively relaxed pace of passengers on the concourse. Best known for a series of crashes and hijackings in the 1970s, Aden International now had its fair share of uniformed security officers, some of them eyeballing Grimaldi and Bolan from the moment they entered, making their way toward Customs and Passport Control.

Thanks to Grimaldi's flight plan, there had been a stretch of tarmac waiting for the Hawker on arrival. Nothing fancy, like a hangar, but the jet could stand some desert sun, and Grimaldi had said thieves were less likely to attack it in the open, than if it were under roof and tucked away behind closed doors somewhere.

Despite the circling soldiers with their AKMS rifles, Bolan and Grimaldi cleared their various official hurdles without setting off any alarms. Their rental car was a Toyota Yaris four-door, right-hand drive, in silver that could pass for gray. It had a spacious trunk, a 1.5-liter 1NZ-FXE engine under the hood, front-wheel drive and a five-speed manual transmission for outrunning heavies—or running them down, if they got in the way.

It wasn't hard to find a street where guns were sold in Aden. Once they'd cleared the airport, Bolan drove northwest to find the N1 highway and approach a sprawling plot with many trees, identified on a web search as Al-Kamasri Fun Park. At the northeast corner of that property, an open market occupied the street, with scores of stalls peddling something for everyone. Bolan paid up for parking in advance, and walked back to the gun stalls with Grimaldi.

Unlike some cities, where he arrived unarmed and had to find the only dealer, choosing weapons from a small stash, Aden had *too much* on offer. Bolan counted twenty-four distinct and separate stalls, packed to the rafters with small arms of every description—and some not so small.

He passed on a couple of mortars, the Russian 2B14 Podnos, and declined various medium and heavy machine guns, represented by samples from various nations. Bolan finally settled on a pair of AK-47s for Grimaldi and himself. He field-stripped both with the stall's proprietor watching, found both weapons serviceable, and backed them up with a pair of twin Glock 22 pistols in .40 S&W. For heavier fireworks, he stuck with the familiar RGD-5 frag grenades that were so plentiful throughout the Middle East. The whole lot cost him one million Yemeni rials, a bit under five grand US, with extra magazines and plenty of ammo included.

Bolan had watched for followers between the airport and the fun park, spotting none amid the traffic which, as in Sudan, appeared to follow no set rules of conduct. Bikers took their chances in a stream of vehicles, reminding Bolan of the bumper cars he'd seen at county fairs when he was young enough to think that crashing into strangers was a form of entertainment without consequences. Somehow, they avoided accidents and got back on the N1 headed north, toward Lahij and their prey.

Three more terrorists were waiting for the Executioner, though, hopefully, they didn't know it yet.

Lahij, Yemen

"BEFORE WE START AGAIN," the interrogator said, "I give you one more chance to speak without persuasion, yes? It's only fair, don't you agree?"

Naseem Damari raised his head, an effort in itself, and viewed the man through his good right eye. The left was swollen nearly shut. He said nothing but spit a little blood, missing the man's boots and khaki trousers by a foot or more. The interrogator cocked his head and smiled.

"We know you are police," he said. "You asked about us at the marketplace in Aden. Very nosy of you, but you'll say it is you job, yes?"

Damari lowered his head, letting his chin come to rest on his chest. He was weary and hurting. His head seemed to weigh fifty pounds. Yet when his tormentor placed two fingers, sheathed in a rubber glove, underneath his chin and his sagging head again, it felt weightless.

"What's this?" the man asked, his free hand dangling a red plastic whistle in front of Damari, tied to a string.

Damari thought he recognized the whistle. Was it his? Something he carried with him on a daily basis? And if so, what for?

The man tried to help with his next question. "Do you

think that if you blow this long and hard enough, your friends will come and save you?"

When Danari said nothing, the interrogator raised the whistle to his lips, leaned forward, fingers still beneath Danari's chin and blew a shrieking note out of the whistle, holding it until his breath ran short. When he was done, he sat and waited, his eyes rising toward the ceiling.

"Anyone?" the man asked. "I don't think so."

Damari made the only move he could, with arms and legs all tightly bound. Tipping his head, he tried to bite the man's fingers, catching just a taste of latex as the hand whipped out of range.

And came back as a fist, striking his swollen eye again.

"Bad dog," the man scolded him. "You should not bite the hand that holds your life. Now you require more discipline. What should it be? Perhaps some electricity?"

The man left his chair and walked around somewhere behind Damari, coming back a moment later, trailing a small handcart with a car battery and thick, looping jumper cables attached. Their copper jaws resembled those of hungry moray eels. Damari could imagine how they'd feel, biting his flesh.

He found the strength to speak, although it cost him further pain from battered ribs. "No...please."

"Ah, so polite now," the monster man said. "I'm afraid it will not help you, dog. You must be punished for your rudeness. Then you'll have another chance to answer questions, yes?"

"I'll tell you...whatever...you wish to know."

"I have no doubt of it," the man said. "But first, you have to learn a lesson."

Reaching up with blue-gloved hands, the man ripped

Damari's shirt open, baring his chest. He studied the expanse of flesh, as if deciding where to start.

"I think one minute should be adequate," he said at last. "I warn you, though, it may seem like an hour."

"Please!"

"Hush now," the man said, and raised the alligator clips, their jagged jaws agape.

CHAPTER TWELVE

North of Aden

The N1 highway started in Aden, on the gulf, and ran from there through San'a and beyond, until it turned into the P1, forty miles below the Saudi Arabian border. Bolan wasn't traveling that far—just twenty miles, in fact—but he'd already hit a snag that was about to cost him precious time.

He saw the oily smoke first, rising from a point about two miles ahead, and then the cars in front of him began to slow, eventually coming to a halt. By then, Bolan and Grimaldi were close enough to see the tanker truck where it had jackknifed and exploded, with a crumpled van of some description pinned beneath its flaming wreckage.

"Good luck getting out of that alive," Grimaldi said. His tone and face were grim.

The stink of burning gasoline pervaded everything, but underneath it, Bolan caught a whiff of something else, like roasting flesh. Whoever was responsible for the collision and explosion wasn't about to walk away from it.

"How long, do you think?" Grimaldi asked.

"The fire brigade will likely come from Aden," Bolan answered. "We're ten minutes out, but you can see the cars lined up behind us. Even with the lights and sirens, call it twenty, twenty-five minutes to get here, minimum."

"Then another thirty, *if* they're packing foam," Grimaldi said.

Water would only spread a gasoline fire far and wide, perhaps involving other vehicles now stopped on either side of the flaming roadblock. They'd be very lucky if the fire was doused in only half an hour, once the trucks arrived.

And then, they could start waiting for a crane to shift the wreckage, letting traffic start to flow again. Call that another hour, minimum, once all the heavy gear and personnel arrived from Aden. Two hours, at the very least, before the wreckage of the truck and van were hauled aside and traffic cleared to move again.

"You think this is an omen?" Grimaldi asked.

Bolan shook his head. He had no faith in omens, signs or portents of the future. While he'd had some pointed out to him with earnest warnings in the past, they'd never interfered with anything he planned to do. If someone had deliberately caused this wreck—to stage an ambush, for example—that would mean something. Most of the time, though, accidents were simply that, resulting from a human's negligence or an equipment failure.

"If they got wind of a problem," Grimaldi pressed on, "this mess could hurt us, time-wise."

"Could," Bolan agreed. "Or they could be long gone by now, a wasted stop as far as we're concerned."

"And how do we bounce back from that?"

"Zermatt," Bolan replied. "We have an address from the phone trace there."

"And what if *they've* cleared out?"

To that, there was no answer but another head shake. If they lost the Swiss connection, he had no idea where they should look next for the remnants of God's Hammer. The group had left Jordan with sixteen men, and six of those were dead now, leaving ten. The world—even the Middle East—was large enough to hide ten men forever if they did the smart thing, went to ground with new identities and kept their heads down, found some other way to occupy their time than murdering Americans.

But *could* they stop?

Based on his hard-earned knowledge of fanatics, Bolan didn't think so. If their only motivation had been money, say a ransom kidnapping, they might have walked away and thanked their lucky stars for still being alive. Fanatics, on the other hand—whether religious zealots or political extremists dedicated to a bloody cause—had different wiring in their heads. They would proceed until somebody stopped them cold.

And that was Bolan's field of expertise.

Lahij

"THIS IS NOT WORKING," Khalid Kamel said.

"You question me?" Tareq Talhouni heard the sharp edge in his own voice.

"It was not a question," Kamel answered back. "I said—"

"And do you have a better plan?" Talhouni challenged. He was sweaty, and his skin itched, both sensations he had felt before when handling an interrogation. It disturbed him in a way, and yet, if he was honest with himself, he drew a sense of pleasure from inflicting pain.

"My plan would be to kill him and be done with it," Kamel said.

"And the information he possesses?"

"He has said nothing because he *knows* nothing, Tareq. He's a policeman. All they do is question people and solicit bribes."

"He asked about God's Hammer specifically," Talhouni said.

"Because we're in the news. The whole world talks about our mission in Zarqa, which makes it a success. He also asked about al-Qaeda, yes?"

"I have no interest in them," Talhouni said.

"And *he* had no real interest in *us*, as long as he could go back to his masters at day's end and tell them he'd been asking questions in the marketplace. *We* made him dangerous by snatching him and bringing him back here. He's seen our faces now, and where we hide. He needs to die."

Talhouni bristled at the challenge. He had been appointed leader of their three-man team by Saleh Kabeer, their founder. It was not Kamel's place to debate or second-guess his orders.

"He will die when I am finished with him," Talhouni said. "Not a moment sooner."

Kamel stepped in closer, lowering his voice. "He knows nothing, Tareq. At least, until we brought him here, he *knew* nothing. Each moment that he spends among us places us in greater danger, to no purpose. We are jeopardizing our next mission for…what is it? Personal amusement?"

Shivering with anger now, Talhouni kept his clenched fists at his sides, fighting the urge to strike Kamel and keep on striking him until he begged for mercy. "You forget yourself," he said through clenched teeth.

"*You* forget our purpose," Kamel retorted. "Yemen

was meant to be our refuge, not another battleground. Instead of keeping quiet and avoiding notice, now we have a cop screaming in the back room."

"He is gagged."

"And squealing like a pig at slaughter. It was a mistake to bring him here, a worse mistake to let him live this long."

Kamel was making sense, but that meant nothing to Talhouni at the moment. He responded to a challenge as his father had, with rage that prompted actions he regretted later. To be called out in the midst of an interrogation and chastised by a subordinate was galling. No, it was intolerable.

"Saleh placed me in charge," Talhouni said.

"Even the greatest of us makes mistakes," Kamel replied, with something like a smirk lifting one corner of his mouth.

"You wish to challenge me for leadership?"

"I wish to *reason* with you. Is that possible?"

"You have insulted me."

Kamel blinked once, then dipped his head a fraction of an inch. "If so, Tareq, then I apologize. My first and only interest is in our greater mission."

"If police are hunting us—"

"They hunt us *everywhere*, from Jordan to Hong Kong and Montreal. One raid, and we've become a legend. We are jeopardizing that by keeping this pig in the house."

Talhouni felt his anger start to fade, although the sweaty itch remained. "I only have a few more things to ask him," he replied.

Kamel nodded and said, "All right, then. But for our security's sake, be quick about it."

Zermatt, Switzerland

SALEH KABEER THOUGHT he could learn to love the mountains, with their snowcaps, evergreens and skirts of bright wildflowers. All his life, the desert had surrounded him, demanding Kabeer's loyalty, but Switzerland had given him a taste of something different. It suited him, and yet...

He had been watching the Al Jazeera news channel when the report came from Sudan. Police believed three members of God's Hamme had been killed in Kassala, with some local hangers-on. No names had been released yet, but Kabeer knew who they were and what their deaths meant to his mission. He and the survivors of God's Hammer were being hunted down and killed like animals.

Kabeer did not intend to die that way, without a fight. Without leaving his mark.

The mission in Geneva could not be advanced, as his targets held the cards in that respect, but Kabeer wondered if he might call in his last survivors from outside, a day or two ahead of time. They could be perspicacious, leave the hunters sniffing after cold trails far away from where the next great blow would fall. And after that...

In truth, Kabeer had not thought far beyond Geneva while he planned the strike. Part of him hoped he would survive to fight again, of course, but martyrdom held no terrors for him. A death in battle—or in prison, for that matter—guaranteed his place in Paradise for all eternity. His Lord would smile on him, if he could only kill enough high-ranking leaders of the enemy before he fell.

Weapons were not difficult to find in Switzerland,

boasting the world's third-highest civilian gun owner-ship rate, with some eight hundred thousand SIG SG 550 assault rifles kept in private homes and others circulat-ing on the street via black market dealers. Neutrality had spawned a militia culture, with young men subjected to mandatory marksmanship training, many of them then allowed to store their military arms at home in case of an emergency. Explosives were more difficult to come by, naturally, but Kabeer had found a source for Semtex and expected fifty pounds to be delivered well in time for the triumphant day ahead.

The problem now was when to call the remnant of his troops from Yemen to join him in Switzerland for the attack. The flight alone, he knew, was sixteen hundred miles—four hours on a plane, including delays for takeoff from Aden and landing in Geneva—then a hundred fifty miles by car over unfamiliar roads to reach Zermatt for final preparations. Call it seven or eight hours total, to be generous, followed by final planning sessions, then the relatively short return trip to Geneva for the main event, in three days' time.

Kabeer thought he would call them later on that night, have them make reservations for the following day on the first flight they could catch from Yemen to Geneva, and arrange the rest accordingly. If they came now, when danger might be hanging over them, he worried that the danger would fly with them and disrupt his grand, apoc-alyptic plan.

If that threat was ephemeral, he lost nothing by wait-ing to transmit the order. On the other hand, if it was real…well, he might lose three more of his soldiers, but the trail should end in Yemen. There would be no time for enemies to track him down, well covered as he was in his Swiss hideaway, before Kabeer had struck his killing blow against the top Crusaders of the West.

Feeling a little better now, Kabeer poured himself a tall glass of wine. Surely God would overlook one small transgression by his loyal disciple on the eve of holy war.

Lahij, Yemen

IT TOOK LONGER to find a crane and clear the N1 highway than expected. By the time bodies had been extracted from the smoking wreckage and the blackened hulk was hauled aside, discarded in the desert for someone else to remove at leisure, more than two hours had passed. Grimaldi felt frustration mounting in him, but he tried to cover it by feigning sleep, his cap pulled low over his eyes. Bolan had switched off the Toyota's engine, saving gas, but that had killed the air-conditioner, as well. They made do with the windows down, sweating like everybody else waiting in line, until the sluggish wrecker crews arrived to do their job, clearing the way.

For just a second, Grimaldi imagined what would happen if the Yaris wouldn't start when Bolan turned the key—stranded halfway between Aden and Lahij, with the two of them obstructing traffic now, an arsenal behind them in the backseat, barely covered by a blanket—but the engine started instantly, and they were off, the welcome air-conditioning roaring into life again with force enough to chill Grimaldi's face.

Better.

He had agreed with Bolan on the need to stop off here, tie up "loose ends" before the title match in Switzerland, but Grimaldi was having second thoughts now. Nothing serious, the kind of nagging little voice that might cast doubt on any personal decision, great or small. If anything went wrong on this lap of their journey—if they both went down for dirt naps, say—would Stony Man be able to pick up the pieces in Zermatt, before Kabeer and his remaining troops pulled off another stunt? Maybe the summit meeting in Geneva?

If they *did*, would it be Grimaldi's fault, Bolan's or a simple twist of fate?

Lahij was disappointing, after what he'd seen of Aden. With Bolan at the wheel, the pilot took in palm groves, houses made of stone, and side streets paved with more. The central feature of the town appeared to be a mosque standing beside a graveyard where the stones were placed erratically, some of them leaning in obeisance to age and gravity.

The N1 skirted Lahij to the west, or left, of town, but the address they had extracted from Nour Sarhan lay to the east, beyond the main drag access road that branched off from the N1 south of town and then rejoined it to the north. That took them past more shops and market stalls, their wares including fruit, clothing, hand-beaten copper implements, curved daggers and more guns. The shoppers eyed them with a mix of curiosity and frank hostility, likely believing they were tourists passing through en route from Aden to Ta'izz.

As for cops, Grimaldi hadn't seen one since they put Aden behind them, but he knew that Lahij was the main city within a district of the same name. Bolan had advised him that, since May, Yemeni troops had been involved with the police, pursuing terrorists in the vicinity, but showing poor results.

Maybe their stop would be a wake-up call.

But knowing Bolan's self-imposed restrictions when it

came to dealing with the law, Grimaldi hoped they could avoid official contact.

Otherwise, he thought, this grubby town might be the last one that he ever saw.

Robert F. Kennedy Department of Justice Building, Washington, DC

It was Brognola's turn to make a call. He'd thought about it for a while, considered skipping it and waiting until he had the final score, but knew the Man was waiting for results and taking heat from his opponents who found fault with every move he made—or, in this case, as they imagined, *didn't* make. Brognola had observed the ritual as it was reenacted time and time again in Washington. Whatever happened in the city or the world at large was *his* fault, automatically attributed to the man in the White House. Paying more for gas today than last week? "Illegals" crossing from the south as they had done for generations? Ups and downs on Wall Street? Mayhem in the Middle East? Let's blame the President!

The funny bit, if you could call it that, was when the opposition killed their own pet legislation, just because the White House had endorsed it. Brognola imagined that the Man could wipe out gridlock if he told the country drinking poison was a bad thing. Overnight, a fair percentage of his enemies might kill themselves, to prove him wrong.

But that was wishful thinking. At the moment, Brognola had real news to deliver—with a plea that it be held back from the media until the final act played out.

That would be problematic, sure. Washington lived on leaks, and keeping secrets was the hardest job in town.

Brognola made the call, after he'd doused the acid in his stomach with a couple of pills, waiting while his private line rang through. There was no operator on the other end. The Man was either in, or he was not.

Three rings, then the familiar voice answered. "So soon?"

"There *is* some news, sir," the big Fed replied, a leap into the deep end. "But I'd like to offer it with a proviso."

"News first, then provisos."

"Yes, sir." There was no point cutting off the call. He would have Secret Service agents at his door before the antacid kicked in. "The good news is, we've taken three more players off the board."

"Sudan? You mentioned that."

"Yes, sir. And I have men en route to three more as we speak, in Yemen."

"That's a tough one," the Man replied. "They claim to be cooperating, but it's always touch and go. One little drone strike on al-Qaeda, and you'd think that we were in there attacking the government."

"This should be deniable," Brognola said.

"*Should* be?"

"Will be, unless you choose to take it public, sir."

"And that, I would presume, is your proviso? You want me to keep it quiet for…how long?"

"That's *part* of the proviso, Mr. President. There's more."

"Let's hear it."

"We have one more stop to make—at least one more—before we have this all cleaned up. Unfortunately, sir, that stop appears to be in Switzerland."

"Don't tell me."

"I'm afraid so, sir. It may just be coincidental, but

with the intel we have, I can't discount the possibility God's Hammer may be looking for a big win in Geneva at the summit."

"Damn it!"

"Yes, sir."

"Wrap it up, Hal. Pedal to the metal. What else can I tell you? Setting up this meet has taken six months of negotiation, and we haven't even started in on the agenda topics yet. It will not—I repeat, *will not*—be canceled. Not for any reason short of Armageddon. Get it?"

"Got it, sir."

"The next report should be an all-clear. Work your magic, Hal. I'm counting on you."

"Yes, sir," Brognola said, as the dial tone drilled into his ear.

Lahij, Yemen

"THAT'S IT?" GRIMALDI ASKED.

"Unless Sarhan was feeding us a line of bull."

"It's not likely."

"No. I didn't think so, either," Bolan agreed.

The safe house looked as if it had been constructed fifty or sixty years ago, at least. Its stone walls needed chinking, and its roof of corrugated metal—likely not the first—was rusted through in spots. Its front door was a slab of faded wood, its lower panels gray from water damage, facing on a street riddled with potholes, where the elements and passing traffic had eroded paving stones.

"This is the worst dump yet," Grimaldi said.

If it's the right dump, Bolan thought, but didn't let his mind pursue that course. If Nour Sarhan *had* managed to deceive them, then their time in Yemen was a total waste, and Bolan didn't want to think about that with a doomsday clock ticking inside his head.

Two days remained until the VIPs began to gather in Geneva, and if Saleh Kabeer passed up that golden opportunity, when he was only one hundred fifty miles from target acquisition, there was something seriously wrong with God's Hammer.

Something other than religious mania, political fanaticism and a thirst for blood, that was.

"One time around the block," Bolan said. "Eyes peeled."

"Roger that."

They'd scoped the safe house to the highest definition possible on Google Earth, before it blurred out to obscurity, and come up short on likely access routes. The door in front was obvious, and Bolan's cruising circuit found another at the rear as he'd expected, but the roof was out, too thin and rusty for a stealth approach of any kind.

When they were back on neutral ground, a street with no direct view of or from the safe house, Bolan parked and asked Grimaldi, "Do you want to flip a coin?"

The Stony Man pilot shook his head. "I took the front last time. Might as well switch it up."

"Suits me," Bolan replied.

The street was empty as they stepped out of the Yaris, made adjustments to the weapons slung beneath their raincoats and secured the car. It didn't seem that odd to Bolan, no one stirring in late afternoon, with men still working and their wives preparing meals that he could smell from where he stood, cooking in houses up and down the street. At any other time, the mixture of aromas might have piqued his appetite, but Bolan wasn't hungry at the moment.

He was in a killing mood; no need to question any of

the targets they had come for, though it might be helpful if he got the chance, unlikely as that seemed. Unfolding circumstances would determine how much time they had to spare, and Bolan guessed it would be slim to none.

"I'll see you," he told his partner, and heard its echo—"See you"—as Grimaldi turned away, taking his own path to the killing ground.

CHAPTER THIRTEEN

Naseem Damari was about to die. He knew that, and despite the hours of torture, wishing that he could die sooner, now his mind rebelled against surrendering the final spark of life. He calculated that the terrorists would shoot him where he was, bound to the straight-backed wooden chair, the concrete floor beneath him speckled with his blood. But if they tried to move him first, he was resolved to fight with whatever pathetic bit of energy remained to him.

At least, he'd told the interrogator nothing, chiefly because he had nothing to tell. His lieutenant had assigned him to patrol a portion of the weapons stalls in the market, alert for any customers he deemed suspicious—which of them were not?—and making futile inquiries about arms sales to terrorists, as if a vendor in his right mind would admit to such a thing. It had been a foolish, time-wasting assignment, and now it had wasted the rest of Damari's life.

It shamed him that he would have told his captors anything to stop the pain they were inflicting on him. Thankfully, pure ignorance had spared him from that last humiliation. If his superiors had known—or truly cared—where foreign terrorists were buying weapons, they could easily have gone directly to the source and shut it down. Futile assignments to the lower-ranking officers presented an appearance of activity without result.

The interrogator was returning, telling one of his companions, "Yes, I know. Don't rush me." As he stepped into Damari's field of vision, the policeman instantly discovered that the man had removed his latex gloves.

There was to be no further contact, then. This was indeed the end.

"You've disappointed me," the man said.

"I'm glad to hear it," Damari replied, fairly certain he would not be struck bare-handed. And if he was wrong, what of it? He could bear another bruise or two before he died.

"I give you credit for your courage," the man said. "Naturally, I cannot release you."

"Naturally." Somewhere deep inside, Damari found the strength to force a smile, despite the pain it cost him from his split and swollen lips.

"You're not afraid?" the man asked.

Of course Damari was afraid, but he was not about to let this bastard see it in the final moments of his life. "Get on with it," he said, doing his damndest to project contempt.

"So be it."

As Damari watched, the man reached around behind his back and drew a pistol from his belt or some concealed holster. Damari recognized it as a SIG Sauer, although he could not guess the caliber or model number. This one's muzzle was a half inch longer than the usual, and threaded to accept a silencer. No great surprise, then, when the man drew one from his left hip pocket and attached it to the gun with three swift twists.

"Any last words?" the man asked him, smirking.

"None that I would waste on you." Damari answered.

"Good. Defiant to the end."

The man raised his pistol, aiming at Damari's forehead. At the last second, the policeman closed his eyes—well, one of them—deciding that he would not try to watch the bullet hurtling toward his face. Perhaps it was a lapse into cowardice, but—

When the shot came, it was *loud*, a great surprise considering the silence, and yet it seemed to issue from some other room nearby. Damari's one good eye snapped open, and he saw the man turning to face the source of unexpected noise.

"Khalid?" he called out, through the open doorway to his right. "Yusuf? What—"

The explosion swallowed whatever the man meant to say or ask his friends. Its shock wave rattled through the house and tipped Naseem Damari's chair, slamming his body to the bloodstained concrete floor.

GRIMALDI HAD CIRCLED around behind the house, watching for neighbors all the way and seeing none. No dogs announced his presence as he left the pavement, moving on to private property. Half crouching, doing what he could to make himself obscure in unforgiving daylight, he eased the AK-47 from under his raincoat and thumbed off its safety, ready to rip when Bolan gave the word.

Default instructions for a backdoor entry were to wait and see what happened out in front, unless an order came to change it up. Based on their last experience with God's Hammer, in Kassala, there was no way to predict how many shooters might be hiding in the house. Collecting local radicals or mercenaries might be standard operating procedure for this bunch, and while they hadn't been in Lahij very long, money and tough talk had a way of drawing thugs.

So he would hope for three and try to be prepared for three or four times that many once the party started. They would have to hit and git, identify as many of the fallen as they could for a report to Stony Man, and then get out of there before police or soldiers made the scene. Above all else, in Grimaldi's mind, was the need to stay alive.

He stood at the back door of their target, waiting for the Bluetooth earpiece to announce his next move.

"Knocking now," Bolan said. They'd agreed a somewhat casual approach was better than a smash-in from the street side of the house, and now that theory would be tested.

"Somebody's coming," Bolan told him, barely whispering.

"Ready on this side," the Stony Man pilot replied.

Grimaldi had his index finger on the AK-47's trigger, muzzle pointed at the door before him. Arabs didn't seem to care for peepholes in their doors, a quirk that pleased Grimaldi as he stood exposed, rifle in hand, waiting to make his move. There were no windows near enough for anyone to glimpse him without leaning into the backyard, and so far the pilot had seen no ripples in their curtains.

This would have been the time for praying, if he'd been religious, but Grimaldi had no time for dusting off old rituals that hadn't made much sense when he was learning them the first time, back in catechism class. Whatever happened in the next few seconds, he'd be going it alone, no one but Bolan standing by to help him.

"Going…now!" Bolan announced, and Grimaldi picked up the sounds of scuffling through his earpiece. When the first shot echoed through the house, he recognized a pistol's bark, nothing at all like the Kalashnikovs he and his partner carried.

"Coming!" Grimaldi advised his headset, just before he kicked the back door open and charged into hell.

TAREQ TALHOUNI LANDED on his left side when the world tipped on its axis and upended him. His shoulder made a cracking sound on impact with the concrete floor and drove a spike of pain into his upper chest, but he kept a firm grip on his SIG Sauer pistol as he fell. The clatter of a chair falling behind him warned Talhouni to make sure his prisoner was still secure, and while the move cost him some pain, he was relieved to find Damari still bound, hand and foot.

A relatively small explosive charge had caused the blast, maybe a hand grenade, preceded by an unmistakable gunshot. He'd been prepared to blame one of his cohorts for the first noise, clumsy as they were, but why would either of them be handling a grenade, much less removing its pin?

The enemy, Talhouni thought, but did that mean police, Yemeni soldiers or the damned Crusaders who had killed his comrades in a series of attacks over the past two days? No matter, he decided, struggling to all fours, then rising on his shaky legs. Whoever was attacking them, Talhouni had work to do.

He found Damari, the policeman, still bound to his chair, though it had toppled over and was lying on one side. He thought perhaps the man had been knocked unconscious when he fell, a bonus, since he could not call for help in that condition. It would be an easy thing to kill him now, a muffled gunshot to the head, unnoticed in the racket echoing throughout the house around him, but it also struck Talhouni as a waste of time. Attackers were *inside* the building, maybe one or both of his companions injured, and he might have only seconds to assist them.

Or escape.

There was no window in the room where he had grilled Damari in a futile quest for answers, but the next room over, just behind him as he stood facing the fallen cop, had one he could open, scramble through, and run as if his life depended on it.

Which it very likely did.

Could he do it? Would deserting under fire shame him beyond redemption in the eyes of Saleh Kabeer? But how would anybody know, if he escaped and his two comrades both died fighting?

It was worth a try. And should he kill Damari first, before he fled?

Why bother? If the captive was not dying from his injuries, he could impart no knowledge of Talhouni to his rescuers, whoever they might be. The smart thing was to run, immediately, while he had the chance.

"Good luck," Talhouni muttered, leaving the prisoner sprawled where he'd fallen, and retreating to the exit. He clutched his SIG Sauer tightly, index finger on its double-action trigger.

If he had to fire, the pistol's silence would help Talhouni, masking his position in the house from any lurking enemies. If audible at all, it would be heard only by the ones at whom he fired, and even they might well be deafened for the moment, by the previous explosion and the gunfire still continuing inside the house.

Trembling, Talhouni reached the doorway, checked both ways along the corridor outside, then slipped into the hall and turned right toward the bedroom next in line.

THE SAUDI, YUSUF ZUABI, headed toward the front door of the house to answer Bolan's knock. He was immediately recognizable from just the portion of his face revealed around the door, still nearly closed and held in place by a brass security chain. He asked something in Arabic, then tried again in rusty English.

"What you want?"

Bolan reached out to Jack Grimaldi through his Bluetooth headset, told him, "Going...now!" and threw his weight against the door with strength enough to tear the slim chain from its moorings on the other side. With any luck, the door would knock Zuabi on his rear and leave him dazed while Bolan finished him, a clean shot to the head and on to find another target.

But the wiry terrorist was faster on his feet than Bolan had anticipated. He sprang backward from the door, firing a pistol that he'd held concealed behind it when he answered, his first slug punching through the wood an inch or so from Bolan's head, spraying his cheek with splinters.

No time to think about that now—they'd missed his eye, at least—as Bolan powered through the door, his AK-47 tracking for a target. He was just in time to see Zuabi duck inside a doorway to his left, no more than six feet from the entryway, firing a second shot before he disappeared. That bullet wasn't even close, a ceiling-scraper, but whatever kind of semiautomatic he was packing, Zuabi likely had at least six rounds remaining in its magazine.

Bolan crouched in the empty foyer for a moment, hoping that Zuabi would come back and try another shot, expose himself to killing fire, but no such luck. Hearing a shout from somewhere toward the rear, immediately

followed by an automatic weapon's clatter, Bolan knew
he had no more time to spend on waiting. He edged forward, toward the open doorway, following the muzzle
of his folding-stock Kalashnikov.

And got there without opposition from Yusuf Zuabi.
There were two ways to approach the entry, and he chose
the safer of them, unpinning an RGD-5 frag grenade
and lobbing it into the room where he had seen his adversary disappear. Three seconds later, more or less, its
detonation shook the house, spewing a cloud of smoke
and plaster dust out through the doorway. Bolan kept his
back turned to it, his eyes shielded, then moved before
a shooter caught on the receiving end could pull himself together.

Too late. Yusuf Zuabi was in pieces and beyond repair.

Bolan supposed he had to have planned an ambush but
had skimped on cover, settling for a low table he'd overturned to crouch behind. It hadn't saved him from the
blast or shrapnel, one arm nearly severed at the shoulder,
while his chest was leaking like a sieve. Zuabi's shattered
jaw had been pushed backward, likely severing his wind-
pipe on its way to meet his spine. Whatever went down
as the final cause, he was irrevocably dead.

And that left two, at least, dueling with Grimaldi
somewhere deeper in the slaughterhouse.

As soon as Grimaldi told Bolan that he was coming,
he'd stepped back a pace and fired a 3-round burst into
the back door's knob, not taking any chances that a lock
would slow him. From there, he rammed the door full-
force, snapping some kind of flimsy chain inside and
nearly spilling to the concrete floor beyond, as his momentum took him through.

There was no one to greet him on the other side, but Grimaldi didn't have to wait long for a target to surface. Two doors down and on his right, a head popped out, together with a slim arm clutching a machine pistol. The Stony Man pilot just had time to hit the floor before a spray of bullets chipped the walls on either side of him and plaster started raining down.

He'd barely glimpsed the shooter's face before he ducked back out of sight, but thought it might have been Khalid Kamel. Names weren't that important at the moment, as Grimaldi fired a short burst in reply, then started worming toward the doorway on his belly, like a soldier crawling under concertina wire.

The shooter tried again, just seconds later, lowering his sights a little for the next barrage, but still fanning the dusty air above his adversary's head.

Grimaldi answered with a burst that chipped the doorjamb, driving his opponent back and out of sight. He took advantage of the momentary lull, advancing in a painful rush of knees and elbows, made it to the open doorway and stopped there, taking a chance to rise and stand erect.

A stray burst through the plaster wall could drop him now, Grimaldi realized, but he couldn't creep around the doorjamb fast enough to keep the gunner on the other side from nailing him. He needed speed, agility, and that meant moving.

He counted down from three, then bolted through the doorway, diving headlong as he cleared the threshold. Muzzle-flashes started blinking at him, bullets tracking him a step behind their mark. Grimaldi hit the concrete floor and slid, no carpet to arrest him, firing toward the enemy huddled to one side of the doorway, on his right.

Khalid Kamel—yes, it *was* him—took most of it,

reeling backward as Grimaldi's slugs ripped through his scrawny chest. Whether he died before he hit the floor or seconds afterward, it made no difference. The operative word was *dead*, as in stone-cold.

Grimaldi scrambled to his feet again, took time to breathe, then turned back to the exit from the killing room. He cleared it just in time to see another shooter stepping from a room downrange and recognized Tareq Talhouni, carrying a pistol lengthened by a silencer. Talhouni saw him at the same time, more or less, and raised his weapon, shifting sideways in a dueler's stance that minimized his body mass and profile for incoming fire.

It didn't help him as Grimaldi held down the AK's trigger and let it rip, burning through the better part of half a magazine to chop Talhouni down. The hot 7.62 mm full-metal-jacket rounds blew Talhouni off his feet and over backward, triggering a single muffled shot into the ceiling as he fell. Grimaldi watched him twitching for an endless moment, boot heels drumming on the floor, then he lay still.

Two were down on the pilot's side of the ledger, and he had to look for Bolan now. Before he had a chance, though, the Executioner's voice was in his head again.

"Jack, if you're clear, come in. We've got a prisoner alive."

THE DAZED MAN lying on his side, bound to a chair, was a surprise. Bolan had come up empty in his search for other targets, after taking down Yusuf Zuabi, but he hadn't been expecting a survivor trussed up like a Christmas turkey ready for the oven.

Only this one was alive.

Barely, it seemed, at first. Someone had worked him

over big-time, beating him and burning him with—what? A glance around the makeshift torture chamber showed Bolan the battery attached to jumper cables, shoved into a corner after they had done their gruesome work. The guy needed a medic, soon, but he still had a pulse, and he was breathing raggedly through torn lips and a broken nose. One eye managed to open after Bolan cut him free and eased him from the chair that had become his torture rack.

"Jack," Bolan spoke into his Bluetooth, "if you're clear, come in. We've got a prisoner alive."

"Incoming," his partner replied, and in another moment he was on the threshold, checking out the scene before he joined Bolan, kneeling beside the prisoner.

"Has he said anything?" Grimaldi asked.

"Not yet."

The captive's one good eye cracked open, focused on the faces leaning over him, and seemed to pick up on the fact that they were speaking English. In a croaking, nearly breathless voice, he said, "Police."

"I don't think we should call them right now," Grimaldi said.

On the floor, the stranger tried to shake his head. It cost him, but he still managed to tell them, "I…police."

"Well, damn."

"You're safe now," Bolan told the bruised and bloodied man. "Is there a hospital in Lahij?"

That produced an obviously painful nod. "Mustashfa 'Ali Jahis."

"Is that the name of it?" Bolan inquired.

"Yes. Name."

They hadn't seen a hospital when they were driving in from Aden. Bolan turned to his partner and asked, "You want to check that out?"

Grimaldi dug his smartphone from a pocket, went online and started tapping keys. A moment later, he said, "Got it. Right downtown, maybe a half mile south of where we're standing. Listen, if we're going…"

"Right," Bolan agreed. "Let's get him to the car."

"Ambulance run," Grimaldi said. "Go figure."

The two men righted the chair, then Bolan cut his bonds with his a penknife.

He took the captive's left side, started hoisting him, stone-faced against the groaning that evoked, then Grimaldi was on his right, providing more support. The policeman's arms weren't broken, so they each took one across a shoulder, slinging him between them as they might a drunken friend after a long night on the town. Except this friend wasn't enjoying it, and he might well be dying as they guided him out of the room where he'd been tied up and abused.

Grimaldi glanced across the sagging head toward Bolan. "If you plan on going in with him…"

"I don't," Bolan said, cutting off that line of thought. "We'll drop him off outside the ER, if they've got one."

"He could give us up."

"We saved his life."

"Cop logic," Grimaldi replied. "Can't always trust it."

Bolan knew that well enough. "We're done here, anyway," he said. "The docs will have to work on him a while. Before he starts describing anyone, we can be in the air."

"You hope."

"What's the alternative?"

"Leave him. Call 911 or whatever it is here. Cops can pick him up. They're likely on their way already."

"No."

"Okay, then. I'm just saying."

"Understood." Bolan had another motive, too. "Maybe," he said, "we'll get some information from him on the way."

CHAPTER FOURTEEN

Naseem Damari tried to pull himself together on the short ride from his former prison to Mustashfa 'Ali Jahis hospital. He occupied the backseat of a new four-door sedan, with duffel bags of weapons at his feet, and had no thought of reaching for them to arrest the strangers who had saved his life.

The pain he felt had lessened somewhat, since his benefactors had extracted him and guided him through relatively fresh air to their waiting car. Along the way, he'd seen the monster who had tortured him, sprawled out in blood, but lacked the energy to kick or even spit on him. There'd been no time to waste, in any case, as they heard sirens closing when they pulled on to the road southbound.

His comrades were rushing to reports of gunfire, unaware that one of their own brothers was involved. Damari was already working on an explanation in his head, trying to craft a story that would make sense at his next interrogation. It was difficult, given the throbbing in his skull, but he could always feign amnesia, buy more time that way, until he came up with a tale he thought might fly.

From the front seat, the taller of his two American rescuers spoke. "While they were holding you," he said, "did they say anything that indicated any future plans?"

English was troubling at the moment, with Damari's mind all out of joint, but he translated it to Arabic and gave the halting answer back in their own tongue. "I hear something about Geneva," he replied.

Up front, the two men exchanged glances, frowning in the dashboard's light. "Can you remember any more of that?" the tall one asked.

"A great day coming, one said. Death to the Crusaders."

"Did they mention any time frame?" the driver asked.

When Damari tried to shake his head, he side-slipped to the brink of consciousness, riding a wave of pain. Through clenched teeth he replied, "No. Nothing else."

"We're on the right track, anyway," the tall one told his friend.

"I'd say," the driver answered. Then, to Damari he said, "Almost there, I think."

Damari scanned the street scene with his one good eye and said, "Two blocks, then left."

"Got it."

There was a line outside the hospital when they arrived, people awaiting service, some with children, and no room to sit inside the waiting room. Mustashfa 'Ali Jahis was small, but Damari trusted its physicians to repair him, if repair was even possible.

They pulled up to the low curb, and the tall man asked him, "Are you sure you've got this?"

"Yes," Damari said. "And thank you. You have time, but not so much."

"Already gone," the driver said, with something like a smile.

Damari found the inside handle of his door and eased out of the car, got both feet under him and clutched the open door until he was securely balanced on his legs. He closed the door behind him, managed not to stumble on the curb and proceeded toward the ER's entrance in a shuffling zombie walk, not looking back. He heard the car leave, focused on the distant doorway, moving past the other sufferers in line.

They glared at him, of course. Why not? Some had been waiting hours, and Damari was about to jump the line. They would not take his injuries into account, but if accosted, he was carrying his badge and pistol, both retrieved by the men who had saved him, as they left the torture cell.

As he approached the door, Damari took the plastic whistle from his pocket, placed it to his swollen lips and blew a shrill, insistent cry for help.

N1 Highway, Southbound

Driving back to Aden, they encountered no more accidents or other roadblocks. They passed no squad cars rolling north toward Lahij, nothing that suggested any kind of citywide or regional alert.

"You think he'll cover for us?" Grimaldi asked.

"Buy some time, at least," Bolan replied. "One-eyed, with a concussion and the rest of it, he won't have any trouble mixing up descriptions."

"Right. Okay."

"You're worried?"

"Till we get up in the clouds, *amico*," Grimaldi replied. "Maybe outside Yemeni airspace."

"Anyway, we know we're on the right track with Geneva," Bolan said.

"A great day coming," Grimaldi said, echoing their

recently departed passenger. "Death to Crusaders. Yeah, I'd call that pretty definite."

"The summit starts on Monday. All the bigwigs will be flying in tomorrow, schmoozing, sleeping off their jet lag," Bolan said. "Kabeer could put his team into play at any time from early afternoon on Sunday, through the next three days."

"Are we still starting with Zermatt?" Grimaldi asked.

"I'd say we have to, since we have an address there. The only other way to go is having Bear ping the phone again and hope they aren't just drifting aimlessly around Geneva."

Bolan had already done the math. Zermatt had fewer than six thousand full-time residents, packed into a mountain valley fifty-three hundred feet above sea level. Geneva had close to two-hundred thousand citizens, with tourists piled on top of that. The odds of finding seven Arabs in Zermatt were vastly better than prowling Switzerland's second largest city, hoping for a chance encounter on the street.

If he missed them there, at least Bolan knew where the summit's VIPs were staying in Geneva. He could mount surveillance there, try Stony Man and see if Kurtzman could work any magic from long distance—and be ready for a quick eleventh-hour intervention, if it came to that.

The best plan, he'd agreed with his partner, was to locate Kabeer and company, eliminate them well before they had a chance to move on any heads of state, then leave the cleaning up and explanations to somebody else. But if they failed...

The internet had given him a rundown on the summit coming up. Aside from the US President, Britain's prime minister and Germany's chancellor, Geneva was hosting the president of France, Italy's prime minister, and the odd man out, Israel's minister of foreign affairs. Bloggers speculated on the meeting's agenda, bound to include tense discussions of Gaza, but the details were irrelevant to Bolan.

He had one job to do: punish God's Hammer for taking out the Americans at the US consulate in Jordan. If saving half a dozen of the "free world's" leaders from another terrorist assault was part of that, he'd call it icing on the cake.

Provided he could pull it off.

A fumble, with the present table stakes, would be disastrous. Bolan wouldn't get a pink slip in the mail from Hal Brognola, but he would carry an oppressive sense of failure to his final days on Earth—assuming that he wasn't living one of them right now.

Defeatism was like a parasite, gnawing away inside a warrior's brain, propelling him toward the completion of a self-fulfilling prophecy. Bolan would have no part of that, but neither would he minimize the risks involved for all concerned, and tens of millions he would never meet.

And he would worry, sure. Even when they were in the clouds.

Zermatt, Switzerland

KABEER HAD GIVEN up on trying to contact Tareq Talhouni via sat phone. He was ready to assume, now, that disaster had befallen his three men in Yemen, as it had the others in Sudan and Paraguay. Frustration seethed within him, but he still had six good soldiers under his command, prepared to sacrifice themselves if necessary for the cause. They would proceed as planned, with certain slight adjustments, and their glory would be all the greater for succeeding in the face of overwhelming odds.

"No luck?" Mohammed Sanea asked him, as he he heard Kabeer set down the phone.

"We've lost them," Kabeer replied.

"Who told you?"

"No one *told* me. I can feel it."

"Ah."

"You doubt me?"

"No, no." Sanea raised his hands in mock surrender. "If you say they're gone, I take your word for it. What now?"

"Now we go on without them."

"Can we?"

"Would you have us miss this opportunity?"

His second in command managed a shrug. "There may be other opportunities. Rebuild our forces first, and field a larger team next time."

"Or wait like cornered rats until they hunt us down," Kabeer replied.

"I didn't say—"

"This is the time to *strike*! We have the top Crusaders—several of them—collected in one place, four hours on the road from where we're sitting now. Who knows if we will ever have that chance again?"

"You always say we make our own luck," Sanea answered back, "with God's help."

"God has given us this gift. If we refuse it, we are spitting in his face."

"Whoever restrains his anger, God will conceal his faults."

"You're quoting the Koran to *me*?" Kabeer demanded.

"Words of wisdom from the Prophet," Sanea said.

"If I were *angry*, you would be correct. I am *determined*. There's a difference."

"Of course, Saleh."

"Are you afraid, old friend?"

The question went home like a barb, bringing fresh color to Sanea's cheeks. "You think I am a coward, after all we've done together?"

"No. I think that losing our comrades has you considering your own mortality."

"None of us is immortal."

"Not on Earth. But when we get to Paradise…"

"I still enjoy the struggle," Sanea said. "As do you, I think."

Kabeer nodded at that. "But when the time comes to lay down my life, I will not hesitate."

"Nor I. There is a difference, however, between necessary sacrifice and pointless suicide."

"*Pointless?* To strike down many of the top Crusaders?"

"Men they automatically replace within a day, while pouring more destruction on our people."

"Your concern for others does you credit," Kabeer said, making no serious attempt to mask his mockery. "Our people have endured this long, and will continue to endure."

"No doubt," Sanea replied, seemingly resigned. "How will you change the plan, then, to account for losing three more men?"

"I lead, as we originally planned, with Habis Elyan and Faisal Mousa. We adjust the others' infiltration routes to the hotel and have them well in place ahead of time."

"And me, Saleh?"

"You drive the van," Kabeer replied, "taking Talhouni's place."

The van loaded with Semtex, that would be, bearing the logo of a well-respected Geneva catering company that had been hired to supplement the kitchen of the Grand Hotel Kempinski. Sanea kept his face deadpan, but Kabeer saw him swallow with some difficulty, as he got the news.

"It shall be as you say, Saleh."

"I never doubted you, old friend," Kabeer replied.

Aden International Airport

GOING THROUGH HIS preflight rituals, Grimaldi kept expecting sirens and police cars on the tarmac, or a rush of military personnel around the Hawker 400. Aden International doubled as a base for the Yemeni air force's 128th Squadron Detachment, consisting of attack and transport helicopters, with enough security on site to manage an arrest, no problem, if they got the call from headquarters.

And how would that play out?

Grimaldi understood Bolan's feeling on cops—well, *understood* might be too strong a word, given some of the cops he'd personally known while working for the Mob—but he'd seen Bolan fight and kill soldiers in other countries where they'd worked together over time. It wasn't just the presence of a uniform that kept Bolan from wasting crooked law enforcement officers, but something in the oath they took when they were starting out, the ideals most of them brought to the job before it all went south. An army, on the other hand, was organized to do whatever politicians ordered, for whatever reason. Yemen's military had a record of atrocities against civilians, switching sides when civil wars went badly and deserting under fire.

Grimaldi wouldn't trust a one of them as far as he could throw their borrowed jet.

But no one came: no guns, no lights, no sirens. As the moments ticked away, he started to believe the cop they'd rescued might have kept his word and given them a pass.

The pilot had refueled the Hawker on arrival, looking forward to a possible requirement for a hasty getaway, but there was still a list of other things to work through before takeoff. Departure paperwork took close to twenty minutes, then Grimaldi made his walk-around, inspecting flaps and landing gear, securing external access to the lavatory, giving visual attention to the Pratt & Whitney engines, checking oil levels in each nacelle, eyeballing the ventral fuel tank through a handy access hatch in the aft equipment bay. From there, with Bolan snug on board, Grimaldi double-checked the instruments and radioed the tower that he was awaiting clearance to take off.

And this was when he *really* started getting itchy, pondering what he could do if clearance was denied.

Take off without it? Possible, but realistically the Hawker needed time to get airborne. It couldn't just leap skyward like a CG flying saucer in some cheesy sci-fi movie. While he taxied, getting lined up on the airport's only runway, maybe dodging other traffic on the ground, alarms would sound and troops would scramble, racing toward the Hawker, maybe lifting off in one or more of their Mi-28 Russian gunships. Those couldn't match the Hawker's airborne speed, but wouldn't have to if they blasted it to flaming wreckage on the ground, using their 30 mm Shipunov autocannons or 122 mm S-13 rockets.

So, a red light from the tower meant their trip was done, and bailing out on foot would only turn the bust into a comic opera. There were no guns aboard, nothing to fight with but their hands and feet, which wouldn't get them far. Grimaldi didn't feel like standing in front of a firing squad, much less dying in some forgotten cell while jailers used him for a punching bag.

He kept his fingers crossed.

The clearance wasn't quick, but it finally came through. Grimaldi passed the news to Bolan via intercom, fired up their engines, and prepared to take his place in line for lift-off.

The last lap coming up, and it was bound to be the worst.

Robert F. Kennedy Department of Justice Building, Washington, DC

"SAY AGAIN, SIR?"

"Hal, you heard me right. I need you with me in Geneva," the President said.

"But, sir—"

"I understand. You've got a desk job now, and well deserved, but this is critical."

"It's not the desk, sir," the big Fed replied. "We have ongoing operations, and I need to be accessible."

"Sat phone. The whole world is accessible."

"But, sir, this is a diplomatic job, and I'm an old street agent from the Bureau." Emphasis on *old*, he almost said, but kept it to himself.

"And you're in charge of cleaning up this mess with God's Hammer, Hal. You're doing a great job of it so far, and you will have seen that nothing's leaked about it. I received your warning on Geneva, which is why I want you flying out with me on Air Force One in…just over two hours' time."

"Sir, it's been many years since I was fit to guard a body of your caliber."

"I've got the Secret Service, Hal. I know you're not a bullet-catcher. What I need—what I *require*—is you on hand to keep your operatives in the field on track, if anything goes wrong."

Require. That said it all. Brognola watched his options for refusal shrivel up and blow away.

"Of course, sir. Did you say two hours?"

"That's takeoff. Any chance you have a go-bag standing by?"

"Old habits, sir."

"Good man. I'll have a driver pick you up in forty minutes for the ride to Dulles."

"Yes, sir. As to weapons…"

"You're all clear. I *am* the President."

"Yes, sir. I'll see you soon."

Brognola cradled the hotline's receiver, cursed his empty office up one side and down the other, then started preparing for his unexpected jaunt to Switzerland. He had meetings to cancel for the next few days and left that to his secretary, then called home and broke the news to Helen that their weekend had been hijacked. She was used to it, accepting it more readily than he was willing to, but they were both creatures of duty, in it for the long haul.

Finally, he made the call to Barbara Price at Stony Man Farm. She listened, didn't ask him any questions, trusting the big Fed to tell her anything he could. When he was finished she said, "Well, that's interesting."

"It's a royal pain," Brognola said. "That's what it is."

"If you're right about Geneva—"

"Striker has confirmed it from a source in Yemen. I was just about to call you when the Man caught me."

"So you could wind up in the middle of it."

"Could," Brognola stressed. "It might not go that way."

"Meaning it *might*."

"Tomato, tom*ah*to."

"Are you taking anybody with you?"

"Secret Service. POTUS says he won't leave home without them."

"Ha-ha. I meant—"

"I know what you meant. And, no."

"When do you leave?"

Brognola checked his watch. "One hour fifty."

"Okay. I can probably get someone to you. Maybe Pol." Price referred to Rosario "Politician" Blancanales, a member of Able Team.

"I don't have a plus-one on this deal," Brognola informed her. "It's a solo gig."

"I don't like this."

"Imagine how my wife feels. She was making pot roast."

"Can I tell Striker, at least?" Price asked.

"I'll reach out to him if I think it's necessary," Brognola replied. "Just be on standby while I'm gone, and let me know if anything comes up."

"I always do. Stay safe."

"To hear is to obey."

Brognola cut the link and went to fetch his dusty go-bag from the closet, hoping that the suits he'd packed still fit him after—what? Eleven months and change since the last hurry call? That made him think of food, and he began to wonder what they served on Air Force One.

Over the Red Sea, 37,000 Feet

BOLAN CONSIDERED SLEEPING on the flight from Aden to Geneva, but it wasn't working for him yet. He didn't like leaving Grimaldi by his lonesome in the cockpit for a long flight, and he still had lots to think about before the title match in Switzerland.

They would be flying over water for much of their journey, 3,248 miles by actual count from Aden to Geneva International. Call it six and a half nonstop hours in the Hawker, at their top cruising speed, first retracing their path over the Red Sea, crossing into the Mediterranean at Suez, then westward until they hung a sharp right at Malta and angled northwestward toward Geneva. Their flight plan was legitimate this time, and someone should be waiting for them on the ground when they arrived, with wheels and other items courtesy of Stony Man.

He didn't know who would be making the delivery and wouldn't ask. Brognola and the Farm would have arranged that side of things, and it was their job to keep a lid on it while Bolan and Grimaldi went to work.

They were approaching the Sinai from the south when Bolan's sat phone shivered on the meal table in front of him. He picked it up.

"What's up?" he asked.

"Thought I should tip you off," Hal Brognola said. "I got a summons to the summit."

"What?" It took a heartbeat, but he got it. "Not Geneva."

"Roger that. Seems like I'm indispensable."

"You're going with the Man?"

"It surprised the hell out of me," Brognola said. "My ride will be here in a couple minutes."

Bolan thought it through at lightning speed. "Okay. We're still hoping to head them off at Point A, but—"

"No guarantees. I know."

"You're staying at the same place as the others?"

"Grand Hotel Kempinski," the big Fed confirmed. "Sounds cushy."

"If they make it past us on the mountain—"

"Just do what you have to do. You understand priorities."

"I do."

"All right, then. Not to worry. If anything goes down, they'll likely stuff us all together in a bomb shelter, or maybe one of their bank vaults."

"Thanks for the heads-up, anyway," Bolan replied.

"I didn't want to take you by surprise, maybe spot me and think you took a wrong turn over the Atlantic, or whatever."

"What kind of security's in place?"

"The usual, and then some. I already gave the Man an overview. He couldn't call this off."

"If something happens…"

"It'll be like old times. You remember Vegas, with the Taliaferro brothers?"

"Don't remind me."

"It's nothing that we haven't done before," Brognola said.

"Okay."

"About security, you know I can't alert them, and if something hits the fan, they won't be cutting anybody any slack."

"I hope not."

"I'm just saying, so you know."

"Okay."

"But, look. If anything goes wrong…"

"It won't," Bolan said.

"Right. It won't. I'll see you soon, or not."

The line went dead, leaving Bolan to review the latest curve ball fate had thrown them. Hal Brognola was the chief of Stony Man Farm, knew all its ins and outs, but since he'd left the FBI he had been handling administrative work primarily, briefings and plans, the kind of string-pulling that made an operation viable. All vital things, but still a world away from fighting in the trenches, where Brognola had been when he was with the Bureau, chasing mafiosi and the Executioner.

Too different? Too long ago?

Bolan could only hope they didn't have to find that out the hard way.

CHAPTER FIFTEEN

Aboard Air Force One

The aircraft was a Boeing VC-25, with two main decks and a cargo area, having the regular 747's four thousand square feet of floor space reconfigured for presidential duties. Its forward section, dubbed "the White House," was the President's executive suite, including sleeping quarters and two couches that converted into beds, a lavatory and shower, vanity, double sink and a private office from which the President could address the nation via satellite TV.

A long corridor ran along the port side, with a Secret Service checkpoint, leading aft to a conference room for staff meetings. Also aboard the flying nerve center were two galleys equipped to serve one hundred diners, a medical annex complete with operating table, plus a nurse and physician on hand, and a pharmacy stocked for any conceivable emergency. Much of the plane's electronic equipment was classified, but the known list included eighty-seven telephones and nineteen TV sets.

"First time aboard, sir?" asked a Secret Service agent.

"No, son," Brognola replied.

"Ah. Well, if you'd like something to eat, sir…"

"Not just now. The lounge is still back this way?"

"That's correct, sir. Enjoy your flight."

Brognola recognized some of the faces that had come on board ahead of him, from news clips on the tube. They were seen on the sidelines at press conferences, sometimes with their heads together, whispering and being grilled by members of the "loyal" opposition party at congressional hearings. Up close, most of them looked smaller and less important, a trait they shared with lesser humans worldwide, but Brognola knew they had the Man's ear, some of them guiding global strategy in ways the public could barely imagine.

There was power on this plane. If something happened to it in midair...

Unlikely, the big Fed decided. Aside from standard safety features, Air Force One harbored an array of classified defenses designed to withstand air attacks and projectiles fired from the ground, including electronic countermeasures to jam enemy radar and flares to confuse and divert heat-seeking missiles. If the aircraft was forced down on hostile turf, the Boeing's Secret Service team and military personnel could hold the fort with hardware from a well-stocked flying arsenal.

Of course, if they went down at sea...

Forget about it.

Air Force One had never crashed or otherwise been threatened, except in a couple of Hollywood features. To Brognola, that meant the plane was reasonably safe—or overdue for a disaster that would set the so-called Free World on its ear. There was a reason why the Man and his vice president rarely, if ever, took the same flight. "Decapitating strikes" were always barely possible, regardless of precautions taken in advance.

But not this day, Brognola thought. The danger that awaited them was at their destination, not drifting above the North Atlantic waiting for an opportunity to strike. A group of men, fanatics, meant to strike a blow for God and a cause that had scourged the Near East for more than six decades.

Wherever a person stood on the Middle Eastern issue, one fact was incontrovertible: Israel's creation and placement, regardless of intent, had lit a fuse of violence that seemed to have no end. How many lives had been snuffed out in the struggle over the patch of land once called Palestine? Brognola didn't know and hardly cared, beyond the fact that it kept generating war everlasting, to the death.

Something he'd heard before, though on a smaller scale.

The one-man army who had waged that smaller war was waiting for him at his destination, though they might not see each other unless things went very wrong indeed.

Brognola stopped a passing flight attendant and asked, "Any idea where I can get a beer?"

Over Malta, 35,000 Feet

THE FLYSPECK ISLAND far below them was a bit of history surrounded by blue sea. Active as a naval base and fortress over centuries, besieged for the last time in World War II and granted independence from the British crown in the Sixties, Malta had hosted a summit meeting of its own before Bolan's birth, when Franklin Roosevelt and Winston Churchill met without their Russian ally, Josef Stalin, to prevent the Red Army from seizing most of Eastern Europe after V-E Day. They'd failed, and the rest was history, with repercussions echoing into the present day.

Wrong time, wrong war, Bolan thought, turning from the window as Grimaldi put the Hawker through its wide turn, looping toward the European mainland. They would be over Sicily in no time, birthplace of the Mafia and one of Bolan's former battlegrounds. Beyond that lay the Tyrrhenian Sea, then dry land, reaching Italy proper midway between the "foot" and "knee" of its boot-shaped outline.

Bolan had learned geography in school, but only *really* studied it when he became a warrior. He remembered names and places now, not from a textbook, but by who had fought and died there, either in the distant past or modern times. Some of the ghosts were fresh, his friends and enemies from recent battles, gone but not forgotten.

Bolan had followed through on his plan to call Stony Man for a ping on the sat phone they'd traced to Zermatt. It was still in the same place, unmoved, briefly active that morning, then silenced. That call, as far as Aaron Kurtzman could determine, had not been completed.

The caller had reached out to Lahij, now behind them.

So, Kabeer would have some inkling of another strike against his scattered soldiers, if he wasn't certain of it yet. Would that propel him into action prematurely, before Grimaldi and Bolan had a chance to reach Zermatt? God's Hammer couldn't attack the summit meeting too far in advance, before its principals arrived, but they could leave Zermatt, find someplace else to lie low while they counted down to Zero Hour.

What form would the attack take, when it came? Assuming that Kabeer had planned for sixteen soldiers on the raid, his force reduced by half and then some, he would have to modify his tactics. Seven men would find it harder to corral the Grand Hotel Kempinski than the gang he'd started out with, facing down security battalions from the government and those accompanying their targets, but they didn't need a clean sweep to achieve some kind of Pyrrhic victory.

A massacre, as long as it included certain higher-ranking victims, would serve God's Hammer as a bloody legacy—an inspiration to the self-styled freedom fighters who would doubtless follow them. And if Kabeer succeeded in eliminating any Western heads of state, his name would certainly be lionized among the refugees and children who would fill the ranks of future Arab armies.

Heading off that slaughter wouldn't solve the larger crisis in the Holy Land, by any means. Bolan didn't delude himself on that score, even for a moment. But it would allow six governments to forge ahead without the stumbling block of rushed special elections in a crisis, fresh invasions of the Middle East, perhaps retaliation on a scale not witnessed since the early days of August 1945.

That was enough to keep the Executioner in motion and to make him risk his life—again.

He only hoped it wouldn't be in vain.

Zermatt, Switzerland

"Our final comrades have been lost to us," Saleh Kabeer announced. "We shall remember and avenge them."

Seated on their chairs and on the floor around the small apartment's living room, his six surviving soldiers muttered, scowling at the news he had delivered.

"Who has done this thing?" Majid Hayek inquired. His dark eyes, underneath a mob of curly hair, were dangerous.

"Crusaders," Kabeer said. "We know that much. As for their names, and those of their commanders…" With a shrug and open hands, he left it there.

"America!" Kamal Bakri declared, while nervous fingers tugged a corner of his spotty beard.

"Most probably," Kabeer agreed. "They are our enemy, beyond a doubt."

"Jew-lovers!" Faisal Mousa said with a sneer.

"Christians!" Habis Elyan spit, as if the word had left a foul taste in his mouth.

Kabeer loved their enthusiasm, but he needed them to focus now. "Remember," he instructed them. "The best way we can wound our enemies is by eliminating those who lead them. Killing random Jews in Israel or the West Bank is a game for children now. True warriors recognize the targets that have value and eliminate them at all cost."

Ali Dajani, always practical, chimed in to say, "We are shorthanded now."

"But not defeated, eh?" Kabeer replied. He pointed to a floor plan of the Grand Hotel Kempinski spread before him on a coffee table. "We adjust our plans and make allowances for their security precautions. Kamal, do you have the uniforms?"

"Five jackets and the black pants to go with them," Bakri said. "In the confusion, they will not be counting busboys."

"Excellent. And all the radios?"

"Prepared," Mousa said, "with fresh batteries."

"Mohammed, when you have the van—"

"I know," Sanea replied, interrupting. "I approach the loading bay in back, with access to the kitchen. If the charge is great enough—"

"It will be," Kabeer told him. "Three pounds of Semtex is enough to level a two-story building. Fifty pounds should be enough for any grand hotel."

He smiled at that, the others joining in, except for Sanea. Kabeer guessed his second in command was nervous about his assignment for the raid, although he faced no greater risk than any other member of the team, and less than some.

"Would you prefer I drove the van?" Kabeer asked him.

"No, Saleh. I am pleased with my assignment."

"Well, then, you all know the signal?"

They nodded, more or less in unison, but no one spoke. After a silent moment, Kabeer said, "So tell me!"

"When I see you in the hotel lobby," Kamal Bakri said, "you raise your mobile phone as if to make a call. I signal two blips on my radio to all the others, and we move in."

"Security shall try to stop you," Kabeer said.

"We won't allow it," Dajani replied.

"Mohammed?"

Sanea met Kabeer's eyes, holding them with his. "I listen for the shooting, counting down five minutes. If security approaches me, I blow the van immediately. If the time elapses and I see no one come out the back way, then I leave and detonate the Semtex by remote control."

"And you bear witness to our sacrifice," Kabeer reminded him.

"Indeed."

"Once more from the beginning, then," Kabeer ordered, "before we pray."

Over Florence, Italy, 36,000 Feet

"Weird," Jack Grimaldi said. "I'm surprised the President is dragging him into the field."

Seated beside him in the Hawker's cockpit, Bolan said, "He isn't calling it field work. Something about 'consulting' on the case and 'supervision.'"

"With the President."

"And a command performance, yet. What's that about?"

"He didn't specify. My guess would be the Man is nervous, and he wants someone to blame if anything goes sideways."

"That's a politician for you. Can't just thank the grunts. And God forbid he'd miss a photo op."

"They've got big issues on the table," Bolan said. "So I'm told."

"Uh-huh."

Grimaldi didn't have much use for politicians, left or right. He automatically suspected anyone who craved authority over the common folk and questioned anything they said in the pursuit of an elective office, where he found that most of them spent all their time trying to *keep* said office, while soliciting somebody else's hardearned cash.

Still, politicians *were* elected in America, no matter what Grimaldi thought of sheep who cast their votes for grinning hucksters, and the worst they'd ever done paled by comparison with terrorists and anarchists who tried to burn the system down. Who was it that had called democracy the worst form of government, except for all the other kinds? Some British guy, he thought, and let it go.

"Does this change how we handle it?" he asked.

"Not yet," Bolan replied. "Bear says our target's still in Zermatt—or, anyway, his sat phone is. If we can tag them there, it's done. If they get past us, we'll just have to play the rest of it by ear."

"With Hal smack in the middle."

Bolan smiled at that. "He'd be relieved to know you rate him higher than the President."

Grimaldi shrugged. "I didn't vote for this one. Or the last two, either."

Truth be told, Grimaldi hadn't voted in so long he couldn't peg the last election where he'd taken the time. He usually had other matters on the go. Sure it was his civic duty, yada-yada, but he'd never thought his solitary ballot made a difference, particularly when he saw one candidate receiving money from the same fat cats who bankrolled his opponent.

If he had to dig a little deeper, underneath his trademark cynicism, Grimaldi believed he made a greater difference working for Stony Man year-round than spending thirty seconds in a voting booth some Tuesday afternoon. Each time he risked his life for strangers whom he rarely met in person and would never see again, Grimaldi cast a vote for civilized society over the jungle occupied by human predators. So far, he thought he'd cast those votes for the right side—at least, since Bolan had yanked him from his old life with the Mafia and turned his life around.

Not a moment too soon.

"We're half an hour out from touchdown in Geneva," he told Bolan. "I'll be talking to the tower pretty soon."

"You want me in the back?" Bolan asked.

"It doesn't matter," the pilot replied. "The whole plane lands at once. You'd better buckle up, though, if you're staying. Just in case."

While Bolan handled that, Grimaldi thought about Brognola's news. If things went sour in Zermatt, it put the big Fed at the center of a free-fire zone. That made him wonder if Brognola ever practiced at the range these days, or if he would be packing heat at all on what was meant to be a strictly diplomatic jaunt.

Consult and supervise my ass, he thought.

There would be *other* shooters in Geneva, though, no doubt about it: Secret Service, maybe SAS for England's guy and similar contingents for the rest. Add God's Hammer to the mix, and it could be a bloody free-for-all, with everyone firing at Bolan.

And at me, he thought.

Another quote came back to him from something he'd read once, supposedly a grizzled old marine sergeant in World War I, taunting his greenhorn privates when they balked at Belleau Wood.

Come on! You want to live forever?

Grimaldi, personally, thought that immortality would be a drag.

That didn't mean that he was psyched to die this day.

Zermatt, Switzerland

AFTER THEIR LAST verbal rehearsal of the Grand Hotel Kempinski raid, Mohammed Sanea left the rented flat and found a small bench in the building's courtyard. He was smoking his third cigarette when Saleh Kabeer found him.

"You still have doubts about the mission," Kabeer said, not asking. "Or at least, your part in it."

"No doubts," Sanea said.

"But you're unhappy with it."

"I was supposed to *lead* it with you," he replied. "Not park a van and skulk away while all the glory goes to others."

"All the glory goes to God," Kabeer said. "Have you forgotten that?"

Instead of answering by rote, Sanea said, "You know exactly what I mean, Saleh."

"Of course. You seek a martyr's end. And you may have it yet."

"Not if I run away before I detonate the van."

"In that case, you survive to tell our story and rebuild God's Hammer. That is the honor I've reserved for you, my friend. There is your glory, in addition to the countless infidels you send to Jahannam."

"You're right, of course," Sanea said, agreeing out of habit.

"Think about the others," Kabeer stated. "Who else among them would I choose as my heir and successor? They're all earnest and devout, of course, but none have your intelligence, your vision for the movement and the future. No. It must be you. I truly hope you will survive."

"I'll do my best," Sanea said, sounding less petulant this time.

"I have no doubt. May I have one of those?"

Tobacco was forbidden under orders issued by Islamic clerics, while in other jurisdictions it was merely something to avoid. The difference was critical to worshipers who deemed themselves devout, but Sanea took it one day at a time. This was the first lapse he had witnessed on Kabeer's part, but he passed the pack and held his lighter.

"I never understood the ban on tobacco," Kabeer said. "So many contradictions, and so many more important things to think about."

"Perhaps the cancer?"

"Probably the cancer. But why not eradicate other diseases that we can control?" Kabeer smiled at his own jest as he added, "Zionism, for example."

"Bitter death to all of them," Sanea answered, as expected.

"And to all martyrs, the open gates of Paradise."

Kabeer finished his cigarette in three long drags and ground it out beneath his heel, leaving a black smudge that would surely irritate the landlord.

The day was coming, and Sanea meant to prove himself. Whether he lived or died, his saga would be written out in blood.

Approaching Geneva

GENEVA SEEMED SMALL from the air, at thirty thousand feet. And it *was* small, beside the lake at whose southwestern end it sat, a tiny blip of human habitation next to 224 square miles of blue, frigid water. From on high, the city did not resemble Earth's ninth most important financial center, European headquarters of the United Nations and the International Federation of the Red Cross, or a year-round tourist draw.

Looks were deceiving, Bolan knew, at this or any other altitude.

He hoped Geneva would be no more than a transit point, as planned from early on, but he was ready if they had to chase the battle there, after Zermatt. He had already memorized approaches to the Grand Hotel Kempinksi, off Quai du Mont-Blanc, with its view of Geneva's lakefront. Ferries ran all day and well into the night, but access to the hostelry was strictly via dry land.

Bolan had experience piercing the minds of savages, fanatics, lunatics and worse, but he could not predict what Saleh Kabeer might do if he escaped Zermatt after a visit from the Executioner. A wise man might bail out and try to put some distance in between himself and his opponents, but religion and political extremism could change the game, as they inevitably changed a person. Terrorists weren't born, they were created—by their families or other circumstances that propelled them to a life of violence.

That wasn't an excuse. It was an explanation, but it didn't help him second-guess Kabeer's Plan B. Much would depend on whether the founder of God's Hammer had enough men for the job, but if his hatred for the world ran strong and deep enough, he just might try a solo operation.

Commonly called a suicide mission.

And if Kabeer's men escaped Zermatt before Bolan even arrived there, then what?

Same drill. What he *couldn't* do, even with Grimaldi to help him, was to search Geneva door-to-door, looking for leads to God's Hammer. He could have Brognola tip local authorities and start them searching, with their vastly greater numbers, but that only worked if the cops believed Brognola, and they'd still be wasting precious time.

Kabeer and company, if they could bridge the one-hundred-fifty miles between Geneva and Zermatt, would ultimately show up at the Grand Hotel Kempinski. Bolan's one and only backup plan was to confront them there and take them down, before they turned the holiday resort into a charnel house.

But could he stop them, even then?

The only way to find out was to try.

Grimaldi raised Geneva's tower on the Hawker's high

frequency radio, identifying their aircraft by its tail number. In the tower, an air traffic controller already knew where they were and how fast they were closing, watching their blip on a radar screen as it approached.

Geneva International had two runways—one made of concrete, pushing thirteen thousand feet, the other grass and earth, one-tenth the other's length. Grimaldi drew concrete, together with his final ETA, and started lining up.

"There are two flights ahead of us," he said. "We're almost there."

Bolan could see the airport now, a couple of miles from downtown, to the south. Already buckled in—the last time he'd be really safe until they lifted off again—he watched the ground slowly ascend to meet their hurtling plane.

CHAPTER SIXTEEN

Geneva International Airport

High-flying traffic had to wait as Air Force One approached Geneva International, looped once above the airport, then eased into its approach. Hal Brognola heard and felt the landing gear as it was deployed somewhere below him, ready to touch down and bear the plane's four hundred tons without letting it belly flop and spill its guts like candy from a huge piñata.

The landing was smooth, all things considered, and they taxied toward the nearer of two terminals, though no one on the aircraft planned to go inside. From his small window on the port side, Brognola saw military and police vehicles standing by, with fire trucks and an ambulance.

The big Fed knew without inquiring that the terminals would be on lockdown, more or less, until the Man and those attending him had left the airport in a motorcade of armored limousines and SUVs. There would be snipers from the Swiss Land Forces on each rooftop, covering the various approaches, while patrolmen made sure that no other sharpshooters had scaled those heights. Inside the terminal, members of the Federal Criminal Police unit would be keeping gawkers well back from all windows facing the runway, also helping officers of Geneva's cantonal police scan the concourse for crazies, drunkards, anyone at all who might create a scene.

Brognola wished them well and waited as the crowd on board began to thin, four Secret Service agents and a couple of Marines descending via air stairs, followed by the President and his aides in approximate order of rank. Brognola took his place near the end of the line, content with anonymity and hoping that reporters, held behind a cordon well removed from contact with the Man, would overlook him altogether.

He'd been told to leave his go-bag on the plane. It would be waiting in his hotel room or turn up shortly after Brognola checked in, no sweat. If anything went wrong, he figured he could restock from the hotel's shops and charge it to his room. Let Uncle Sam pick up the tab.

Three black stretch limos waited on the tarmac, bookended by SUVs and cop cars that looked gaudy by comparison, white with Police painted in black on bright orange door panels. Brognola figured that he would be relegated to the last limo in line, but he was wrong. Already headed off in that direction, he was intercepted by a Secret Service agent who rerouted him, steering him toward the lead car with its little fender flags beating the presidential seal.

"The President would like to speak with you en route," the agent said.

"Okay," Brognola said, as if he had a choice.

He found a jump seat waiting for him in the limousine—a Lincoln Town Car stretched to twenty-eight feet overall—that placed him to the Man's right, with two others sitting in between them.

Turning to an aide immediately on his left, the President said, "Ray, would you mind switching with my friend there, for a minute? We've got something to discuss."

Ray didn't seem to like it, but he moved without protest, Brognola filling in his spot just as the Lincoln started moving forward.

Turning to Brognola, the President lowered his voice to an approximation of a whisper and inquired, "Where do we stand?"

Stony Man Farm, Virginia

"Is it working?" Barbara Price demanded.

"Absolutely," Akira Tokaido replied. "I designed it, didn't I?"

"That's why I'm asking."

"Ouch!" Tokaido flashed a grin, the headphones draped around his neck whispering heavy metal like a sound of distant screams.

"It's five by five," Aaron Kurtzman said, parked behind Tokaido in his wheelchair, his right hand clutching a ceramic mug of freshly brewed swill—or what he referred to as coffee.

"So, where is he?" Price inquired.

"They landed in Geneva twelve—make that thirteen—minutes ago. The presidential party is en route to their hotel. No problems yet."

In front of Price, a twenty-inch Samsung LED-backlit LCD monitor displayed a street map of Geneva, Switzerland, four thousand miles and change to the northeast where they stood in Stony Man's Computer Room. A small red dot was moving over surface streets and getting closer to the lakefront by the second.

"No one knows he's carrying the homer?"

"Nope," Tokaido said. "*Hal* doesn't know he's carrying."

That much was true. The homer—activated by remote control from Stony Man for situations such as this, rare as they were—had been inserted in Brognola's go-bag without telling him.

"I thought the Secret Service would have scanned their luggage," Price replied.

"I say again," Tokaido answered back, "the toy is *my* design."

"Smart-ass."

"You got the *smart* bit right, at least."

"Let's focus, people," Kurtzman interjected. When he blew lightly across his steaming coffee mug, its odd aroma tickled Price's nostrils.

"How you drink that stuff," she said, "I'll never understand."

"It's nectar of the gods," he said.

"Yeah, maybe Hades."

"Philistine."

"Whatever. We can only track his bag, right? We've got nothing if he exits the hotel without it."

"True," Tokaido admitted. "If I'd had the time and access to his house, I could've tracked his suits, his shoes, his skivvies—"

"Never mind," Kurtzman cut in. "We've got the meeting's whole agenda. They're not taking any day trips from the hotel, no boating on the lake, no nothing. Noses to the grindstone for the three days they're in Geneva."

"That's a gaping window for the other side to crawl through," Price reminded him.

"Assuming that they ever make it to Geneva from Zermatt," Kurtzman replied.

"Uh-huh. How are we doing on that end?"

"Our last ping on the sat phone showed no movement."

"When was that?" she pressed him.

Kurtzman hesitated, then said, "Four hours and twenty-seven minutes ago."

"Damn! What if they left the phone behind?"

"Why would they?" Tokaido asked.

"You're right," Price said, as if trying to make herself believe.

Except, she thought, they've got nobody left to call outside Geneva, that we know about. Striker had taken down the other members of God's Hammer, scattered around the globe, before they could regroup for what was shaping up to be their main event. Their leader, Saleh Kabeer, was running short on manpower, and all of his remaining men were with him now, in Switzerland.

Would he suspect, by any chance, that someone might have traced his phone? If so, would he have used it for another call as recently as Kurtzman claimed? She couldn't answer either of those questions, and the damned uncertainty had Price's nerves on edge.

"Striker and Jack?" she asked.

There was another homer in the jet, which only told her where the Hawker was. Better than nothing, by some small degree.

"Inbound," Kurtzman said. "They'll be on the deck in ten, maybe fifteen."

"And someone's meeting them."

"Hal set it up."

Price hated situations that were not within her own immediate control, and this was one of them. Hell, half her life was spent observing actions far beyond her reach, hoping the latest well-laid plan didn't disintegrate.

It was a miracle that she wasn't turning gray.

Geneva International Airport

Two guys were waiting for Bolan and Grimaldi as they passed through Customs, with nothing to declare. One of them was a six-foot-something blond, his hairline creeping backward from a worried forehead. His companion was a stocky five-ten, with a dark buzz cut and a bristling mustache. Their suits were off the rack and likely cost less than their matching sunglasses. The shorter of the pair held a piece of cardboard with COOPER printed on it, watching passengers stream past him, at a loss to spot the travelers he'd come to meet.

"I'm Cooper," Bolan said, and left it there. He didn't introduce Grimaldi and received no names from either member of the welcoming committee.

"We're in the garage," the tall man said. "This way."

It was a relatively short hike through the terminal and down a hallway to the parking garage labeled P1 on walls and supporting pillars. The escorts led them to a navy blue Volkswagen Jetta, parked between one of the pillars and a black Citroën C4 Aircross compact SUV. The taller man produced a set of keys and popped the Jetta's trunk lid. Inside, underneath a blanket, he revealed their hardware, neatly laid out for inspection, saying, "Hope these suit you."

The long guns were SG 552 Commando carbines, with folding stocks and 8.9-inch barrels featuring open, three-prong flash suppressors. The Commandos, smaller versions of Switzerland's standard-issue SIG SG 550 battle rifle, packed its parent's same firepower, feeding 5.56 mm NATO rounds from 30-round box magazines. Like the full-size rifles, these were also capable of selective fire at the shooter's pleasure.

Keeping it local, the greeters had also packed two SIG Sauer P226 MK25 pistols, each fitted with a Sure-Fire X300 Ultra flashlight mounted on a Picatinny rail to pick out targets in the dark and tell combatants where their shots were meant to land. The pistols, Bolan saw, were chambered in .40 S&W, meaning they carried magazines with fourteen rounds and one more up the spout. Extended, threaded muzzles would accommodate the slim sound suppressors nestled next to each handgun, with adjustable shoulder holsters.

Last came the stun grenades, a dozen of the M84 model, weighing in at half a pound each, detonated by M201A1 time-delay fuses allowing the thrower an average 1.5 seconds to duck out of range. "Okay?" the short man asked.

"Have these been tested?" Grimaldi queried.

"We keep our stock in perfect working order," the taller guy stated.

"We're good to go, then," Bolan said, taking the Jetta's keys.

"Good luck," the taller man said, palming another key that made lights flash and an alarm chirp briefly on the Citroën parked next to it.

Bolan and Grimaldi stood waiting for the men to climb aboard their vehicle, back out and exit the garage, before they leaned into the trunk, hiding their hardware from surveillance cameras. They checked each pistol's magazine and chamber, holstered them, keeping the rigs down low until they both were seated in the Volkswagen, then slipped them on and covered them with windbreakers against the nippy air outside.

"Zermatt," the Stony Man pilot said, from his position in the shotgun seat.

"Zermatt," Bolan agreed, and put the Jetta into gear.

Zermatt

SALEH KABEER WATCHED as the Great Satan's commander in chief deplaned at Geneva International Airport, welcomed by a small brass band and many security officers. The television flickered—something in the atmosphere, perhaps, or plain old age—but he could see enough. The slim Crusader's smile, all arrogance, as he waved to a crowd restrained by waist-high barriers and armed police. Kabeer wondered if he could read some of the signs they waved at him, or if he thought the slogans all were complimentary.

An ambush at the airport would have been impossible, even with RPGs if they had any. And besides, what was the point in killing just one leader of the mythical "free world," when he could take out six at once?

Grand gestures had been few and far between since 9/11, in the war against Israel and its supporters. It was high time for a greater, even more impressive strike that would demoralize the West for years to come. Perhaps, at last, they would take time and reconsider their commitment to an outlaw state that drained their resources and offered nothing in return except continual headaches.

Kabeer studied the president—or POTUS, as they called him; what a foolish nickname for a head of state, more like a vegetable—as he approached the first of three stretch limousines, giving the crowd a final wave. Kabeer knew certain members of the presidential entourage by sight, from CNN and Al Jazeera broadcasts, but the rest were strangers to him, walk-on players in the drama he had scripted, simply present to enhance the final body count.

"He's here, then," Mohammed Sanea said, having entered without knocking at the parlor's open door.

"All safe and sound," Kabeer replied. "For now."

On screen, the band stopped playing, and the motorcade rolled out, led by police cars and black SUVs, with more trailing behind. A talking head for a local news station came on, describing the scene in French for those too stupid to use their own eyes, inserting some gibberish about the world's "high hopes" for resolution of long-standing tensions in the Middle East.

You may be right, there, Kabeer thought. Once God's Hammer had its say, some in the West might finally decide the price of keeping Israel at the trough was too high for their liking. Or, they might retaliate with overwhelming force against the usual third parties, mouthing platitudes of justice.

Either way, if still alive, Kabeer would be well satisfied.

Mayhem inflicted on the innocent for "crimes" committed by small groups of dedicated freedom fighters was the norm, where Israel and its various supporters were concerned. Why should this time be any different? Each blow they struck against civilians, each home that they razed in Gaza or along the West Bank, brought the armed resistance more recruits.

"The van is waiting for us," Sanea said, his voice calm but devoid of enthusiasm.

"Excellent. You have my every confidence."

"God will guide our hands."

"Undoubtedly."

"I'll leave you to it, then."

Kabeer switched channels, turning to M6 Suisse for another view of the primary target's arrival. Watching the Crusader, he could only smile. It might well be the last time that a global audience would see his enemy alive.

On the A40 Motorway, Switzerland

GEOGRAPHY COMPLICATED TRAVEL by car and rail in Switzerland. The Alps did not cooperate with engineers to grant straight rights of way from one town to another. The last leg of their long campaign, Grimaldi hoped, would take some three and a half hours nonstop, winding around mountain peaks, ducking in and out of tunnels where multilingual signs warned drivers to lay off their horns. Naturally, there was at least one clown in every concrete passageway who had to break the rule and blare away, trailing Doppler echoes behind him.

They were headed for Täsch, a village of fewer than fifteen hundred souls that marked the end of the line for drivers approaching Zermatt. Täsch lay three and a half miles north of Zermatt, and some five hundred feet closer to sea level, featuring tourist hotels and restaurants, plus parking for those continuing on toward the summit. Zermatt itself had banned combustion engines to minimize air pollution, thus preserving its view of the Matterhorn. All cars and buses in the higher town were electric and nearly silent, aside from emergency vehicles and a handful of municipal garbage trucks.

Clean air, great scenery, a date with death.

"I would've thought they'd look for someplace closer

to Geneva," Grimaldi said, as they entered yet another tunnel through the latest mountainside.

"It might have seemed too risky," Bolan theorized. "Kabeer likely wanted someplace to hide, while he was hatching plans."

"He's an ambitious prick, I'll give him that," Grimaldi said.

"Nobody ever made it big by thinking small."

"Still, do any of them think they'll walk away from this? Even a clean sweep leaves them dead, along with everybody else."

"That may not enter into it," Bolan replied. "Outfits like this are all about the gesture, even if it takes them down."

"So, this could be like Oklahoma City with a bunch of suicide commandos."

"If we let them get that far."

"Let's not."

"My thought, exactly."

"The address you got from Stony Man," the pilot said. "Is that some kind of rooming house?"

"It isn't labeled on the aerials, like hotels and the Matterhorn Museum. It could be a rooming house, maybe a smaller hostel or a B and B."

The logo *Blood and Breakfast* surfaced in Grimaldi's mind. He shrugged it off and focused on light at the end of the tunnel, a hundred yards distant but closing.

"I guess we're bound to ruin someone's day," he said.

"Bet on it."

"And they've got police up there?"

"A small detachment, mostly for the tourist beat and climber rescues."

"Too bad we can't fly in," Grimaldi said. "It would make a quicker exit."

He was thinking of the funicular railway from Täsch to Zermatt, not a long ride at fifteen minutes one way, but time enough for SWAT to gather at the bottom when a fugitive was in a hurry. All dressed up and nowhere to go, when they got to the terminal.

Terminal?

Bad choice of terms. Shake it off.

Grimaldi stretched as best he could and said, "You want a break, I'm good to drive."

"I'm fine," Bolan replied. "We're nearly halfway there."

Grimaldi didn't want to raise the subject that was nagging at him: What if God's Hammer had come down the mountain in advance, to be on hand before the summit formally got underway? There was nothing the two of them could do about it, barring redirection from the Farm, but it was troublesome. To come this far and miss the show…

Not happening, he thought, just as they cleared the tunnel and another one came into view. It was as if the mountain highway had been built by giant moles, rather than men and their machines.

No matter. They'd have ample daylight soon enough, before the pristine sky was fogged by battle haze.

Täsch

BOLAN HAD BEEN to Zermatt before, when he was wrapping up a mission that began with an airline hijacking, himself among the captive passengers. He had pursued the men responsible halfway across Europe and faced their ringleader almost within the shadow of the Matterhorn.

He had been lucky then, but would it hold?

From what Bolan recalled, security around the funicular depot in Täsch had been light last time, a couple of cops, no bomb- or drug-sniffing dogs. He and Grimaldi had their carbines packed in oversize gym bags, the extra magazines and stun grenades divided between them, padded with clothes to keep them from clanking together. He hoped they'd fit in well enough with other tourists hauling luggage, climbing gear and squalling children. Add the normal drunk or two, and Bolan thought they had a decent chance to pass unnoticed.

Otherwise, if they were stopped and searched, the campaign ended here.

Bolan parked the Jetta in a designated long-term slot, retrieved a ticket from the nearby vending machine and left it on the VW's dashboard. He and Grimaldi went into the depot, bought their passes for an open-ended round trip and had five minutes to kill before the next train started on its uphill grind.

Two cops, no nosy dogs. So far, so good.

The call for boarding came, and in another moment they were seated on the second car of four in line, their lethal luggage stowed beside their feet. The haul up to Zermatt was estimated to take twenty minutes, much of it bored through the mountain in the steepest tunnel they'd encountered yet.

It was a strange phenomenon, in Bolan's personal experience, that people tended to keep their voices down on trains. It helped that many of the travelers sharing their train seemed weary from the drive to Täsch from wherever they'd started out that morning. That, together with the novelty of chugging through a mountain tunnel at an angle close to forty-five degrees, kept riders peering through the windows at stone walls illuminated every twenty yards or so by caged fluorescent lights.

"This narrows down the getaway," Grimaldi said, leaning a little closer in his seat.

"Unless they catch a ride with Air Zermatt," Bolan replied.

It was the only helicopter service authorized to operate topside, available for cargo transport, sightseeing, and mountain rescues as the need arose. He thought the odds of God's Hammer booking helicopter service would be slim. Shave them to zero if they had to make a sudden exit on the run and under hostile fire.

But if you brought a pilot with you…

Bolan had to smile at that. He didn't plan on any skyjacking today, although the notion echoed how he'd met Grimaldi in the first place, long ago and far away. That was the way of fate, sometimes. You walked around a corner, maybe stepped off an elevator, and your whole life changed.

Or it ended.

Fate didn't always deal the hand you hoped for, obviously. Sometimes, by the time he saw which way the cards were running, all a guy could do was call or fold.

"There's daylight," Grimaldi announced, sounding relieved.

Another tunnel cleared. How many left to go?

CHAPTER SEVENTEEN

Grand Hotel Kempinski, Geneva

The hotel was a five-star colossus, stretching along Geneva's lakefront, advertised as a "veritable oasis in the heart of the city," offering something for everyone: a thirteen-hundred-seat theater; three gourmet restaurants; an "elite" spa and fitness center; Geneva's largest indoor swimming pool; and one of the city's trendiest nightclubs. Brognola's room had a sweeping view of the lake, with yachts and ferries drifting past, and a fruit basket that could have fed a family of three for two days.

The big Fed wasn't in his fourth-floor room just now, however. He'd been called to the Geneva Suite—largest in Europe according to the Kempinski's brochure, at 1,080 square meters, nearly ten times the size of the hotel's plain old Presidential Suite. The Man was holed up there, with pride of place, presumably because the joint was hosting six world leaders and he had the biggest army, or the biggest checkbook.

By the time Brognola made it, passing four guards on the door, the rest of Air Force One's exalted passengers were there ahead of him, eating pâté, sausage and various cheeses with fruit on the side, wolfing down everything within reach as if they'd forgotten they had a five-course banquet coming up in four hours. The man from Justice contented himself with a flaky croissant and a bottle of mineral water that tasted like thin olive oil.

Good times.

The President was busy, naturally, but he raised a hand to Brognola and gave that little half smile so familiar from his TV interviews. Someone from State was giving him the lowdown on whatever, gesturing with a six-inch piece of kielbasa for emphasis. It reminded Brognola of a political cartoon, but for the life of him he couldn't come up with a caption.

He'd been watching for an ambush since they touched down at the airport, knowing there wasn't a damned thing he could do about it. Sure, he'd packed his sidearm and was wearing it to the buffet—a subcompact Glock 26 loaded with ten 9 mm rounds, holstered at the small of his back to keep it unobtrusive—but he also knew that if God's Hammer came party crashing, they would have to deal first with the Secret Service and the local gendarmes standing watch outside the Geneva Suite.

What were the Man's guards carrying? SIG Sauer P229s were standard-issue for the Secret Service these days, chambered in .357 SIG for extra stopping power, but roughly one agent in three would also be carrying heavier firepower: Heckler & Koch MP5K machine pistols perhaps, maybe a Mini-Uzi or two. So the party ought to be secure. In which case, why couldn't Brognola relax?

Because he knew what was coming if Bolan and Grimaldi missed their targets in Zermatt, which was a four hour drive from Geneva. Hell, for all he knew, the birds had flown before his guys landed in Switzerland and were already on their way to make the summit meeting a reprise of the Munich Olympics massacre. It was what they lived for—and would die for, given half a chance.

Why not?

Watching the President, Brognola thought he seemed at ease, absorbing what was told to him, nodding along with the kielbasa guy before he interjected something on his own. A casual observer wouldn't know that everyone in the Geneva Suite was under threat of death right now, but that was SOP for White House occupants these days.

The big Fed hoped he would be ready if the ball dropped.

Zermatt

EMERGING INTO SUNLIGHT from the spotless modern station where their train was prepping for its journey back downhill to Täsch, Bolan shouldered his bag of clothes and weapons, standing with Grimaldi as they scanned the picturesque town laid out before them. For transport, they had a choice of electric shuttles or horse-drawn carriages bearing the names of various hotels, but since they hadn't booked a room, they wound up walking three blocks to a gingerbread boarding house that advertised both *vacance* and *Vakanz*.

The proprietress was middle-aged and open-minded. She had nothing against two men sharing digs, as long as they presented cash up front: Swiss francs, euros or US dollars, it was all the same to her. She led them to a second-story room with double beds, en-suite facilities and a smallish window overlooking a street lined with touristy shops, leaving them to their own devices once she had been paid.

"Nap time?" Grimaldi quipped.

They had agreed to find a room, if only to deposit their mundane belongings, and as someplace to retreat to, if they had a chance. Outside, the day was clear but brisk enough to justify the coats they'd packed, to hide their military hardware as they circulated through the streets. Guns might be common in this neutral nation, ringed by various belligerents from days gone by, but the Swiss weren't keen on America's recent open-carry fad, particularly if the people packing heat were foreigners.

According to a street map Grimaldi had purchased at the railway depot, they were roughly half a mile from the short street where Stony Man had pegged their targets' sat phone being last in use. It was an easy walk, in spite of narrow, steeply sloping cobbled streets where homes and shops pressed close on either side, with window boxes full of blooming flowers mounted overhead.

They unpacked the SG 552 Commando carbines, leaving their skeletal stocks folded off to the right-hand side, double-checking their magazines and pocketing the spares. Cheap nylon slings secured the weapons over one shoulder, while their suppressor-equipped pistols rode armpit rigging on the other. When the small room's full-length mirror told them they were reasonably squared away, they donned coats, locked the door behind them and descended to the first floor.

The landlady was waiting below, reminding them that they were on their own for meals, suggesting a café nearby that probably kicked back for word-of-mouth promotions. Both men thanked her, and they stepped out just as a red electric shuttle passed, with tourists' faces pressed against its windows.

On the street, based on the faces Bolan saw and languages he overheard, Zermatt was more like the United Nations than a simple Swiss village. Granted, it had all the outward charm of someplace from a children's fairy tale—or, on the darker side, a 1930s Gothic horror film from Hollywood—but catering to members of what once was called café society had stolen something from the scene. Bolan's eyes swept over Asians dressed as Alpine hikers, backpackers with scruffy beards and dreadlocks, and a host of plump pink specimens who didn't seem to do well in direct sunlight, all a contrast to the hearty peasant types and roly-poly tavern keepers that the scenery might have suggested.

Some of them were about to suffer hitches in their vacation plans, through no fault of their own. As Bolan turned left from the rooming house and started on his trek uphill, he hoped that all the innocents would make it through the afternoon alive.

"The trousers are too short," Kabeer advised Faisal Mousa. "You'll have to wear them lower on your hips."

Mousa nodded and tugged his pants down, underneath the navy velvet blazer that completed his disguise, topped with a matching bellman's hat like those worn by the Grand Hotel Kempinski's servant staff, secured by a strap beneath his chin. He wasn't happy with the uniform, but it made no difference, as long as he fit in.

The next in line was Kamal Bakri, in a blazer too large for his slender frame. His pants, by contrast, seemed to be a perfect fit, but Kabeer frowned while peering at his feet. "You need to shine those shoes," he said. "The bell captain won't let you on the floor looking like that."

"Then I will leave *him* on the floor," Bakri replied, smiling as he mimed slitting someone's throat.

"You think this is a farce?" Kabeer snapped back at him, then ranged along the line, including all of them. "Who thinks this is a joke? Show me your hands!" None rose, but he was not placated. "We are on our way to strike a blow for God. If you mock the mission, you are mocking Him!"

Bakri lowered his eyes and muttered an apology. Some of the others followed suit, although they had done nothing to offend Kabeer so far.

"Ali," he said, reaching Dajani, "you must brush your hat. The lint makes you resemble an old man who's going bald."

The joke fell flat. They were afraid to laugh.

"All right," he said, addressing all of them at once. "Remember that the hotel staff does not arrive in uniform. They have a locker room for changing out of street clothes, which you'll share."

"We don't have lockers," Majid Hayek said.

"I've told you they are not assigned," Kabeer replied. "Since servants work in shifts around the clock, the lockers are first-come, first-served. No one should question you, since shifts are often traded. Even the bell captain should accept it, if you tell him you were transferred unexpectedly. And by the time he gets suspicious, *if* he does—" Kabeer raised both hands, palms up toward the ceiling "—it will be too late."

The five fake bellmen nodded, more or less in unison.

"Now, are there any final questions?"

No one answered.

"Excellent. You all know your positions and assignments. If you're told to go somewhere or do something, agree at once, then keep to the arranged schedule. It's not as if the manager can fire you, after all."

Kabeer's smile at his own wit signaled that it would be safe for them to laugh, but only two joined in. The others were preoccupied with thoughts of death.

"Remember we must leave at four p.m., in time to make the train's final descent at five. Go separately. Is there anyone who needs money for tickets?"

Once again, silence.

"Aboard the train," he told them, stressing what they knew already, "do not speak or sit together if it is avoidable. We meet below and take the hired cars. On the road, we stay in touch by radio. Questions?"

None.

As satisfied as he could be, Kabeer dismissed them all to change their clothes and spend the next four hours as it pleased them, conscious of the fact that this might be their final night on Earth.

"NICE PLACE FOR a vacation, I suppose," Grimaldi said.

"It is," Bolan agreed.

He could have said the same for countless other places, from Hawaii to the shores of Acapulco, the Bahamas, London, Paris, Rome and Tuscany—you name it: sites and cities that drew anyone from lovers on their honeymoons to seniors who had saved enough to travel in their so-called golden years. Places to get away and live it up in style.

For Bolan, they had all been battlegrounds.

Zermatt was quaint, almost a village out of time, like Brigadoon. Surrounded by the Swiss Alps, it maintained a flavor of the nineteenth century, until you scrutinized the merchandise on offer in its shops: TAG Heuer watches, smart phones, iPad tablets, fashions by Marianne Alvoni, Consuelo Castiglioni, and Albert Kriemler. Alongside classic fare, the restaurants included Japanese, Tex-Mex and Thai cuisine.

A horse-drawn carriage clip-clopped past them as they

climbed the sloping street. Inside it, two tourists, maybe man and wife, slurped ice cream cones and ogled shops along the way. Proprietors stood watching through their windows, willing passersby to step in and divest themselves of cash. One raised a hand to Grimaldi and Bolan as they walked along, then let it drop and lost his smile as they passed on.

When they had covered half the distance to their target, Bolan made a left-hand turn into an even steeper side street, this one paved with cobblestones instead of asphalt. Bicycles would have a rough go of it, heading uphill, but the ride back down would be a howler, risking life and limb. Plants trailing from a row of window boxes overhead came close to grazing Bolan's scalp as he trudged up the hill, starting to feel it in his thighs and calves.

"I should've spent more time on the stepper," Grimaldi said.

"The good news," Bolan told him, "is that going back, it's all downhill."

Their target was one block west of Bahnhofstrasse, near the Rifflealp Resort hotel. Aerial photos showed only rooftops, leaving Bolan to discover for himself if it would be a private home, a boarding house or a hotel. In any case, he couldn't get a floor plan and had no idea precisely where his enemies might be inside the building.

That was, if they *were* inside.

Kabeer and his men had to know the President was in Geneva now, the other summit members close behind, if not already on the ground and rolling toward their rendezvous. It would have made sense for the team to get a jump on things, move out ahead of time and be in place, but Bolan only had the sat-phone fix to go by, courtesy of Stony Man.

And if that failed him…what?

Reach out to Brognola first, in Geneva, then the Farm, to see if Aaron Kurtzman's cyberteam could give him any kind of update on Kabeer's location from some other source. That seemed unlikely, in the final run-up to a major operation, when they would be using every trick at their disposal to avoid detection, and that brought him back to the alternative he favored least: the Grand Hotel Kempinski, hosting a cast of global VIPs and who knew how many tourists, all of them oblivious to terror waiting in the wings.

Bolan thought he should keep his fingers crossed, but that made it more difficult to shoot.

Täsch

ONE MEMBER OF the God's Hammer team *had* gone ahead, in fact. Mohammed Sanea caught the train down from Zermatt at one o'clock, en route to fetch the van that waited for him in Geneva, parked in a long-term garage on Rue de Monthoux, near the railroad yards. The key, he had been told, would be secured inside the left-rear wheel well, in a small magnetic box.

And what if someone happened by to steal it first?

The person would be in for a surprise if he or she attempted to unwrap the van's cargo.

Sanea took a pistol with him onto the funicular, a Heckler & Koch P30 in 9 mm Parabellum. It amused him that the depot had no real security in place, not even a metal detector for passengers boarding the train. Were the Swiss so naive that they believed neutrality protected them from contact with the world beyond their borders? In any case, it worked to his advantage now, and would allow the other members of his team to reach their vehicles at the appointed time, with no untoward incidents.

The terminal in Täsch boasted twenty-one-hundred parking spaces, acres of asphalt and steel, but Sanea knew precisely where to find his hired Renault Twingo, its parking pass still on the dashboard. He paid dutifully at the depot—there was no point in courting trouble now, of all times—and was soon back on the winding mountain highway that would take him through its many tunnels to Geneva, in about four hours.

That was ample time to think of what lay waiting for him when he reached the city. Still not pleased with his assignment, even though it offered him a fair chance of surviving the attack, Sanea wondered if it had been rigged in some way to deceive him. Why would Saleh Kabeer not take the prime position for their raid, with a potential for escaping to reconstitute the movement if his last troops fell in battle?

Could it be some kind of trick? If so, *what* kind?

Sanea had already racked his brain in search of answers to that question and had come up empty. He saw no way in which Kabeer could profit from a leading role in the attack, where he was almost certain to be slain. A martyr's death would certainly enhance his reputation with the faithful, but despite his lectures on God, Sanea found Kabeer more commonly concerned with earthly matters than with things divine.

The riddle stumped him, so Sanea concentrated on his driving as another mountain tunnel loomed ahead. The Twingo had daylight running lights and thus required no action on Sanea's part as he drove in and out of darkness on the path back to Geneva. He was troubled more by other drivers, speeding past him in a manner that reminded him of motorists in Riyadh, where he'd come from, heedless of their own safety and anybody else's.

He could match their speed, but what then, if he caught the eye of a policeman with a quota of citations to be met? Sanea's driver's license was a forgery, and not the best at that. If he was ordered from the car and he resisted, pulled his pistol, it would end in death for someone, and the outcome worked against him either way. Dead, he was useless to his comrades. Hunted by police for killing one of them, he posed a greater danger to the cause than if he was shot down.

So he made sure to watch the speed limit, his rearview mirror and the dashboard clock that told him time was slipping past. However this night closed, Mohammed Sanea knew his life would never be the same.

Zermatt

FROM STREET LEVEL, the target looked like any other building on the block. Its front door was a vibrant red, while those of neighbors had been painted other party colors, and the flowers in its window boxes gave a spark of individuality. Otherwise it had a steep roof, its ground floor walls were made of bricks, the upper stories constructed out of wood, same as the others lining both sides of the street. A small brass plaque beside the door labeled it as a *Familiengästehaus* or *Pension de Famille*.

"Is that what I think it is?" Grimaldi asked.

"Family guesthouse," Bolan said.

"Could be trouble," the pilot observed.

"We're after seven men," Bolan replied. "I don't see any landlord in Zermatt packing them all into one room."

"Seven could nearly fill a place this size," Grimaldi estimated.

"Or, they could be spread all over town."

"But if the sat phone's here…"

"We've likely got Kabeer, at least."

"I don't suppose we can just call him up and see who's home."

"So we just drop in."

"Looks like it."

Bolan had already cocked his carbine in their room, and it was ready for whatever waited on the far side of the red door facing him. The question now was how to get inside without alerting any targets on the premises before he had them lined up in his sights.

The guesthouse was a place of business, but did that mean anyone could walk in off the street to ask about a room? He saw a doorbell, but if Bolan raised the landlord, what was his next step? Kabeer and company would not be registered under their own names, surely, and Brognola's files had not provided any likely pseudonyms.

"Cold call?" he asked Grimaldi.

"I'm with you," his partner replied, reaching beneath his coat and switching off his carbine's safety.

The doorknob turned when Bolan tried it, well-oiled hinges giving off no sound, but then a bell mounted inside, above the door, jangled to warn the landlord of a new arrival in his foyer. Bolan reached up overhead to still it, but a man's voice was already calling out from somewhere to his left.

"Guten tag! Wilkommen!"

The landlord had a thin halo of white hair and well-waxed handlebar mustache that compensated for whatever thinning he'd suffered on top. His ruddy cheeks bespoke a cheerful disposition or perhaps a love of alcohol.

Bolan decided it was worth a gamble. "You speak English?"

"But of course, my friend. How may I help you this fine day?"

"We were supposed to meet some friends here," Bolan told him. "Middle Eastern fellows, six or seven of them."

"Certainly! They are my guests. May I— But wait! Here comes one of them now!"

Bolan followed the landlord's sweeping gesture toward a nearby staircase, where his eyes locked on to those of Faisal Mousa, one of the Jordanians still unaccounted for. Mousa froze on the stairs, then started to retreat, reaching for something that could only be a weapon.

In a flash, the jolly landlord lost his smile, and it all went to hell.

CHAPTER EIGHTEEN

Saleh Kabeer was dozing when the battle started. He had set his traveler's alarm clock for three-thirty before stretching out upon the sofa, fully dressed except for shoes, the gym bag that he planned on taking with him to Geneva resting on the floor beside his couch, within arm's reach.

The bag contained a Russian Bizon submachine gun, a unique variation on the classic Kalashnikov design chambered in 9 mm Makarov, fed from a 64-round helical magazine mounted below the hand guard in line with the weapon's barrel. Three more magazines were also packed in the bag, with half a dozen frag grenades, although Kabeer was not convinced he would live long enough to reload when the action started in Geneva.

He had begun to dream of something, a landscape he did not recognize immediately, when the first shots shocked him out of sleep and snapped him upright on the sofa, reaching for his pistol on the nearby coffee table. For an instant, Kabeer thought the gunfire might have been within his dream, until it was repeated and he heard one of his soldiers shouting from the corridor outside his room.

"Crusaders! They have found us!"

Kabeer set his pistol down and fumbled with his shoes. They were slip-ons, with elastic wedges on the sides, and only caused him to blaspheme one time as he was grappling with the left one. He rose, picked up his pistol and the bag of weapons, stood and listened to the rising gunfire for a moment, then proceeded to the nearest window with his mind set on escape.

They had rehearsed evacuation of the guesthouse shortly after moving in, a common-sense precaution that Kabeer demanded of his men at any "safe" location. Each of his soldiers knew precisely where to go and what to do in the event of an attack, without him leading each one by the hand. They knew their mission in Geneva took priority above all else, and that they should spare no effort to flee the guesthouse, flee Zermatt, if anything went wrong.

Beyond that, they were on their own.

More shooting echoed through the stairwell leading to Kabeer's room on the second floor. He reached the window, freed its latch and flung it open to the cool breeze of an alpine afternoon. With the gym bag slung across his back, its strap across his chest, Kabeer secured his pistol in a pocket of his khaki cargo pants and peered out at the drop below him.

Call it fifteen feet between the windowsill and cobblestones, closer to eight if he could manage dangling by his fingers from the sill before he dropped. A headlong fall would damage him severely, maybe break his neck and leave him dead or paralyzed, but he'd rehearsed the exit in his mind and had no fear of heights per se.

A fear of *falling*, now, that was another thing entirely.

The exit proved more awkward than he had imagined, leading with his right leg, clinging to the window frame for dear life as he turned around—his groin scraping painfully across the windowsill—and brought his left leg out over the drop. From there, he had to let his straining fingertips slide until they gripped the sill alone, bearing the full weight of his body while it dangled over empty space, the street below invisible no matter how Kabeer might crane his neck.

He pictured tumbling down atop some *hausfrau* or a family of tourists passing by, and wondered whether they would break his fall. Almost smiling at the image, Kabeer loosened his grip and plummeted, remembering to tuck his legs and roll on impact with the hard, smooth cobblestones. He started rolling down the steep side street but managed to arrest the tumbling with an outflung arm, escaping from the drop with nothing more than painful bruises to his back, hips, knees and palms.

More gunfire echoed from within the guesthouse as Kabeer rose and ran.

BOLAN WISHED THERE had been time to draw his silenced pistol, but Faisal Mousa was fast, allowing none. It came down to the carbine, starting with a 3-round burst that caught Mousa as he was multitasking, reaching for his gun and trying to retreat upstairs at the same time.

One of the 5.56 mm bullets missed and chipped a handrail bolted to the wall on Mousa's left. The other two went in on target, more or less, though slightly lower than intended, punching home above the slender gunman's belt line, dropping him to one knee on the stairs. He grimaced at the sudden pain, but kept on groping for the weapon he was after, his teeth clenched in grim determination.

Bolan let him have another short burst, to the chest this time, stopping his heart and turning both lungs into useless bags of blood. Mousa slumped backward on the stairs and started sliding down to meet his killer, muscles slack in death. The gun that hadn't saved him, a Beretta, tumbled down ahead of him and struck the floor at Bolan's feet.

The Executioner was on the move by then, aware of pounding footsteps overhead, Kabeer's men scrambling for their weapons, shouting warnings back and forth in Arabic. The landlord wailed out something from below, Grimaldi shoving past him, and it didn't take a mind reader to know that he'd be howling for the police as soon as he could reach a telephone.

Bolan pushed on upstairs, nearing the second-story landing, slowing there as it went quiet in the guesthouse, no running, the initial shouting silenced. That brought either one of two scenarios to Bolan's mind: an ambush or escape, both fairly well rehearsed.

"I'm going up," he warned Grimaldi, in a whisper.

"I got you covered," his partner replied, his carbine raised, his voice barely audible.

Bolan attacked the few remaining steps as if they were the last yards separating him from a decisive touchdown in the last game of a winning season. He lunged forward as he reached the landing, sliding belly-down on the carpet, which released a little puff of dust on impact. He was ready when an automatic weapon chattered at him from the far end of the hallway, through an open bedroom door, its muzzle-flashes blinking at him, then cut off as suddenly as they began.

Bolan returned fire, just to keep the shooter's head down, while he pushed up on all fours and scuttled to his left, pressing his back against a wall papered with a complex chintzy design. It made a little whisper of its own as Bolan slid along the wall, advancing toward the shooter's den and watching two more doors that opened off the short hallway.

The Executioner didn't look back to see if his partner was covering him. A Grimaldi promise was as good as gold—or body armor, as the case might be. More shooters might spring out in front of him at any second, but with Grimaldi behind him, Bolan had no fear of back shooters.

A few more yards remained before he had an angle on the open doorway. Bolan strained his ears for any sound of movement from within the room but heard nothing. It was a death trap, obviously, but this was what he'd come for.

Creeping, step by silent step, Bolan advanced.

"COME ON!" ALI DAJANI snapped at Majid Hayek.

"Go!" the man seethed back at him. "I'm right behind you!"

In rehearsal, it had all seemed so much easier. Of course, they had not actually leaped from any of the guesthouse windows while discussing their emergency escape plans. If the truth were told, Dajani thought the whole thing was a waste of time, preparing for a raid. How could Crusaders find them in Zermatt?

And yet, they had.

Now he was peering at the steep street below him from a third-story window, thinking what an idiotic plan it was to clamber out and drop through space as if he were invincible, not just a fragile thing of blood and bones wrapped up in skin. The very least Dajani could expect was broken ankles, if he landed wrong. At worst, he would be killed as surely by the fall as by a damned Crusader's bullets, but without the chance to take someone with him.

It was idiocy—but despite the fear inside of him, Dajani felt he had no choice.

"Well, are you jumping out or not?" Hayek demanded, standing close behind him.

"Yes! I'm going!"

And he did.

First thing, Dajani had to take the flower box some fool had bolted to the wall outside his window and dislodge it, hammering the corners with a lamp until it cracked and tumbled to the distant pavement, spilling dirt and lilies. Next, flinging the broken lamp aside, Dajani had to struggle through the window backward, Hayek helping him until he hung suspended from the windowsill, his dangling feet some eighteen feet above the cobblestones.

And then he let go.

The drop was giddy, terrifying, but Dajani landed on his feet, flexing his knees as he'd been taught in training, rolling backward to disperse momentum from the fall. That saved his legs, but jammed the satchel with his weapons and bellman's disguise into his left kidney, sending a bolt of white-hot agony up from his waistline to his skull.

Dajani barely moved in time, before Hayek crashed down on top of him, a perfect four-point landing on his toes and fingertips. The Lebanese eyed him and asked, "Are you all right?"

"Just help me up," Dajani answered, grimacing with fresh pain as Hayek assisted him in standing upright.

"If you cannot walk—"

"I can!" Dajani snapped at him. "You lead the way."

"All right. But if you cannot make the train—"

"Just go!" Dajani snarled.

Hayek set off downhill, jogging with gravity to aid him, and Dajani followed, gasping from the pain at first, then breathing more evenly as it slowly eased. He might be passing blood that night, but it was of no consequence. Unless a miracle occurred, they'd all be dead before another sunrise, anyway.

Running to reach the railway depot—hobbling, in Dajani's case—they met locals and tourists, none of whom seemed interested in the odd pair passing by. The locals were accustomed to outlandish visitors, Dajani thought; the tourists, meanwhile, cared for no one but themselves.

Plodding along, he wondered if Kabeer or any of the others would escape. And if they didn't, should the action in Geneva still proceed? What would Mohammed Sanea say when he arrived, driving the vanload of explosives, if he found only two comrades ready to proceed? Would they go ahead or call it quits?

They could discuss that, he decided, on the drive back to Geneva. For the moment, all Dajani cared about was getting to the depot and aboard the next funicular to Täsch.

OUTSIDE THE BEDROOM DOORWAY, Bolan dropped to all fours once again, then lay prone on the dusty carpeting. He knew the tendency of shooters cornered in a single room to fire through walls around the entrance, normally around chest height, in hopes of taking out their enemies before a hopeless final rush. It sometimes worked—Bolan had done it once or twice, himself—and he preferred to stay below the common line of fire if possible.

That made it difficult to charge the room, but he was ready with a fair alternative. He palmed one of the small M84 flash-bang grenades, crude in appearance, like a perforated five-inch pipe bomb, and removed its double pins—one pull ring circular, the other one triangular—while keeping a tight grip around its narrow safety lever.

A quick countdown, and then he made the sidearm pitch, immediately clamping his hands over his eyes, which were shut tightly, and turning away from the doorway in front of him. The stun grenade's short fuse allowed his enemy no time to duck and cover before blinding light and thunder filled the small bedroom, unleashing more dust from the carpet under Bolan and the ceiling overhead.

He hit the threshold running, no real smoke to speak of interfering with his vision in the tiny room. Before him, writhing on the carpet with a hand over his eyes, lay Kamal Bakri, one of four young Palestinians who'd pledged themselves to God's Hammer and its war against the West.

The kid was hurting now, and dazed, though not severely injured. Medics could have treated him for any damage to his eardrums, but it wasn't in the cards. As Bakri crawled toward a handgun, Bolan aimed his carbine and fired.

One more portion of the tab settled for Zarqa, with another five outstanding.

Bolan doubled back and found Grimaldi clearing rooms along the second-story hallway. He'd done two and was emerging from the third when Bolan met him in the corridor.

"Nobody home," the pilot said. He nodded toward the doorway just behind him, adding, "There's a window open here."

"A bug-out?" Bolan asked him.

"Couldn't say."

"Okay. Third floor."

Bolan hated to think of anybody getting out, but his first job was to secure the rest of the guesthouse before police arrived, then worry about stragglers in the wind. He reached the final flight of stairs and started climbing once again, cursing a step that groaned beneath his weight as he ascended. Anybody waiting for him on the top floor might have heard it and be zeroed on the landing, ready to unload on any target that revealed itself.

But no one fired as Bolan stepped into the open, facing four more rooms, two doors on either side of yet another hallway. And all four of the doors were shut.

"Cops ought to be here anytime," Grimaldi said.

"Can't help it," Bolan replied, and stepped out toward the first door on his left.

SALEH KABEER SAT waiting in the railway depot, his gym bag resting on the seat beside him, his right hand resting near the unsnapped pocket of his cargo pants that held his pistol. Waiting for the train to come, unload its passengers and start back down the mountainside, he watched the street for any sign of enemies approaching.

If they tried to take him here, his choices were to fight and surely die, or to attempt escaping down the tracks on foot, perhaps stumbling along the way and tumbling three miles down to Täsch—or meeting the funicular as it returned and being ground to bloody pulp beneath its wheels.

So, death, in either case.

And if the train arrived in time to carry him away... then, what? Would someone call ahead and have police waiting to seize him at the lower depot? That would also mean a firefight, doubtless ending in his death. Kabeer's sole hope, in that event, would be to take a few Crusaders with him as he fell, sending their rotten souls to Jahannam while his flew off to Paradise.

But if he reached one of the waiting cars and made it out of Täsch alive, Kabeer still clung to hope of pulling off his greatest move against the leading politicians who supported Israel in its war on Islam and descendants of the people it had dispossessed in 1947. He could not change history, but Kabeer reckoned he could write a new chapter in blood.

And in that chapter, he would be the star.

Nine endless minutes into waiting, he was startled by the sight of two familiar faces pushing through the depot's swinging doors. Ali Dajani and Majid Hayek spotted their leader seconds later and approached him, Hayek moving briskly, while Dajani lagged behind and kept a hand pressed tight against his lower back.

Without a word, the winded soldiers settled into seats on either side of their commander, Dajani with a sigh of sweet relief at getting off his feet. Kabeer surveyed them briefly, then turned toward the street again, to see if they had been pursued.

"The rest?" he asked.

Dajani shrugged and winced. Hayek said, "We don't know. Someone was shooting in the guesthouse when we jumped."

"And the police?" Kabeer inquired.

"No sign of them while we were there," Hayek replied.

Kabeer had heard no sirens yet. They still might have enough time to escape. "Go buy two tickets," he told Hayek, handing him a small wad of Swiss francs.

"How long until—?"

"Five minutes," Kabeer interrupted, "if the timetable is accurate."

"The Swiss are always accurate," Dajani offered through clenched teeth.

"How are you injured?" Kabeer asked him.

"Something in my back, perhaps the kidney. When I jumped, I landed on my bag. The weapons…"

"But you're capable of fighting?"

"Yes, sir." Dajani sounded less than confident.

"Mohammed will be waiting for us in Geneva," Kabeer said. "Success is still within our grasp, if we but persevere."

Dajani nodded. "By the time we get there, I'll feel better, certainly."

"And then—"

Kabeer stopped short at sight of Habis Elyan just entering the depot. Calling out to Hayek, halfway to the ticket window, he said, "Majid! Make it three."

Hayek glanced back, saw Elyan and signaled understanding as he hurried toward the window.

And he had to hurry now, because he heard the funicular approaching, still concealed within its tunnel as it labored up the mountainside, but drawing nearer by the moment.

We can make it, he decided. We can still succeed.

And drown the top Crusaders of the world in their own blood.

BOLAN CLEARED THE last room on the third floor of the guesthouse, stepping out to find Grimaldi in the hallway with a glum expression on his face. "Two out of seven sucks," the pilot said.

"The only place the rest of them can go from here is down," Bolan replied. "That means the depot."

"Right."

They stormed downstairs through silence tinged with gun smoke. On the ground floor, almost at the exit with its tinkling bell, the red-faced landlord shouted after them, *"Die police kommt! Sie warten dort!"*

"Halt die klappe!" Grimaldi replied, before the door slammed shut behind them.

Jogging down the sloping street toward downtown, weapons stowed, Bolan asked, "When did you learn German?"

"I can say 'shut up' in six or seven languages," Grimaldi answered.

Bolan focused on the streets in front of them, watching for cruisers or a foot patrol in uniform, his ears straining for the sound of sirens racing toward the guesthouse. Nothing yet, but what did that prove? They were in a mountain town, cut off completely from the outside world except by two railways, one running down to Täsch, the other headed up to Sunnegga, a ski resort at higher altitude.

Going that way would only place Bolan and Grimaldi a few miles farther from their rented car, while Saleh Kabeer and his survivors made a run for it—and likely for Geneva, to complete their mission. Whatever else was said about Kabeer, no one had yet called him a quitter. Bolan thought the man would try his best to see the job through, even if he had to do it on his own; and with another four members of God's Hammer unaccounted for, they still might do sufficient damage for a grim footnote in history.

They reached the railway depot just in time to see

the train pull out and disappear into the tunnel's maw. Grimaldi cursed, while Bolan did the mental calculations. Twenty minutes down, another ten or so for disembarking passengers and loading new ones, twenty minutes back up to Zermatt, more unloading and loading, then another twenty back to Täsch. Kabeer and company, assuming they were on the train, had gained more than an hour's head start toward Geneva, and he couldn't do a thing about it.

Nothing, that was, but attempting to avoid arrest.

Bolan dismissed the image of his quarry hiding somewhere in Zermatt. It would be risky to the point of sheer insanity, once the police began to search for Arabs whom the guesthouse landlord could identify. And if the local cops followed Bolan's logic, would they not be headed for the depot, once they'd heard the landlord's story blurted out in breathless bits and pieces?

"Let's go shopping," Bolan said.

"Say what?"

"We have the best part of an hour to kill, before the train comes back," Bolan explained. "We're sitting ducks in here. The least we can do is hit some shops and change our look a little. Drift back here with five or ten to spare, and come in solo, so we don't stand out."

"I get it," Grimaldi said. "Going tourist."

"Right."

"Okay, let's do it. Shopping till we drop."

CHAPTER NINETEEN

Grand Hotel Kempinski, Geneva

Brognola caught a break after the meet-and-greet broke up, two hours wasted in his estimation, but the VIPs seemed to enjoy grazing at the buffet while they were warming up for dinner. He had glimpsed some famous faces and been introduced to no one, thereby signaling his status on the diplomatic totem pole.

What am I doing here? he wondered, not for the first time, as he was waiting for the silent elevator to deposit him on the hotel's fourth floor. He still had no idea what he'd been added to the roster at the Man's direct command, but curiosity was leading him along dark mental corridors as he tried working through the riddle, looking for a clue.

The President had claimed he wanted Brognola close by to "keep his operators in the field on track," but that was bull. The Man knew Brognola was an administrator these days, that he had no more to do with a specific action on the firing line than an army general would have with privates in a combat rifle company. It had to be something else, and all Brognola could come up with was a not-so-subtle warning that whatever happened to the President while he was in Geneva would be happening to him, as well.

Which begged the question: If the Man was doubting his ability to lead, what was awaiting Brognola in Washington if all of them survived their present jaunt? Brognola wasn't worried about being canned. He had his twenty in, and then some, with a decent pension waiting for him come what may. Getting the boot would be an insult, sure, departing Justice on the worst of sour notes, but he could definitely live with that.

What troubled him was the idea of being sucked into the blame game, if the summit fell apart and any of the bigwigs came to harm. Brognola had nothing to do with site security, but there were ways of twisting things, as he had learned while working for the FBI, and later at the helm of Stony Man. Before he knew it, a congressional committee could be asking him exactly why in hell he'd let a pack of rabid terrorists go through the summit meeting like a dose of salts—and while they plastered him across Fox News, what would be happening to all his people at the Farm?

Exposure was the kiss of death to Stony Man and every member of its team. Brognola was prepared to take the hit alone, rather than sacrifice a single member of that tight-knit family. But would that be his choice?

He let himself into his room facing the lake, and saw that someone had come calling in his absence. The big Fed's go-bag did not include a tux, but now he found one laid out on his bed: Joseph A. Bank, immaculate inside its sheath of plastic. Someone on the Man's team prepping him for dinner in the banquet hall downstairs, assuming—rightly—that he'd turned up on short notice, unprepared.

Brognola's first reaction, as an old campaigner, was to search his room for any other signs of tampering while he was out. His go-bag had a combination lock, four digits, still set on the number where he'd left it, but he opened it and checked its contents, anyway. When he found nothing out of place, his only other thought was that someone might try to bug his room—but why, when he was staying on his own? To eavesdrop if he called room service in the middle of the night?

There was the sat phone, but he'd already decided any call he made to Stony Man would be made on the move, outside his room, to frustrate uninvited listeners. Besides which, he regarded "checking in" for no good reason as a sign of weakness and avoided it whenever possible, letting the team he trusted work without his hot breath on their necks.

Brognola needed sleep before the evening's big do, but first, his curiosity was nagging at him. He would have to try the tux for size, and if it fit, decide whether he should be pissed that some smug stranger had correctly guessed his height and weight.

Zermatt

GRIMALDI CAME BACK to the train station with five minutes to spare. He'd bought a gray felt alpine hat, complete with perky little feather in the band, and backed it up with shades resembling those favored by the late Ray Charles. His scarf, bright red, was decorated with a hundred mini-Matterhorns, each likeness of the killer mountain showing different shaded contours. He'd swapped his jacket for a royal blue hoodie, carrying the jacket and his carbine in a spacious shopping bag displaying the national colors.

All in all, he was a tourist who would set most locals' teeth on edge.

Grimaldi went directly to the depot's ticket counter for a one-way ticket down to Täsch. He'd ditched his round-trip ticket, now potentially incriminating, while he shopped for his disguise—as if a piece of cardboard could be more accusatory than the weapons he was carrying. Police were on the prowl downtown, but none of them had stopped him as he moved from one shop to another, likely looking for a shifty duo act, rather than one geek seeming casual.

If he could jet get on the train...

Grimaldi didn't look for Bolan until he had the ticket in his hand. Turning, as if to scan the depot for an empty seat, he spotted Bolan in a corner near the door, from all appearances reading a true-crime magazine printed in German. Bolan wore a long-billed cap, bearing a red cross on its front panel, above a pair of sunglasses with iridescent lenses. The jacket he'd been wearing was reversible, its lining inside-out now, for a look the guesthouse owner likely wouldn't recognize. The canvas shopping bag he'd chosen to conceal his hardware was jet-black, bearing a red-and-white logo that read: I ♥ ZERMATT.

Grimaldi picked a seat as far away from Bolan as the depot's layout would allow. He'd brought nothing to read, so he pulled his hat down and pretended to be snoozing, all the time watching for cops through the dark screen of his eyelashes. Just as he heard the train approaching, groaning on the last leg of its uphill run, a young lieutenant stopped outside the depot, speaking briefly to the officers on duty there, heads shaking as he questioned them and then moved on.

Grimaldi didn't dawdle when it came to boarding, but he let Bolan go first, then chose another car. He wound up sitting on the aisle, beside a dark-skinned older man wearing a turban, maybe Sikh or Hindu, who looked worn out from whatever job had drawn him to Zermatt. Behind them, two Japanese girls chattered, punctuated with ecstatic giggles, while the train reversed and started chugging back downhill.

We made it, the pilot thought, then winced at the thought of cursing their escape. They would be clear when they were on the highway to Geneva, not before. And after that, God only knew what was awaiting them.

On the A40 Motorway, Westbound

SALEH KABEER WAS starting to relax. An hour from Zermatt, with no sign of police behind them yet, told him that they were not being pursued. It was a temporary fix, of course—the men he'd lost in the resort town soon would be identified and linked to God's Hammer, which in turn would launch a nationwide manhunt—but he would take advantage of the time remaining to them, pushing toward their goal.

Their hired car was a Volvo XC90 midsize SUV crossover, gray, with a five-speed automatic transmission and a 2.5 L 210 hp turbocharged engine. Majid Hayek had the wheel, with Kabeer in the shotgun seat, Elyan and Dajani riding in the back. Dajani, thankfully, had ceased complaining about his discomfort once he'd settled in his seat, and now sat with his eyes closed, his head against the padded pillar next to him, as if asleep. The others had been hyped up, chattering, until Kabeer had silenced them at last, a few miles outside Täsch.

He needed time to think, and silence to accomplish it. Kabeer had tried to call Mohammed Sanea on his sat phone, once they had a head start on the motorway, but it had gone to voice mail and he'd left a cryptic order for a callback. As it stood, he didn't know whether Sanea had been able to retrieve the van, or if he had decided to forsake them, driving off to parts unknown.

Kabeer wanted to trust Sanea, but they had not parted on the best of terms. He knew Sanea questioned his assignment to the van carrying the explosives, although he claimed it was because he did not want to be the last man standing when the smoke cleared in Geneva, much less the commander of a new God's Hammer; but might that disaffection lead Sanea to desert the cause entirely?

If the van was not in place when they arrived, the raid would come down to four men—one of them injured—facing scores of bodyguards and soldiers, armed with nothing but the small arms they had salvaged from Zermatt. The massacre resulting would most likely be of his men, rather than the targets Kabeer intended. If that turned out to be the end of his grand enterprise, would he be wiser to forget the whole thing, drive out of Switzerland and find a place to hole up while they made new plans from scratch?

No.

He could wait a lifetime for another opportunity like this, and in the meantime, how many more Palestinians would die or suffer at Israeli hands, cut down by bombs and bullets paid for by America? How could he think of safety for himself, when his Islamic brothers lived in daily fear of death, displacement and the loss of everything they owned, such as it was?

Kabeer glanced at his watch. He'd cracked its face while leaping from his bedroom window at the guest-house, but it still kept time. They had three hours left, perhaps a little more, before they reached Geneva and approached their target. Based on the agenda broadcast by the media, he thought the top Crusaders should be sitting down to dinner in the Grand Hotel Kempinski's banquet hall when he arrived, with or without Mohammed Sanea and the van. Perhaps they would be on the appetizer course, or salad.

Unknown to the men who ruled the world, a late addition to the menu would be sudden death.

"THEY'VE GOT AN hour's lead, I figure," Grimaldi said.

"Sounds right," Bolan agreed, pushing the Jetta west on the A40 Motorway. The same parade of mountain tunnels lay in front of them, seen from the other side this time, no changes since they'd passed that way a few short hours earlier.

"Want me to call Hal with a quick heads-up?"

"We don't know who he's with or what he's up to," Bolan countered. "Better tip the Farm instead, and let them run with it."

Grimaldi used the sat phone, Bolan listening to his side of the conversation from the driver's seat.

"It's me…No, on the highway heading for Geneva… No…Two off the board…Mousa and Bakri…Yeah, I *know* that still leaves five…Okay, sorry…No…Striker thought you ought to call him, if you think the time's right… Yeah, okay. Later."

"No joy in Mudville," Grimaldi announced, when he'd cut the link. "They'll get in touch with Hal ASAP."

Bolan wasn't a brooder, but Grimaldi sensed his dark mood, adding, "It was just dumb luck, you know. Missing the rest."

"I know. It doesn't help."

"It's not too late to tip the cops," Grimaldi said.

"And tell them what? We don't know what Kabeer's people are driving, or how many vehicles they have. We don't know what they're planning, other than a massacre. Geneva already has people on the scene, along with armed security from half a dozen other countries. They're prepared for anything Kabeer might try, in theory."

"But you're worried."

"Sure. Aren't you?"

"Hell, yes. I'm picturing another Oklahoma City, or a mini-9/11. If they've got a pilot with them, access to a private plane stuffed full of RDX or something similar, I don't see how hotel security could hold them off."

Bolan wondered how many guests were registered at the hotel that day, if some of them were sitting down to dine or sweating in the gym, swimming or getting a massage, browsing among the shops or watching some new movie in the theater. How many lives would be snuffed out or changed forever if he didn't stop Kabeer in time?

It was a question Bolan asked himself each time he took a new assignment from the Farm. The stakes were always life and death. Only the scale varied from one job to another, while the human cost remained identical for individuals caught up in Bolan's endless war. Some didn't even know the war existed, but it sucked them in and chewed them up, regardless.

"When we get there," Grimaldi said, "are we heading straight to the hotel?"

"It's all that I can think of," Bolan replied. "We'll have to play it cagey, with the timing and the layers of security in place."

"We might spruce up a bit and try to check in," Grimaldi suggested. "Get a foot inside, at least."

"Might want to call about a reservation, if we're doing that," Bolan replied. "And we'd still have to think about the hardware."

"I can get the phone number online for reservations. Do you think they'd scan our luggage, checking in?"

"With six heads of state in residence? I wouldn't doubt it."

"Right. And if we leave them in the car…"

"They're inaccessible."

"Damn it!"

"Hold off on phoning," Bolan said, "and try to find a floor plan and service entrances. Turning invisible might be a better way to go."

"I'm on it," Grimaldi replied, and bent over his sat phone, leaving Bolan to the long, dark tunnel of his thoughts.

Rue de Monthoux, Geneva

THE VAN WAS waiting for Mohammed Sanea when he reached the cavernous parking garage. He spotted it, then left his Renault Twingo on another level, walking back to reach the van while checking shadows high and low for any sign of enemy surveillance. One hand on his pistol, he retrieved the van's key from its hiding place, unlocked it, climbed inside and locked it once again so no one could surprise him while he checked its cargo.

Semtex was invented at Prague Technical University in the 1950s, and was odorless until the Lockerbie airline disaster of December 1988 persuaded its primary manufacturers to make work easier for bomb-sniffing dogs. Otherwise, its stable compound would pass through airport scanners as easily as a pair of socks. Sanea frankly didn't care if there were dogs at work around the Grand Hotel Kempinski, or a team of psychics picking up on danger vibes. He had a relatively simple job to do: arrive on time, park at or near the hotel's spacious underground loading dock, and wait to see whether the raid went down as planned or not.

If so, he was to walk away, trigger the charge remotely and claim credit for the devastating blast with CNN as soon as possible.

If not, should he be cornered or the plan should fall apart somehow, the small remote control device that waited for him in the glove compartment would become his ticket to the Elysian Fields of Paradise.

But was he ready for the end?

In theory, certainly. Sanea's training with al-Qaeda, then with God's Hammer, had strengthened the belief he shared with every fellow Muslim, of a grand reward beyond the veil of death for God's loyal disciples. Many differed on the context of that loyalty, excluding those who waged the long *jihad*, and that had troubled him at times. If the Koran was true, how could *imams* vary so radically on their interpretation of the text?

Sanea counted bricks of Semtex, plastic wrapped, each one weighing a kilo more or less. The detonators were in place, but disconnected from the battery that would, on cue, send voltage sparking to their blasting caps and turn the van into a massive fireball, slamming its destructive force through the selected target, rending flesh and bone along with glass, concrete and steel.

All present and accounted for.

Connection of the battery required only a moment's time. That done, Sanea crawled back to the driver's seat, opened the glove compartment and removed the small remote control. It had two switches: one to arm it, and the other to direct its deadly signal through the air by line of sight, within one hundred yards of where its user stood. Sanea flipped the arming switch, saw the green light come on and turned it off again for safety's sake.

Ready.

The van started immediately, and he backed out of its parking space, wound slowly through the circuits of the vast garage, until he reached the street, then turned and headed for the lake.

Grand Hotel Kempinski, Geneva

IT WAS NEARLY DINNERTIME, and Brognola admitted to himself, if grudgingly, that he looked sporty in his borrowed tux. He could have used a trim around the ears, but balked at going down to the hotel's salon. Sometimes, with a command performance, the commander had to take his players as they came.

There'd been no time to fit the tux jacket precisely, so he still had room to hide the small Glock 26 behind his back, no bulge to speak of. If the Secret Service challenged him, he would refer them to the President, and if the Man turned thumbs down on his being armed, Brognola thought he might as well go back up to his suite and order room service. He had no role in any of the talks that might start over dinner, and if he was stripped of any minimal protective function, it was all a waste of time.

In fact, nobody seemed to notice he was packing. In the elevator, riding down with members of the German party, Brognola stood off to one side, catching stray words here and there, without a hope of stringing them together. I'd have been a lousy spy, he thought, more

suited to administration in the new world where so many
threats were global and the players represented every
color of the human rainbow.

On the ground floor, Brognola stood back and let the
Germans off, then trailed them toward the banquet room.
Local police and Secret Service had the door, checking
IDs, but they had left their scanning wands at home and
weren't inflicting any pat-downs on the guests. If any
Arab states had been included in the gathering, Brognola
thought Kabeer or someone from his clique could have
obtained an invitation, slipped inside without much fuss
and been in place to try some dirty work, but this turn-
out was virtually lily-white.

Brognola wasn't seated with the Man or other po-
tentates, up on the dais at the head of the long dining
room, which put his nerves a little more at ease. Dining among the great and near-great could be harrowing
enough, without three-quarters of the room watching
each bite he forked into his mouth. Seated with lesser
members of the US team who had trouble remembering his name, the big Fed focused on the menu, reading through the courses that included double appetizers
chosen from a list of twenty, a palate-cleansing sorbet,
an entrée making no allowance for potential vegans in
the crowd, and a choice of five desserts leaning toward
chocolate. He said farewell to any semblance of a diet
and prepared to chow down like a hog.

If this was going to be Brognola's last meal, he might
as well enjoy it—though he could have wished for better company.

Sommeliers were circling, offering a sip and sniff of
wine to those who viewed themselves as connoisseurs.
Brognola knew the difference between a red and white,

but still had trouble matching them to their respective dishes, so he started with a glass of claret, wishing it was beer.

Bon appétit, he thought. Here's hoping we all make it to dessert alive.

CHAPTER TWENTY

Mont-Blanc, Geneva

"There! I see it!" Habis Elyan called out from the Volvo SUV's backseat.

"We *all* see it," Kabeer replied, more than a touch of acid in his tone.

"Of course. I just—"

"Drive past it slowly," Kabeer told Majid Hayek, at the Volvo's wheel. "One pass to check it out, before we stop."

The Grand Hotel Kempinski lived up to its name, at least in size and its display of lighting now that night had fallen over Lake Geneva and the waterfront. Reflections of its sign, its countless lighted windows, and its port cochere all shimmered on the lake, casting moored ranks of yachts and smaller powerboats in stark relief. Behind the vast facade, he knew, there was a courtyard with a giant swimming pool and outdoor dining area, three-quarters covered by a glass roof said to be unbreakable.

Tonight, that theory would be tested.

The hotel filled a whole city block, boxed on the north by Rue de la Cloche, on the south by Rue de Monthoux, on the east by Rue Philippe-Plantamour, and on the west by Quai du Mont-Blanc, where Kabeer's SUV cruised past at a leisurely speed, Hayek ignoring the drivers behind him. From all outward appearances, they were another group of rubbernecking tourists taking in Geneva's sights.

Hotel brochures advertised public parking "available on site," but the hotel concealed it well—below ground, as Kabeer knew from the floor plans he'd obtained in preparation for this night. The entry to that subterranean garage was on Rue de la Cloche, near the hotel's northwest corner, also serving the separate loading docks that would have jammed the hotel's border streets with traffic otherwise. Deliveries were not accepted from the giant trucks that served outlying restaurants and "big-box" stores, but rather limited to tidy vans—such as the one Mohammed Sanea should be driving toward the scene right now, if he was not already in his place. The underground location was ideal.

"Turn left," Kabeer ordered, as they approached the intersection of Quai du Mont-Blanc and Rue de la Cloche.

He was imagining the sheer destructive force unleashed by fifty pounds of Semtex, bursting upward from the man-made cavern underground, propelling steel and concrete toward the sky, through the hotel's eight floors and out its roof. It would resemble a volcano's blast, he thought, in a mountainous land where eruptions had never been seen.

Magnificent.

But would he be inside when that occurred? And if so, would he already be dead, cheated of seeing it?

"And left again," he said, spotting the entry to the hotel's secret world below ground. Hayek signaled for the turn, let two oncoming cars pass by, then swung their SUV on to the entry ramp.

Two guards were waiting there, one in the garb of a hotel employee, his companion some kind of policeman with a pistol and a walkie-talkie on his belt, a Brügger & Thomet MP9 machine pistol slung across his chest, its stubby muzzle angled toward his boots.

The hotel man addressed them, asking, "How may we help you tonight, gentlemen?"

"Four for dinner," Hayek said, as they had rehearsed. "The FloorTwo Lounge. We have a reservation."

"Ah."

The hotel man studied their faces for a moment, then checked out their clothing, suitable for dining in the lounge where business was conducted at all hours of the day and night. He could have asked to check the car, but glanced back at the well-armed officer instead and got a lazy shrug in return.

Kabeer pegged that one as a moron whose career would not advance beyond this night, assuming that he lived to see another sunrise. He was perfect.

"Excellent," the hotel man decreed. "Enjoy your time at Grand Hotel Kempinski, gentlemen."

"We will, I'm sure," Kabeer replied, before Hayek pulled away and left the two guards at their lonely station, unaware that they had made the greatest—and perhaps the last—mistake of their lives.

Quai du Rhône, Geneva

A LONG, THIN island lay beneath them as they crossed the Rhone, then took the off ramp onto Quai des Bergues, along the waterfront. Bolan was concerned about time but handling it, Grimaldi restless in the passenger's seat to his left. They'd made up some time on the highway from Täsch, taking chances with speed and police through the mountains and racing through tunnels if there was no traffic, trying to shave Kabeer's lead.

Was it enough?

Quai des Bergues turned into Quai du Mont-Blanc where it met Rue de la Servette, three hundred yards south of the Grand Hotel Kempinski. Rolling northward, Bolan kept his eyes turned to his left, hoping he wouldn't see a roiling cloud of smoke with flames leaping inside it, or a swarm of helicopters circling the scene of some other disaster, dreaded flashers winking on the street.

Nothing.

"You think we made it?" Grimaldi inquired.

"We're here," Bolan replied. "The question is whether we made it in time."

"That's what I meant."

"Only one way to find out."

They'd researched the hotel's layout in advance, knew where to park and had absorbed the message that no reservations were required for hotel visitors to park their vehicles. Whether that still held true with half a dozen leaders of the "free world" gathered in the banquet hall still remained to be seen. If not, Bolan would drop the Jetta anywhere he could get it off the street, without creating traffic hazards.

They'd changed on the drive, more or less, shedding the wilder tourist duds to avert police attention at the railway depot. Going in, they would seem average enough to pass, he hoped, but failing that, the aerials on Google Earth revealed what seemed to be a vacant lot immediately west of the hotel, across Rue Philippe-Plantamour and Rue Abraham-Gevray. They could walk back a hundred feet or so from there and find another way inside, with any luck.

"They don't exactly have the place closed off," Grimaldi observed.

Good news, as far as that went, but they had to think about an exit plan, along with getting in. Whatever happened at the Grand Hotel Kempinski, Bolan hoped to survive it and drive—or walk—away when it was done. Parking below ground put a crimp in any plan to flee the scene, since underground garages were notoriously easy to seal off, but getting close was more important at the moment than an easy getaway.

He saw Rue de la Cloche, turned left and hoped that they weren't too late.

Grand Hotel Kempinski Banquet Room

THE SMALL SCOOP of sorbet was raspberry. It was refreshing after Hal's two appetizers—stuffed prosciutto with mixed greens and parmigiano shavings, followed by smoked salmon, horseradish, crushed peas and caviar—but it was small enough that Brognola could have wolfed it in a single bite. He took his time, though, mimicking the other diners, making sure he used the right miniature spoon to make it last.

Next up, if nothing interrupted them, he had a roasted pork chop with crispy anchovies, baby artichokes and lemon thyme jus on the way, followed by homemade tiramisu for dessert. The big Fed was already leaning toward full, but when in Rome—or in Geneva, as the case might be...

The speeches wouldn't start until the crowd had dined,

stuffed and high enough on wine to make the same hot air they'd heard before more palatable. Everybody on the dais hoped for peace and justice, yada-yada, but Brognola saw the head of the Israeli delegation flicking eyes over the audience, preparing to deliver the same show of defiance that had been his stock in trade for years. There would be no concessions to "the enemy," no pullback from occupied lands, no relenting on "self-defense" tactics that struck some other nations—and the UN Security Council—as aggressive acts of war.

Same old, same old.

The only thing this summit meant to Hal Brognola was a prime target for terrorism, with himself at ground zero for once. He didn't like it there, but it had not soured his appetite.

His table's sommelier was making another round, topping off glasses. The big Fed considered passing this time, then decided he should take the fill-up, use his own willpower if he didn't feel like drinking any more, but keep the wine handy in case the later speeches dragged. He had begun to think that Bolan and Grimaldi had to have nailed down God's Hammer in Zermatt, although he'd had no bulletin to that effect from Stony Man. The cell phone in his pocket, set to vibrate, had been silent as the grave since he'd put on his tux.

Which meant precisely nothing, one way or the other.

Terrorists were like the water babies in Charles Kingsley's old fairy tale. Just because you don't see them, that doesn't mean they don't exist. You have to see them *not existing*, first.

And in Brognola's world, that generally meant you had to see them dead.

Grand Hotel Kempinski Loading Docks

MOHAMMED SANEA WAS surprised how easily he was allowed to pass the slack guards on the entrance to the hotel's underground complex He thought it had to be all those generations of neutrality, where all sides worshiped at the altar of Swiss banks, that made them feel invincible.

But they were wrong.

And this night he would prove it.

Sanea did not drive directly to the loading dock where other panel trucks were parked, unloading linens, groceries and liquor. It was safer, in his estimation, to maintain a healthy distance from the center of activity, knowing a few yards either way would not affect the ultimate destructive force of his own cargo. Nearly centered underneath the Grand Hotel Kempinski, when the Semtex blew, the underground garage would not contain it.

Physics would win out.

Sitting in the van, he played the radio on low volume, not caring if the battery ran down. Whether he managed to survive the night or not, the van was going nowhere. It had reached its final resting place. Sanea found an English-language news channel, the best that he could manage in Geneva, where there were no Arabic broadcasts, and listened to the weather forecast, followed by some boring news of sports events, until the headline stories were recycled on the hour.

There'd been nothing on the drive from Täsch, but now he heard it, a preliminary bulletin reporting murders in Zermatt. Two victims, not identified by name, were said to be of Middle Eastern ancestry. That could mean anything to casual observers, but Sanea knew they had to be his comrades.

Which ones? Guessing was futile, so he did not try.

The brief report described gunfire and an explosion at a guesthouse, with translated comments from the landlord and the town's ranking policeman. Two men, unidentified, had barged into the building with automatic weapons, killing two boarders, while several more apparently escaped through upstairs windows.

And again: *Which ones?*

If Saleh Kabeer was dead, Sanea had to question whether the survivors would proceed as planned. He knew them fairly well and trusted their commitment to the cause, but also thought that they required a guiding hand, the motivation of a leader prodding them to risk the final sacrifice for brothers of the faith whom they would never meet in life. Without Kabeer, they might lose heart and scatter to the winds.

Leaving Sanea…where, exactly?

In a basement, sitting on a load of Semtex with a solitary duty to perform.

He had a cell phone with a single number programmed into memory. If he dialed that number, would he reach Kabeer, or had police retrieved the other phone? Sanea didn't think a brief call could be traced, particularly if he shut his phone off afterward, even removed its battery. He could dial in, listen and hang up without speaking if he did not recognize the voice that answered him.

And if there was no answer, then what?

Cursing his own indecisiveness, Sanea let the radio play on but tuned out its noise, trying to decide if he should flee or wait awhile to see what happened and decide if it was time for him to live or die.

BEFORE THEY LEFT the Volvo, Saleh Kabeer's surviving soldiers double-checked their bellman uniforms. Each had already worn a white dress shirt, some of them smudged or slightly damaged in their scramble to escape, but nothing that would show once they had donned their blazers in the locker room. The rest they had in shopping bags, together with their weapons: black slacks, pillbox hats and the hotel's red trademark blazers. Black clip-on bow ties completed the ensemble, and the three would soon resemble any other servants of a great hotel where rich men gathered to discuss the fate of peasants.

Of the three, only Ali Dajani seemed to have any lasting discomfort from their skirmish in Zermatt, and he'd assured Kabeer that he could still perform as planned, to carry out his part of their design. That plan had changed somewhat, with the loss of two men, but its basic object was the same. Dajani, Habis Elyan and Majid Hayek would obtain carts from the hotel's kitchen, claiming they were needed for some task the concierge had ordered, then conceal their weapons on the carts and head directly for the banquet hall. If stopped outside its doors, they would employ whatever force was necessary to proceed, then unleash bloody havoc on the celebrated diners while they stuffed themselves with gourmet fare.

Kabeer, from his position in the lobby, would call—and spill the breaking news of justice being meted out to foul Crusaders at the Grand Hotel Kempinski, claiming credit for God's Hammer. That done, he planned to exit on to Quai du Mont-Blanc and place one final call, telling Mohammed Sanea it was time to blow the Semtex charge.

One problem: when he'd tried to reach Sanea on the drive from Täsch, his calls kept going to voice mail. Kabeer had tried a cryptic text, as well, without result. At present, he had no idea whether Sanea was on station, waiting in the loaded van, or if he had kept driving on from Täsch to parts unknown.

"All ready?" he inquired, receiving affirmation from his soldiers. "One more moment, then," he said. "I need to try Mohammed's phone again."

"He has deserted us," Dajani opined sourly.

"Mohammed wouldn't do that," Elyan replied.

"Then he should have answered."

"We don't know what has happened. Maybe he is in a dead zone for the cell."

"This is Geneva," Hayek chimed in, "not the middle of the desert. If he's here, he can make calls. He can receive them."

Stubbornly, Dajani shook his head. "I don't believe it."

"Quiet, all of you!" Kabeer ordered. "I'm dialing now."

Sanea's phone rang once, twice—and was answered on the third ring by a strong, familiar voice. "Saleh?"

GRIMALDI THOUGHT THE two guards on the entrance to the Grand Hotel Kempinski's underground garage would turn them back, or at the very least demand valid ID. In fact, they didn't even have a clipboard, and it seemed that only one of them—some kind of cop—was armed. The other was a minor hotel greeter, asking general preliminary questions before waving them along with hopes that they enjoyed their stay.

"Too easy," Grimaldi remarked, when they were out of earshot from the checkpoint. "I expected more."

"The hotel's open. It's a business," Bolan answered.

"Still."

"I hear you. Anyone could be inside."

"Bingo."

There was no way to confirm it without searching. Never mind the subterranean garage. They didn't know what Saleh Kabeer was driving, whether his men had left Täsch in one car or several, each terrorist boosting his odds of a clean getaway. They could have kept in touch while traveling with cell phones, two-way radios, whatever. All that mattered now was whether they were somewhere in the huge hotel, preparing to raise bloody hell.

"The banquet room?" he asked.

"It must be," Bolan answered, "if tonight's the night."

Grimaldi got that, sure. If God's Hammer let their targets finish eating, listening to speeches, sipping cognac, they would have to take their marks one at a time, battling security at each VIP suite while the hotel's alarms went off and law enforcement swarmed the scene. That was a stupid way to go. Better to skip the first night altogether, try the following day or the one after that during sessions of the conference or when they broke for lunch and everyone was back together in one place.

"So, are we really checking in?" he asked.

"No point," Bolan replied. "It's either on tonight, or isn't. If we keep a sharp eye out, maybe we'll spot them on the sidelines, gearing up. If not, there's still all day tomorrow and the next day."

"I was never fond of guessing games," Grimaldi said.

"Me, either. But it's what we've got to work with."

"Overnighting in the car won't work."

"Agreed. We'll have to stay awake or nap in shifts, maybe take in a late show at the theater."

"Any idea what's playing?"

Bolan smiled at that and let it go. "You ready to go up?"

"Let's do it."

Standing by the Jetta, screened from CCTV cameras behind a massive concrete pillar, they switched jackets for longer coats that did a better job of covering their shoulder-slung carbines. The coats had inside pockets, too, for stashing extra magazines and M84 stun grenades. They wouldn't make it through a pat-down, much less any kind of metal detector, but it was the best they could do.

Security wasn't impressing Grimaldi so far. He knew the summit VIPs were prone to travel light, maybe a dozen guards apiece in quiet countries such as Switzerland, but these were extraordinary times. The local cops, if nothing else, should have increased their presence at the Grand Hotel Kempinski—though, for all he knew, plainclothesmen could be as thick as fleas inside and roving on the grounds.

Another obstacle to watch for, once they were inside.

They found an elevator one row over from their parking slot, punched in, waited, and rode the car with a quirky instrumental take on Elton John's "The Bitch is Back."

"They shouldn't tamper with the classics," Grimaldi commented.

"Classics?" Bolan asked.

"Don't get me started."

That was good advice, and Bolan took it. They were headed for the mezzanine, midway between the hotel's first and second floors, accessible by elevator, escalator and old-fashioned stairs. It was a compromise, giving them time to scope the lobby, have a look around and see if any faces from Brognola's file were hanging out in the vicinity, instead of stepping from the elevator car directly into line of sight for all the officers and agents standing watch outside the banquet hall.

Good intentions, right.

But were they good enough?

Five men, well armed, could still wreak bloody havoc, even if they never reached the world leaders they hoped to kill. Bolan remembered the Utøya massacre, with sixty-nine killed by a single gunman, and Virginia Tech, where another lone shooter had slain thirty-two, wounding twenty-three more. Five men with automatic weapons, maybe with explosives, could put those grim death tolls in the shade.

Most people, in the present circumstances, would have blown the whistle to security. Of course, that meant detention and interrogation, officers from half a dozen agencies wanting to know how Bolan and Grimaldi knew the summit was at risk, and why the two of them were armed. From there, ballistics tests were just a step away, linking their weapons to the carnage in Zermatt. They would be disavowed by Washington, and when the murder charges landed, that would mark the end of Bolan's life.

Switzerland didn't execute convicted killers. In fact, of all developed countries in the West, only the USA still practiced capital punishment. The law wasn't a factor when it came to Bolan, though. Once caged, somehow, before too long, he'd have a price tag on his head, a target on his back. He would defend himself, but in the end, prison meant death.

And Grimaldi? Depending on the circumstances, Swiss law punished homicide with prison terms ranging between five years and life. Add terrorism to the list of charges, and the best that the Stony Man pilot could hope for was to totter out of jail someday, when he was old and gray—if not a broken man, one left to live from hand to mouth by menial pursuits, disgraced, an outcast.

Those were all familiar risks, and understood by anyone who worked with Stony Man, but Bolan personally would prefer a clean death in the heat of battle if it came to that.

But better yet, he would prefer to leave his enemies in body bags and move on to another contest, on another battleground.

As soon as he had finished up on this one.

CHAPTER TWENTY-ONE

Saleh Kabeer sat inside a men's room stall, just off the lobby of the Grand Hotel Kempinski, wishing the commodes in public lavatories came with solid lids like those installed in private homes. It would have been more comfortable, waiting for the first reports of gunfire, when he would emerge and step into the lobby with his cell phone, to make history with the announcement of a major coup as it was happening, before the massive hostelry was blown sky-high.

But for the next few minutes, he could only sit and wait, pretending to relieve himself while others came and went, answering calls of nature, scrubbing hands, drying their fingers with the droning hot-air blower. No one tarried long enough to notice Kabeer in his stall, or realize how long he'd been in place.

Five minutes? Ten? It felt like hours, sitting with his phone in one hand, pistol in the other, while his backside started to go numb.

It would have been too dangerous for him to simply loiter in the lobby, where the concierge or check-in staff might log him as a stranger who was neither registered at the hotel nor seeming to go anywhere within it. If he was accosted, had to use his weapon prematurely, that could jeopardize the more important strike against the banquet hall.

At least, after his conversation with Mohammed

Sanea, Kabeer knew the Semtex was in place, ready to blow upon command. A weight had lifted from his shoulders when he heard Sanea's voice affirm that he was on the scene and ready to proceed. If both of them survived the night, they would have much to celebrate.

And if not, they would celebrate in Paradise.

Kabeer glanced at the cracked face of his watch and saw that thirteen minutes had elapsed. Not long to work a miracle, but he was champing at the bit, eager to do his part and leave. That was no cowardice, he told himself, but dedication to a cause with no one other than himself quite fit to lead it.

He shifted on his plastic seat of pain, was just about to rise, restore the circulation to his lower body and be done with it, when gunfire crackled, distant but still loud enough to register. Kabeer immediately tucked his pistol out of sight, behind his waistband, covered by his jacket. Flushed with sudden energy, he marched directly to the lavatory's exit, hands unwashed, pushed through the swinging door—

And instantly collided with a cop.

The impact startled both of them. Kabeer was on the verge of reaching for his pistol when he caught himself, apologized and held his phone up for the officer to see.

The cop said something to him in German.

It was totally incomprehensible, but Kabeer smiled and nodded, stepping back to let the man pass. Outside, the lobby lay no more than fifteen feet in front of him: the stage from which he would address the world.

"NOBODY HOME," BOLAN SAID, when he'd scanned the lobby twice without detecting a familiar face from Hal Brognola's gallery of God's Hammer terrorists.

"Ditto," Grimaldi replied, after another sweep around the mezzanine. "Plan B?"

"Affirmative."

They'd seen cops standing at strategic places, decked out in ballistic vests, half of them armed with MP5s, all packing pistols, pepper spray and other weapons on their belts. The officers weren't stopping anyone, or even blocking access to the second floor, since there were other meeting rooms up there and business had go on for the hotel to turn a franc. As Bolan and Grimaldi drifted toward the escalator, feigning small talk, no one in authority appeared to spare a second glance for them, but Bolan would have bet their faces had been filed away for future reference.

That was a risk, but Bolan had this visit slated as his last trip to Geneva for a good long while. He didn't like to play a venue twice, if he could help it, though some cities in the States had lured him repeatedly. Outside his home turf, when it came to places like Geneva and Zermatt, repeated stop-ins had been few and far between— some of them when he'd used his birth name and worn another face.

They reached the second floor and turned right from the escalator, following the unobtrusive signs toward several meeting rooms, leaving the banquet hall behind them for the moment. Plan B called for them to scout the second floor—or *first* floor, as it would be known in Europe, where the *ground* floor didn't count—and see if they could intercept Kabeer's gunmen before they crashed the summit's opening event. Failing in that, they had agreed to split up and to mount roaming surveillance on the banquet room, hopefully without tipping the guards already set in place to watch them.

It was no easy task, trying to be invisible with no disguise and several dozen watchers on alert. Some might have said it was impossible, but Bolan had removed that word from his vocabulary long ago.

They passed two meeting rooms en route to check the kitchen. One was hosting a reception for conventioneers from something called the Church of Rectified Humanity. The other room was wall to wall with people watching color slides of something that appeared to be a giant rotting carcass, hoisted on a crane above a ship's deck, while a narrator described the photographs in French.

The Stony Man warriors reached another corner, rounded it and started toward the kitchen, following its tantalizing aromas toward two sets of swing doors. As they approached, three bellmen cleared one set of doors, their leader empty-handed, while the other two pushed covered serving carts.

MOHAMMED SANEA WOULD have missed the action's startup, three floors down and buried underground, if his cell phone had not chirped in his hand. He answered midway through the first note with a breathless, "Yes?"

"It's starting," Kabeer announced, then cut the link before Sanea could respond.

But what would he have said, in any case?

Sanea set his pistol on the empty seat beside him, with his phone and the remote control to detonate the Semtex sitting less than three feet behind him. If he triggered it right now, would he feel anything before his eyes opened again in Paradise, beholding all the wonders that awaited him?

A niggling voice asked him what he would do if he and all his spiritual teachers had been wrong, that killing even in the name of God was wrong, and he woke up on fire, in Jahannam—or if, in fact, there was no afterlife at all. Again, Sanea had no answer, so he turned the radio back on and found a music station, "easy listening" they called it in the West, which meant songs without meaning, never sparking any controversy.

As a mental exercise, Sanea tried to picture what was happening upstairs. He still had no idea which members of the team had died back in Zermatt, except that Saleh Kabeer had not been one of them. That left three counterfeit bellmen to carry out the mission. They would all be killed in the attempt, of course. The only question now was how many Crusaders would die with them.

And the answer, with Sanea holding the remote control for fifty pounds of Semtex, was: every last one of them.

He waited only for the final word, telling him that Kabeer had cleared the premises. When that was done, Sanea would immediately leave the underground garage on foot, retreating to a safe distance from which to beam a lethal note through space and spark the Semtex detonators. If the pudgy fellow and policeman still guarded the exit, he would act accordingly: two head shots for the policeman, maybe one for the civilian if he did not run away.

Then out, across Rue Philippe-Plantamour, and when he reached the vacant lot there, find something to hide behind—one of the concrete buildings in the southwest corner, preferably—and key his detonator for the biggest blast in all of Geneva's history.

No one was neutral anymore, no one untouchable.

A new day was about to dawn, and none who stood against God were safe.

For comfort, he retrieved his pistol from its place

and held it in his right hand, then took up the detonator with his left, careful not to touch the bright red button that would vaporize the van, himself and most of the hotel. Holding the weapons reassured Sanea, as if he were drawing power from them by osmosis, rather than just sitting in a panel truck, holding two lifeless objects in his hands.

He would be ready to use one or both, when it was time.

And his gut told him that time was coming soon.

HABIS ELYAN HAD expected difficulty, entering the Grand Hotel Kempinski with security in place for the Crusaders, but in fact, no one challenged him as he and his companions left the service elevator on the ground floor, following directions to the locker room. One bellman passed them in the hallway, said in German, "You're late," and swept on past them with a look of satisfied superiority.

"Mos zibby," Elyan replied, knowing the white man would not understand him, and his two companions chuckled their appreciation, even as Elyan cursed himself for slipping into Arabic.

"Quiet!" he snapped, to silence them. Majid Hayek began to say "But you—"

"Enough!" Elyan rounded on them, wild-eyed. "Say nothing. Anyone who ruins this, I cut his throat myself and promise you that he will not see Paradise. Now, follow me!"

The locker room was much like any other Elyan had seen, and held the same stale odor trapped between its concrete walls. Not having lockers of their own, Elyan and his two comrades emptied their shopping bags of bellman garb and started changing clothes: trading their denim jeans for slightly rumpled dress slacks, slipping on the blazers that were oversize except for Hayek's, fastening their pillbox hats in place with straps beneath their chins, and straightening their small bow ties. When they were done, a full-length mirror on the wall revealed three slightly scruffy members of the servant class, prepared to spend another shift slaving for minimum wage.

They left their other clothing where it lay, on the floor or crumpled on hard wooden benches, useless to them now. Each member of the team knew that the Grand Hotel Kempinski would most likely be his final resting place—or, rather, the last place on Earth their eyes would ever see. Beyond it lay an unmarked pauper's grave and history.

When they were dressed, the three retrieved their shopping bags, still heavy with weight of their AKS-74U carbines, extra 30-round magazines and antipersonnel grenades. The spare magazines were a nod toward optimism, in Elyan's opinion, since they were unlikely to have time for reloading once the action started. They were meant to spray the banquet room, focusing on the heads of state who always shared a table at such gatherings, then hurl as many hand grenades as possible before Crusaders cut them down.

That was reality. The rest was only fantasy.

No matter, though. Habis Elyan was prepared to die and thought the others were, as well, although Ali Dajani whined too much about his aching back for someone who did not expect to live another ninety minutes.

Elyan had worried that a concierge might stop them on their way to reach the kitchen, calling them away to other tasks, but no one passing by appeared to notice them at all. The great hotel was bustling with employees, most of them behind the scenes, moving on special staircases and elevators the wealthy guests would never see. Maids in their café au lait-colored uniforms pushed carts piled high with linens, towels and rolls of toilet tissue. Bellmen trudged past with luggage carts of polished brass, taller than they were. Waiters lugging trays for room service trailed the aroma of overpriced food behind them. Elyan and his two cohorts, bent on a mission of murder, were lost in the crowd.

The hotel's kitchen was another beehive of activity this night. A master chef presided over it, his tall hat cocked slightly to one side as a symbol of insouciance, correcting here, tasting there, chastising drones who disappointed him in any way. The drones wore white coats of their own, but most of theirs—unlike the master chef's—were stained with soups, sauces or gravies. One group worked to keep the banquet room supplied, another served the hotel's three gourmet restaurants, while a third kept orders flowing to the FloorTwo Bar and room service. Despite the clatter, chatter and confusion of aromas, it appeared to be a well-oiled, well-directed operation.

No one noticed Elyan or his companions as they found a rank of polished service carts, chose two and cautiously removed their weapons from the shopping bags they carried, carefully arranged them on the carts, then covered them with spotless tablecloths. It only took a moment's time, and they were on their way, Elyan leading, bearing death to cap the great Crusader's feast.

"IT'S THEM!" GRIMALDI hissed at Bolan, as the bogus bellmen made their exit from the kitchen, fifty feet away. Despite their silly costumes, all three faces were recognizable to the pilot from the mug shots of God's Hammer members he'd studied since he came on board the mission. Habis Elyan led the trio, empty-handed, while Majid Hayek and Ali Dajani followed, pushing service carts. The effort seemed to cost Dajani something, as he grimaced in apparent pain.

Bolan was there ahead of him, his carbine rising by the time Grimaldi spoke. One of the bellmen saw the move and said something in Arabic that put the other two on full alert, whipping the linen covers from their carts and grabbing for whatever lay beneath.

Not food, Grimaldi saw, as stubby AK carbines sprang to hand and swiveled toward him, brown plastic magazines seeming longer than the weapons' stubby barrels. The Stony Man pilot dove for the vinyl-covered floor when muzzle-flashes started blinking at him, bullets chewing up the wall immediately next to him, a yard or so above his head.

No sound suppressors, which meant the racket should alert the delegates and bodyguards inside the banquet room. Evacuation could begin immediately, sweeping the assembled dignitaries out of range—unless they ran into another hunting party on the way.

As he began to return fire, Grimaldi's brain was doing basic math. Five minus three left two members of God's Hammer unaccounted for.

And where in hell were they?

Grand Hotel Kempinski Banquet Room

BROGNOLA'S FORK WAS halfway to his mouth, bearing a slice of pork with an anchovy skewered to it, when he heard the sharp *snap-crackle-pop* of automatic fire. It wasn't fireworks, or a backfire from the highway, or a loaded tray someone had dropped while en route from the kitchen. The big Fed knew a Kalashnikov when he heard one, and that meant shit was coming down right freaking now.

Around him, conversations stammered to a halt, while bodyguards moved toward their principals, producing weapons they had managed to conceal under tuxedo jackets, closing ranks. Brognola had been briefed on the evacuation plan, in case of an emergency, and this was it—or one of them, at least.

In fact, there had been several plans, each tailored to a certain crisis. If the place caught fire—unlikely, although not impossible—the diners would be escorted through whichever one of the banquet room's exits was nearest their part of the hall, broken down in advance with a helpful floor plan. If there was shooting, egress would depend upon the source of the attack, using the exits that appeared to be the most secure and farthest from the source of hostile fire. That plan involved a separate escape route for each of four exits, with different routes leading escapees upstairs to their suites or out into the street, as logic might dictate.

The shots Brognola heard were coming from the general direction of the hotel's kitchen, or the entrance nearest to the dais where the VIPs were sitting frozen now, surrounded by the officers in charge of their security detachments. None had risen yet, or made a move to leave, although Brognola saw them fidgeting and arguing with bodyguards who restrained them.

We're wasting time, Brognola thought, but kept his seat, letting the pros have first shot at controlling a disaster in the making. When they started moving people toward the exits, he'd be ready—and to guarantee it, the big Fed reached under his tuxedo jacket, to the back, checking the mini-Glock he'd hidden there.

It wasn't his job, personally, to defend the Man against a terrorist attack, but if he had the chance, Brognola would not hesitate. He'd dropped the hammer on assorted bad guys in his time and lost no sleep over the fact, although it wasn't something that he relished, either. There'd be ample time for feelings somewhere on the other side of action, for the ones who managed to survive.

For those who didn't…well, the story ended, either way.

Up on the dais, Secret Service agents had the Man in motion now, surrounded, and the other heads of state were likewise rising, ringed by guards with weapons on display. The bulk of diners—undersecretaries, aides— were becoming restless, stirring like the surface of a cooking pot about to boil. More guards were circulating through the banquet hall, collecting members of the delegations they'd arrived with, aided by local police.

Brognola followed orders when a Secret Service man approached his table, telling him and the companions he had barely met to follow him. They made a beeline for the exit where the President was headed, picking up their pace upon command.

Moving toward safety, or a one-way ticket to the Great Beyond?

THE FIRST WILD shots missed Bolan as he dropped and rolled, aware of Grimaldi doing likewise, somewhere to his right. The faux bellmen were laying down a blaze of 5.45 mm fire, crouching behind the service carts they'd overturned for cover in the hallway, when they'd spotted Grimaldi and Bolan drawing weapons. They had canvas shopping bags back there, as well, and part of Bolan's mind wondered what they contained, but he was busy at the moment, fighting for his life.

Bolan fired a short burst from his SIG 552 Commando carbine, punching holes along the steel top of the nearest cart, impact resounding with a rapid *clang-clang-clang*. He missed the shooters, though, and one of them—he thought it was Ali Dajani—popped up long enough to answer with an AK burst that plowed linoleum a foot to Bolan's right, chipping the concrete underneath.

The service carts weren't much, in terms of cover, but they still provided more than Bolan or Grimaldi had, sprawled in the open corridor downrange from their opponents. Three weapons against their two, and even in the midst of battle, Bolan understood that left two terrorists still unaccounted for.

Saleh Kabeer and Mohammed Sanea. Where in hell were they right now?

Bolan triggered another burst, aimed slightly to the right of where he'd hit last time and firing for effect. His 62-grain bullets drilled the relatively thin steel surface of the capsized cart, seeking a fleshy target on the other side and finding one. As a cry of pain reached Bolan's ears, he saw an arm flung back, hand empty, quickly dropping out of sight again.

One down, or only wounded while retaining the ability to fight?

The next arm raised was clutching a grenade, lobbing it overhand with no attempt to place the pitch precisely. Grimaldi called out a warning from his place against the other wall, and Bolan fired to keep the shooters down, while trying hard to track the wobbling path of what appeared to be an RGD-5 antipersonnel grenade.

It struck the wall above Grimaldi and rebounded, spinning through the air, sailing some twenty feet past Bolan before bouncing off the other wall and dropping to the floor. He heard a *pop* as the pyrotechnic delay fuse ignited and started to burn. Lying outside the ten-foot "guaranteed" kill zone, Bolan pressed his cheek against the cool linoleum, one arm over his head and waited for the blast.

CHAPTER TWENTY-TWO

Saleh Kabeer seethed with frustration as the switchboard operator at Radio Télévision Suisse put his call on hold, filling his ear with music that reminded him of something from a third-rate science fiction film. He cursed into his cell phone, pacing in the Grand Hotel Kempinski's lobby until he noticed uniformed employees staring at him, whispering among themselves behind the registration counter.

Surely they had heard the same gunfire he had—or was it all in his imagination?

No! There came another sharp, staccato burst, and patrons in the lobby were excited now, milling about and conversing in languages Kabeer could not translate. The desk clerks had forgotten him, their eyes shifting toward the mezzanine and second floor above it, where the sounds of battle echoed down the escalators to ground level.

There still was no human being on the phone line, only vapid New Age music boring into Kabeer's head with all the delicacy of a rusty awl. He snapped the phone shut, dropped it in the left-hand outer pocket of his coat and drew the Bizon submachine gun from concealment with his right hand. He cocked it with his left, and aimed it toward the registration counter.

Somewhere in the lobby, Kabeer heard a woman

scream in German, "Someone has a gun!" while someone else picked up the cry in French.

The gun that so alarmed them was already spitting
death, strafing the registration desk and those behind
it, 9 mm bullets chipping wood veneer and drilling into
flesh as his disoriented targets reeled, stumbled and fell.
Kabeer saw two men and a woman drop before he lifted
off the Bizon's trigger, breathing in the heady scent of
gunsmoke, hot brass crunching underneath his shoe soles
as he crossed the lobby, moving toward the escalator.

Someone shouted after him to stop, and he turned to
face the challenger, a portly older man dressed in the uniform of Geneva's cantonal police. The cop had his pistol
drawn and vaguely aimed, but he had balked at shooting
Kabeer in the back. That mistake cost him dearly as Kabeer squeezed off another burst, ripping a jagged gash
across the policeman's stout abdomen. The cop fired too
late to save himself, his bullet wasted on the vaulted ceiling overhead, and landed on his back, awash in blood.

Kabeer turned from his kill and leaped aboard the
escalator, climbing two steps at a time while the con-
veyor belt propelled him toward the mezzanine, a somewhat dizzying effect that made him stagger when he
reached the solid floor. People were running here and
there around him, most intent on getting to the escalator
that would take them down and out of the hotel to what
they viewed as safety.

Fools.

Kabeer took time to spray the long descending escalator with his Bizon SMG, starting a wild landslide of
lacerated flesh and screams. Pausing to check the helical magazine's indicator holes, Kabeer found that he
had expended forty rounds, leaving but twenty-four to

fire before reloading. Smiling fiercely, he decided that he might as well spend those right where he was, before proceeding to the banquet hall.

His last long burst across the mezzanine sent bodies tumbling, sprawling, as the Parabellum slugs cut through them, spilling pools and streams of blood across the pale Carrara marble floor. More screams accompanied the slaughter, their cacophony encouraging Kabeer, wringing a shout of laughter from his throat.

The Bizon's bolt locked open on an empty chamber, and he hastily removed the weapon's magazine, discarding it. Drawing a fresh one from a pocket, he engaged its forward hooks with pins below the SMG's front sight and snapped the rear end into contact with a spring-loaded paddle catch/release in front of the gun's trigger guard. A quick yank on the bolt, and the Bizon was ready to go.

But not here.

Grinning, feeling invincible, Kabeer ran toward the nearest entrance to the hotel's banquet hall.

THE RGD-5 FRAG grenade exploded, buffeting Mack Bolan in his prone position on the service hallway's floor. Smoke filled the corridor, while fragments of acoustic tile, shot through with shrapnel, rained down from the dropped ceiling overhead. A piece some two feet wide cracked Bolan on the head, tearing his scalp, but he ignored it as the storm of death washed over him.

Physics spared Bolan's life, sending most of the grenade's shrapnel upward and outward, riddling walls and ceiling while sparing objects lying on the floor. He felt one fragment graze his right arm, drawing blood, and thought another might have clipped his left shoe sole before it cut a divot in the nearby wall. Behind him,

Bolan heard Grimaldi gasp in pain and turned to face him through the haze.

"You hit?" he asked.

"A couple stingers," Grimaldi replied, his voice taut. "Nothing I can't live with."

Hoping that he was right, Bolan returned his full attention to the upturned service carts, both scarred by shrapnel now, where two assailants lay waiting to finish the skirmish. As he watched, they fired short bursts from both ends of their cover, their rounds still flying high and wide, brass glittering as it sprang upward from their weapons, then came tinkling back on to the vinyl-covered floor.

It was a stalemate, and they had to break it soon, before the missing terrorists attacked the banquet hall. For all Bolan knew, they could be on the threshold even now, prepared to burst in firing, hurling hand grenades, before the diners and their muscle could react to the chaotic sounds of battle he'd ignited in the corridor serving the kitchen.

Silence fell, then Bolan heard his adversaries whispering in Arabic. He didn't need a translator to know that they were working up a plan to sweep the hallway one last time, then make a run for their primary target when they had eliminated any opposition on that front. But would they rise to do it, or—

He got his answer seconds later, when Ali Dajani rose, snarling, arm cocked to pitch another frag grenade. Bolan and Grimaldi fired simultaneously, bullets ripping through Dajani's face and chest, tipping him over backward with the lethal egg still in his hand. Impact took care of that, as Bolan hugged the floor once more, waiting for an explosion to his front this time.

The blast propelled both service carts toward Bolan and Grimaldi, one caroming off the Executioner's outstretched hand and spinning to his right. The other struck it with a *clang* and both of them stopped dead, wheels spinning, while Bolan peered through a veil of smoke to find his enemies.

All three of them were down now, lying tangled and twisted where they'd shared their meager cover under fire. One of the three—Majid Hayek, he thought—was twitching slightly, clearly dying, while the other two lay still.

Bolan rose to his feet, reached out to help Grimaldi, but the pilot waved him off, saying, "I'm good. Let's hit it."

The Executioner nodded, turned back toward the banquet hall downrange and stepped around the dead.

GRIMALDI GRIMACED AS he kept pace with his partner, limping slightly, still getting it done. He felt blood trickling down the inside of his left thigh from a shrapnel wound—too close for comfort, there—but he'd been hit before, and from the feel of it, he guessed that any medic with a pair of tweezers and a sewing kit could patch him up when they were done.

He reloaded his Commando carbine on the move. He'd been through worse, much worse, and lived to talk about it over cold beers with survivors like himself, who'd walked the wild side and returned to share the tale. Survival wasn't really much of an achievement when he thought about it—skill and luck combined to beat an enemy who came up short in one or both—but it beat hell out of the only known alternative.

Grimaldi figured that their dust-up with the three

shooters would have upset the fancy diners' appetites
and sent them streaming for the nearest exit, under the
direction of their bodyguards. That could be good or bad,
depending on the terrorists still unaccounted for, and how
they'd planned their moves, whether they'd laid an ambush with this very thing in mind, or if they'd conjured
something even worse.

Like bringing down the house.

"Hold up a sec," he called to Bolan.

"What?"

"It strikes me that our pals back there were packing
light," Grimaldi said.

Bolan took no time to connect the dots. "Another
World Trade Centers deal, you think?"

"Could be."

Not 9/11, maybe, but the *first* one, back in 1993, when
Ramzi Yousef and his cronies from al-Qaeda parked a
truck bomb underneath the North Tower with plans to
bring it down. The death toll had been relatively small—
six pulled out of the rubble afterward—but the explosion and resulting fires had left more than a thousand
wounded. Architecture and the limitations of homemade
explosives had kept the damage and the body count from
being vastly worse, but if God's Hammer had access to
more powerful and more sophisticated tools...

"We've got no way to check it out," Bolan replied.
"No one to call, right now. If we get through this, we
can hand it off to Hal."

By which time, Grimaldi thought, it would likely be
too late.

Bolan was right, though: there was nothing they could
do about some hypothetical disaster, when reality was
right in front of them. Three shooters down, two others

still at large, including the ringleader of the plot. It would be idiotic folly to retreat before they had done everything within their power to secure the target VIPs.

Grimaldi was moving even as he spoke. "You're right. What are we waiting for?"

Bolan looked at the pilot's bloodstained pants, frowning. "Do you want to check that out?"

"Later," Grimaldi said. "I'd hate to miss dessert."

MOHAMMED SANEA WAS fed up with waiting. Sitting in the van, below ground, he had no idea what was occurring in the huge hotel above him. Had Kabeer and the others achieved their goal, or had they all been slaughtered by security before they had the chance to fire a shot? For all Sanea knew, he was alone now, with no orders to obey beyond Kabeer's command that he get out alive, then detonate the Semtex before slipping off—to where?

Sanea clutched his cell phone, wishing he could call Kabeer and ask for his advice, some clue to what was happening upstairs, but that would be a futile exercise. Kabeer was either dead or in the midst of speaking to the media, announcing the attack to all the world at large.

The radio!

Sanea turned the van's ignition key and switched the radio back on, tuned in to the English language news channel. The anchor's voice droned on, emotionless, about stock prices and a ferry run aground somewhere in Asia, an airline crash in South America, nothing to indicate that the anchor had been tipped off to mayhem at the Grand Hotel Kempinksi in her own backyard.

What did it mean? Had the police moved in before Sanea's friends could strike? None of them would surrender. He was sure of that, which meant they had to be dead if they were cornered by authorities.

To hell with this.

Sanea put the cell phone in his pocket, grabbed his pistol and the Semtex detonator from the passenger's seat, and stepped out of the van, locking the driver's door behind him. Anyone who tried to search it now would have to beat the locks, and by the time someone attempted that, their moment would have passed. He only had to walk a hundred yards, if that, before he keyed the detonator and left Switzerland a grim reminder that it could not hold the world at bay forever.

He jogged toward the exit, finally seeing streetlights illuminating traffic passing by on Rue de la Cloche. The watchmen on the entrance both had cell phones pressed against their ears, imparting or receiving information. Possibly, if Kabeer and the rest lay dead upstairs, the guards would be recalled, but that seemed doubtful to Sanea. More than likely, officers would search the hotel from top to bottom, seeking any other threats, before the staff and guests returned to any semblance of normality.

Sanea had no time to waste.

He started forward, saw the sentries notice him, the plump hotel man raising one hand as a warning gesture, calling out, *"Sie müssen aufhören, mein Herr."*

To hell with stopping on demand. Sanea raised his pistol, shot the flunky twice and watched him fall. He swung his weapon toward the cop, but his second target proved more agile than expected. Dropping to a crouch, he fired a short burst from his submachine gun, followed quickly by another as he found the range.

Sanea felt the bullets ripping through him, stealing air from ruptured lungs. He hit the concrete floor facedown, gasping and twitching like a grounded fish. His outflung hands released his pistol and the Semtex detonator, each spinning beyond his reach in different directions as he fell.

Lying in blood, synapses firing and misfiring in his brain, Sanea thought the soldiers who had trained him long ago were wrong. Sometimes a man *did* hear the shots that killed him, after all. And what else had they lied about? Sanea closed his eyes and waited to behold the final mystery.

SALEH KABEER WAS nearly there, a few yards from the apogee of his ambition as a freedom fighter for the Holy Cause. Incredibly, there were no guards in evidence outside the banquet room, and he saw one door standing open halfway down the corridor, ahead of him. Had God cleared his path in aid of Kabeer's plan to punish the Crusaders?

He would take that much on faith and strike before the opportunity was lost.

The import of this moment nearly overwhelmed him. After so much planning and so many losses, perseverance had delivered him to the precise point where his destiny demanded him to be. Six major targets awaited, if his men had not already slaughtered them, and if he'd come too late to kill the most important of them, there was still time for Kabeer to make his mark, before Sanea brought the Grand Hotel Kempinski crashing down in ruins.

He was almost to the door, and now a single guard emerged, armed with an Uzi submachine gun, glancing to his right, then freezing as he turned and saw Kabeer almost on top of him. The terrorist leader triggered a short burst, barely aiming, and he felt like cheering when the enemy collapsed, blood spraying from his face and throat. That cost Kabeer the slim advantage of surprise, but nothing mattered to him now, beyond the need to kill as many of his people's foes as possible before he fell.

He hesitated for a moment at the open doorway, then stepped through, his Bizon leveled from the hip, prepared for anything but failure and disgrace. Incredibly, he recognized the top Crusader of them all approaching him, surrounded by a group of stone-faced men, all armed, who had be US Secret Service, since they wore no uniforms. Kabeer's eyes met the American President's, and while he could not hope for recognition, nonetheless Kabeer was pleased to see a kind of grim acceptance there.

He held down the Bizon's trigger and swung the weapon's muzzle in an arc from left to right, then back again, hosing the target's bodyguards with Parabellum rounds, remembering to place his first shots low, in case the drones were wearing body armor under their tuxedos. They went down like weeds before a scythe, a couple of them crying out in shocked surprise and pain, before Kabeer's next sweep ripped into skulls and faces, silencing his enemies for good.

And there he was, the man Kabeer had traveled so far from his homeland to destroy, exposed and walking backward from the smoking muzzle of the Bizon SMG. Before Kabeer could finish him, another man—too old for bodyguard material—leaped from the sidelines, tackling the President and riding him to ground, shielding the top Crusader with his body, even as he swung a small pistol around to fire at Saleh Kabeer.

And missed!

God was truly with him this day. No other answer could explain a miss from less than fifteen feet.

Kabeer stepped forward, quickly checked the ammo level in his weapon's magazine, then leveled it, prepared to give the full remaining load to these men at his feet. It was appropriate that they should grovel for him in the final moments of their wasted lives, as judgment fell upon them from above.

BOLAN HEARD THE high-pitched canvas-ripping sound of submachine-gun fire as he approached the banquet room's rear entrance, with Grimaldi close behind him. It was definitely coming from inside the hotel's lavish banquet hall, but Bolan had no way of knowing whether it was triggered by attackers or some member of the VIP security detachment.

Either way meant lives at risk, including Hal Brognola's and the President's.

But moving in also put Bolan's life at even greater risk. Unknown to any Secret Service agent, much less bodyguards assigned to other dignitaries at the summit, Bolan and Grimaldi would be two more strangers packing guns and nothing more, the kind of targets that attracted fire from anybody with a weapon and a boss to shield from harm.

Match that against the other choice—retreating, leaving those inside the banquet hall to live or die on someone else's whim—and it came down to no alternative at all.

"I'm going in," Bolan said. "You should stay out here."

"Fat chance," Grimaldi retorted.

And that was it. Bolan edged through the doorway, checking out the room that had become a battlefield. All doors were standing open now, a party of Italians slipping through the one farthest to Bolan's right without a backward glance, the way Carabinieri were drilled to cover their principal first and forget about stragglers. Bolan couldn't tell the other milling individuals apart—French, English, German or Israeli—without hearing someone speak, and at the moment they were all focused on action, rather than discussion. Plans made in advance were being carried out with varied levels of precision, with a dash of chaos added now that terrorists had breached the banquet hall.

Make that *one* terrorist.

Bolan picked out the boss of God's Hammer, Saleh Kabeer, directly opposite the doorway where the Executioner stood with Jack Grimaldi. Wreathed in gun smoke, bodies scattered at his feet, Kabeer had cut a swath through Secret Service agents ringed around the President. When Bolan spotted him, Kabeer was about to make the top score of his life—before Brognola threw himself in harm's way, bringing down the Man beneath him, while he fired a wild shot from a handgun, on the fly.

It was a miss, but Brognola shot off another round as he hit the floor, hitting Kabeer's left bicep. Blood spurted from the wound, rocking Kabeer off balance for a heartbeat, but he steadied short of falling, brought his SMG back into line and wore a hungry shark's smile as he poised to make the double kill.

Bolan shot him from eighty feet away, one round to stagger him, and then a long full-auto burst when he'd confirmed the first hit. Kabeer took it all, successive impacts lifting him completely off his feet, driving him backward through the doorway where he'd entered on his killing errand moments earlier.

Brognola glanced up from his place atop the President, ready to fire again, and saw no adversary waiting for him. Turning in the opposite direction, he saw Bolan and Grimaldi, gave the pair of them a nod and waved them off with his gun hand.

Time to get out of there.

Bolan and Grimaldi dropped their Commando carbines where they stood, keeping their pistols under cover for emergencies and left to find the nearest exit from the Grand Hotel Kempinski. Bolan figured they had minutes left before the first wave of police arrived in full SWAT mode, likely with soldiers close behind. Someone would find the Jetta parked downstairs, in time, and after fruitless searching for its driver, would return it to the rental agency.

For now, he and Grimaldi were walking. They could hail a cab after they'd put some ground between themselves and the hotel, decide if they should head back to the airport or locate a small hotel somewhere, to hide out for the interim.

Mohammed Sanea was still missing, to the best of Bolan's knowledge, hadn't joined the final action in the banquet hall—and what did that mean? If he hadn't moved by now…

They came out of the hotel on to Rue de la Cloche, taking their time without appearing to be hurried as they passed the entrance to the underground garage. A white-and-orange patrol car with Police stenciled in blue across its doors sat blocking off the entry ramp, two officers standing over two bodies on the pavement. Farther back, inside, fluorescent lights picked out a third corpse lying on its side, facing the street and freedom that had proved impossible to reach.

"The odd man out," Grimaldi said.

"Looks like it," Bolan agreed, and felt a sense of relaxation overtake him.

Endgame. For this round of play, at least.

EPILOGUE

Stony Man Farm, Virginia

"He just wants to thank you in person," Hal Brognola said. "I already explained that a medal was out of the question."

"You know we don't do meet-and-greets," Bolan replied.

"Yeah, yeah. But it's the President."

"Who ought to know the rules as well as anyone."

"He's grateful," the big Fed said.

"Not a problem," Bolan answered. "You're the one who nearly took a bullet for him, and you winged the shooter, too. Without that shot, he likely would have been too quick for me to stop in time."

"I wasn't thinking," Brognola admitted.

"That's what makes a hero," Bolan said. "And since you're in the public eye already, he could pin a medal on you in the Rose Garden. Nobody would think twice about it. Maybe even put a little something extra in your next pay envelope."

"As if." But Brognola was thinking now, maybe seeing the ceremony in his mind's eye, Helen and the kids at his side for one hell of a photo op.

Bolan changed the subject, asking, "So, they had no trouble with the Semtex?"

Brognola came back to Earth and answered, "None.

Sanea dropped the detonator when he did his face-plant. The responding officers were smart enough to let it be until the techs showed up and told them what it was. From there, they didn't have much trouble tracking down the van."

"With fifty pounds of Semtex," Bolan said.

The big Fed nodded. "Plenty to remodel the Kempinski, if it wasn't flattened like a pancake."

Bolan didn't like to think about the hundreds, maybe thousands, of employees, guests and visitors who might have been annihilated in the time it took for shock waves to drive upward through eight floors, collapsing concrete walls on every side. Rescuers would have been extracting bodies or their remnants from the wreckage for a week or more.

"And God's Hammer?" he inquired.

"Kaput," Brognola answered. "If they've got any members outstanding, no one's been able to identify them so far."

"So, a clean sweep, then," Barbara Price said. She had been sitting on the sidelines, watching Brognola and Bolan spar over the White House issue. "We ought to get some time off, don't you think?"

Brognola nodded. "Well, not me. I'm on the turnaround to Washington in… Damn! Five minutes."

"Thanks for dropping by," Price said.

"I'll leave you to it, then," Brognola said, a final handshake for the road before he left the Farm's War Room to catch his chopper out.

"Alone at last," Bolan remarked.

"I thought he'd never leave," Price said. And smiled.

* * * * *

COMING SOON FROM

GOLD EAGLE®

Available November 3, 2015

GOLD EAGLE EXECUTIONER®
DARK SAVIOR – *Don Pendleton*

Cornered at a mountain monastery in the middle of an epic winter storm, Mack Bolan will need both his combat and survival skills to protect a key witness in a money-laundering case from cartel killers.

GOLD EAGLE DEATHLANDS®
DEVIL'S VORTEX – *James Axler*

When a group of outcasts kidnaps an orphan with a deadly mutation for their own agenda, Ryan and the companions must protect her without perishing in her violent wake.

GOLD EAGLE OUTLANDERS®
APOCALYPSE UNSEEN – *James Axler*

The Cerberus rebels face a depraved Mesopotamian god bent on harnessing the power of light to lock humanity in the blackness of eternal damnation.

GOLD EAGLE ROGUE ANGEL™
Mystic Warrior – *Alex Archer*

Archaeologist Annja Creed must face down a malevolent group of mystic warriors when she discovers an ancient document that could lead to lost treasure.

CNMGE1015

COMING SOON FROM

GOLD EAGLE

Available December 1, 2015

GOLD EAGLE EXECUTIONER®
FINAL ASSAULT – *Don Pendleton*

When the world's first self-sustaining ship is hijacked and put up for auction, terror groups from around the world are scrambling to make an offer. Mack Bolan must rescue the hostages and destroy the high-tech floating fortress before it's too late.

GOLD EAGLE SUPERBOLAN™
WAR EVERLASTING – *Don Pendleton*

On a desolate ring of islands, Mack Bolan discovers that a reactive volcano isn't the only force about to blow. A Russian mercenary and his group of fanatics are working to destroy America's network of military bases and kill unsuspecting soldiers.

GOLD EAGLE STONY MAN®
EXIT STRATEGY – *Don Pendleton*

One reporter is killed by a black ops group and a second is held captive in Mexico's most dangerous prison. But when Phoenix Force goes in to rescue the journalist, Able Team learns that corruption has infiltrated US law enforcement, threatening both sides of the border.

SPECIAL EXCERPT FROM

~~THE~~ **EXECUTIONER**
DON PENDLETON'S

Check out this sneak preview of
DARK SAVIOR
by **Don Pendleton**!

Bolan watched and waited for the signal from Grimaldi in the cockpit, answered with a thumbs-up and leaped into the storm.

The Cessna's slipstream carried Bolan backward, his arms and legs splayed, then the plane was gone and gale force winds attacked him like a sentient enemy. His goggles frosted over almost instantly, which wasn't terribly important at the moment, when he couldn't see six feet in front of him regardless, but he'd have to deal with that soon.

The insulated jumpsuit kept him relatively warm, but it wasn't airtight, and the shrieking wind found ways inside: around the collar, through the eyeholes of his mask, around the open ends of Bolan's gloves. The freezing air burned initially, then numbed whatever flesh it found, threatening frostbite.

From thirteen thousand feet, Bolan had about two minutes until he'd hit the ground below. Ninety seconds before he reached four thousand feet and had to deploy his main chute. If he dropped any lower without pulling the rip cord, the reserve chute would deploy automatically in time to save his life.

In theory.

At the moment, though, Bolan was spinning like a dreidel in a cyclone, blinded by the snow and frost on his goggles, hoping he could catch a glimpse of the altimeter attached to his left glove. Without it, he'd have to rely on counting seconds in his head. A miscalculation, and he'd be handing his life over to the emergency chute's activation device, hoping it would prevent him from plummeting to certain death in the Sierras.

If he didn't survive this jump, it could mean a massacre. A dozen lives, and maybe two or three times more, depended on him without those people knowing it. If he arrived in time, unbroken, and could circumvent the coming siege…

A burst of wind spun Bolan counterclockwise, flipped him over on his back, then righted him again so he was facing the jagged peaks below. He kept counting through the worst of it and reached his silent deadline. Breathing through clenched teeth behind his mask, Bolan reached up to grasp the rip cord's stainless steel D ring.

Don't miss
DARK SAVIOR by Don Pendleton,
available November 2015 wherever
Gold Eagle® books and ebooks are sold.

Copyright © 2015 by Worldwide Library

GEXEXP444